ARCANUS

by Ali K. Eke

Visit author's website at www.arcanustheseries.com
Visit publisher's website at www.amazonpublishing.amazon.com

Published by: Ali K. Eke & Amazon Publishing
Identifiers: ISBN: 979-8-9866307-0-0 (print) | ISBN: 979-8-9866307-1-7 (digital)
Subjects: Science Fiction | Alternate History

Cover design: Ayhan Cebe | www.tactile.tv
Interior design: K. J. Harrowick | www.authorkjharrowick.com
Edited by: Isabella Betita | www.reedsy.com/isabella-betita
Proofreading by: K. J. Harrowick | www.authorkjharrowick.com

TABLE OF CONTENTS

DEDICATION

To my friends and family—specifically my sister and my friend, Chino—without whom I probably would have never finished this passion project.

Probably.

ARCANUS

PROLOGUE

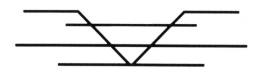

Magic, the manipulation of elements and other mysterious phenomena, is limited only by the stamina and pain tolerance of the individual.

It has been harnessed by humanity to great results and is used daily in industries like agriculture, construction, or even entertainment. But for all the good that magic can do, some use it with far darker and more nefarious intentions.

For magic is a weapon of utmost destruction. A single mage who has unlocked the secrets of the arcane might wield more power than any soldier, army, or weapon.

The rich and noble, using their cultivated magic bloodlines, crushed all opposition—all dissent against them. Wars became nothing more than contests between noble mages, who wished to show their strength through brutal slaughter. And it stayed that way for millennia.

Then the rise of the industrial era ushered in a golden age of innovation.

People built golems that could do the work of ten men faster and better, trains and steel ships to travel across the globe in a fraction of the time it would take any horse or galleon. The new factories of the industrial age worked day and night, booming at full capacity to produce modern comforts and weapons.

But that didn't matter to the haughty and rich elites of Europe, who still held onto the delusions of their supposed power. With those same delusions, they once again declared war on one another, imagining it to be nothing more than a quick skirmish in which they would display the superiority of their magic over their opponents. To them, it was nothing more than a simple competition, a contest. The armies of Europe marched against each other in a war they jokingly called "The

Great War." But these nobles, hidden from the changes in the rest of society, would be brutally reminded of how much the world had changed.

The average soldier could now shower a mage in a barrage of bullets by simply tapping a trigger. A tank could launch a shell at terminal velocity toward a mage, crushing any barrier or defense they could muster. A plane could rain down explosives that would annihilate anyone—mage or not—before they ever knew an attack was imminent.

The illusion of these unbeatable, near godlike wielders of magic, was shattered. And in its wake came the realization that even the most skilled mages, who spent decades mastering their abilities, could be gunned down by a soldier who had never picked up a rifle before stepping onto the field.

The great mages of the past—those who battled entire armies and walked away completely unscathed, whose advanced knowledge and culture pushed the human body to new heights, whose understanding of the arcane was next to none—were reduced to nothing more than a simple weapon, used like any piece of factory produced artillery or machine gun was.

The petty conflict between the Central and Allied powers was drawn out into something far more devastating. Both sides believed it would end within a month, then a year, until more than five years of grueling, brutal, and unforgiving fighting had passed. And both sides, their once supposed trump cards now gone, became more and more desperate, searching for a way to end this terrible conflict.

In this desperate race to end the Great War, they created a weapon that was more powerful, more destructive, more terrifying than anything one could have imagined. The unholy child of science and magic—a magical weapon of mass destruction, or MMD.

Created by the Germans in their desperate struggle to end their war on two fronts, being pushed back by the Russians and British, the weapon combined the power of nuclear fission with the arcane power of magic, creating a destructive capability to wipe out an entire city. As the Germans found themselves surrounded by all sides, they unleashed their bomb into the Russian empire in one final act of retaliation. One final scar upon a ruined land.

With the gruesome end to one of the most savage wars in history, the victors found themselves questioning what to do and how to stop another war from occurring again in the future.

Bastion was their answer.

An international coalition of elite mages funded by the nations of the world, Bastion used the power of its multinational army to regulate magic throughout the world. Their deeds are well known and well respected, and as time goes on, they have become a symbol of unity and peace in the eyes of many.

Yet as tensions between the superpowers of the Commonwealth and the Russian Empire grows, both sides armed themselves with their many superweapons.

As the world draws closer and closer to the edge of destruction and authoritarianism, Bastion is now its last hope.

CHAPTER 1

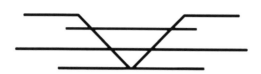

"You disgust me."

Kibo was on his hands and knees. He did not dare to look up.

The air was cold, even by the standards of a Russian winter. It was as if at any moment, it could shatter into a million pieces, never to be put back together again. He gritted his teeth and felt his eyes burn red.

"Look at me."

Kibo refused. The dirt was a lovely alternative compared to—

"Look at me!"

An icy spike shot down at Kibo, missing his hands by mere centimeters. He jolted back. Hesitantly, he looked up into those eyes, that mocking smile. Worst of all, that stupid golden brooch on her stupidly elegant blue outfit. He hated that the most: the symbol of her family's power and her magical proficiency.

Siris Vasilyeva, heir of the Vasilyev family, flipped her hair and dangled the paper in front of his face mockingly.

"Please, give it back!" Kibo shouted. He rushed up to grab the paper, only to be slammed back into the ground once more by a strong blast of ice.

"Let's take a look at this, shall we?" Siris unfolded the crumpled paper and, skimming through it, her voice broke into a piercing laugh. "An application to join Bastion? Gotten rather bold now, haven't we? I didn't even think that someone like you could get your hands on something like this!"

Siris crumbled the application and froze it solid. Kibo clenched his fist, his breathing uneven. The ice mage's smile only widened, her eyes unflinching.

"Even if, by some miracle, you're allowed to take the exam, you wouldn't even come *close* to passing." Siris lowered her face right next to his, her sneering tone a haughty whisper. "Still, I would love to watch you fail. Nothing would bring more joy." Then Siris tossed the paper away. She walked off, mocking him one final time. *Welcome to Bastion.* Good luck ever hearing that.

Kibo reached for the frozen application. Horrified, he attempted to defrost it with his uneven breath. No dice. The ink only became smudged, the paper soggy. Still on the ground, Kibo grit his teeth and aimed his hand toward his tormentor's back. Channeling his anger, he focused with all his might on gathering his mana. It was time to fight back. Yes, he would summon a roaring flame, a dragon's breath that would surely burn the smugness off Siris' face. He imagined the cloak of that fancy uniform going up in flames, singing her coiffed hair, melting that stupid brooch that she so often dangled in front of his every failure.

A pitiful flame puffed from his palm. He tried harder, pushing every ounce of energy within his body to his hand. He could feel his body heat slowly drain as he pushed ever more to make the small flicker of flame into something, anything that he could retaliate with. All it did, however, was cause the small flame emanating from his hand to backfire, sending lashes of fire across his arm.

"Damn it." Kibo grasped his arm in agonizing pain as it grew burning hot. He bit down on his tongue to stifle his scream; it would be worse if Siris noticed him fighting back. After a few minutes, the pain finally subsided. Crumpling the paper in his singed fist, Kibo walked over and sat at a park bench.

Unfair. It was all so unfair.

He thought of Bastion. The international organization was known for its peacekeeping corps, gathering members from across the globe, but most famous of all were their elite mage units. As a child, he had eagerly awaited news of their exploits on the state radio, for they were his only refuge from a bitter reality—Battlemage Grischa, the Crimson Cossacks, and so on. They were all his heroes. Of course it was his dream to join. To keep the peace between nations and travel the world, fighting evil. And to do it alongside his father.

Kibo shook his head. Siris was right. He would never be able to join the elite mages; he had no magical talent.

"Mother, I want to become a mage like my father!"

Those haunting words had followed him all his life.

A couple walked by, loudly gushing over one of those popular Commonwealth mop-haired boy bands, snapping Kibo out of his trance. He got up from the park bench and started to walk home, deciding it was best to get back before dark.

Across the street, he noticed a drab, old recruiting poster from The Great War hanging on the window of an old café, a relic of a bygone era. A serious, red-clad soldier grasped a Kalash rifle with one hand and with the other pointed squarely at Kibo. *Expand the Glory of the Motherland! Enlist for the Tsar!*

But what drew his attention far more was the newly plastered poster right next to it. Pristine and laden with bright and sharp colors, in contrast to the faded hues of the old one. At the very center of the poster stood a well-dressed man wearing a pair of glossy blue robes with silver cuffs along with a wide grin, stretching out an open hand towards Kibo. *Do you wish to spread peace and prosperity across the world? Come and sign up to join Bastion today!*

Slowly, Kibo turned his gaze up to the sky's expansive, violet dome. Yet, at the same time, he felt so claustrophobic, as if the twinkling stars were an audience of laughing onlookers and the moon scrutinized his every step. The freezing air nipped through his sweater.

He tried to relax, but deep down he didn't feel right. His entire body felt numb from a mix of sorrow and hope. Kibo took a last look at the application, hoping for some miracle, but there was none. Melted ice had mixed with ink to the point where the application was a mush of dark blotches and soggy paper.

"I don't need this anymore." He ripped the paper to shreds, tossing them to the wind. Without thinking, he started running. His chest felt as if it would burst, but he held through the pain. Was he just another nobody that would pass unnoticed, forgotten by society and the world? Was he truly another worthless peasant, meant to watch as others soared past him, just because they were lucky? Would he never be a great mage that could help the world, just like his father?

Then he felt something. A sudden pulse of...something washed over him.

Kibo stopped right in his tracks, bewildered.

"What was that?" Kibo looked around for a moment, surrounded by several trees and bushes, along with the chirping of birds and a few crickets. In a blind haze of anger and grief, Kibo had run off deep into the woods, far away from any signs of civilization. He was alone. *Better yet, where am I?*

Then, he was hit by *it* again.

"Ah!" Kibo suddenly tripped back in surprise. He turned his head, trying to catch a split-second glimpse of where he would land.

But he kept on falling. The light around him faded as he slipped deeper and deeper into the void, until he was surrounded by nothing but darkness.

Kibo woke up drenched in sweat and fear.

He gasped for air, glancing around. It was pitch black in every direction. The earth beneath him was cool and moist, with the air cold enough to chill him to the bone. Water droplets hit the ground in the distance, the sound of their impact echoing around him as he got onto his feet and wondered where he'd ended up.

Kibo's eyes slowly adjusted to the darkness. He stared at the wall and ceiling. Stones and crystals faintly glittered all around him. He was in some kind of cave.

"What the hell?"

Kibo slowly got up and started to walk toward the sound of dripping water. Before long, cool drops splashed onto his head. He laid his hand on the ground to feel a small puddle of water, suddenly realizing how parched he was. He fell to his knees, scooping up some water in his palms; it was cold and sweet as it ran down his dry throat. After he drank his fill, Kibo stood up and looked around.

In the distance, a faint blue light flickered in the darkness.

Huh, that light must be the way out of here from the looks of it, probably leads to some sort of crack or exit out of this place most likely. But, why is it blue?

Urged by a mix of curiosity and having nowhere else to go, he walked towards the light. He squinted as he got closer to the increasing brightness. After several minutes, he had finally reached the end of the tunnel where that same flickering blue light shone through a crack in a wall. As he drew in closer to take a look, Kibo leaned his full weight upon the wall.

The wall cracked beneath suddenly the weight of his hand, throwing him face-first into the floor. "Jesus!"

Before him lay a massive vault. The entrance alone was about fifty feet all around. The gate must have been built centuries—if not millennia—ago, judging by the clumps of weed, cracks, and rust. And behind all of that rubble was that faint blue light, the same light that had guided him through this cavern.

"My god, what is this place?" Kibo looked up at the giant vault door in awe. Slowly, Kibo got back on his feet and walked up to the wall, completely mesmerized by its arcane structure.

As Kibo drew in closer to the vault, his foot brushed up against something, breaking the enchantment the wall placed upon him for a single moment. Still, that single moment was all it took.

Dozens of skeletons littered the bottom of the vault, all mixed together over the years. Their bony hands reached and clawed for the door, as though attempting to break through the seal, yet all of them had been unsuccessful. Kibo's body was paralyzed in a mix of dread and panic. His skin suddenly was covered in goosebumps as every hair on his body stood up. His heart beat faster and faster as every part of his body screamed at him to move, to run.

"AHHH!"

Kibo bolted away from the mound of skeletons littering the entrance. His horror overrode all other emotions and reason. Kibo looked back over his shoulder, fearing that the skeletons would rise from the dead and drag him to a fate similar to their own. But in his panic, he lost all sense of direction and caution, and with a single misstep, he slipped.

"Argh!"

He crashed into the floor again, tumbling over a small, inconspicuous rock, his face slamming into the wet dirt below. But it seemed to have also knocked Kibo's senses back into himself. The pain of hitting the earth so violently pierced through the mist of terror that had blinded him.

"*Haaaaa...* Stupid rock," Kibo grumbled. As he tried to look for another way out, he could not see anything. It was pitch black. No matter where he looked, there was no exit, no escape from this earthen prison, save one. Kibo glanced back towards the door with the sinking realization that he had no other path.

Cautiously, Kibo stumbled towards the door, maneuvering around the many decaying corpses that had clawed toward freedom, just like him. His foot crushed the broken remains of one of the many skeletons.

"*Just keep moving, Kibo, don't look down.*" Kibo shuddered. A sliver of doubt started to spread through his head as he looked at the door. It seemed so beautiful, humming quietly as its faint blue glow beckoned all who had become trapped within this cavern. But in the end, it led all of them to a slow and agonizing death. It was nothing more than a fly trap, luring its prey to their untimely death with its sweet light.

Despite that, Kibo kept moving forward until he was eventually centimeters away from the door.

Kibo laid his hand on the wall and grabbed onto the weeds leeching off the light. With a hefty grunt, he managed to pull away some of the weeds. It took most of his strength to uncover the bare metal. The faint blue light was brighter with the plant matter scraped away. Kibo reached deeper and deeper into the thicket of weeds until he managed to grab onto the roots, and with one final rush of strength, Kibo pulled them away from the wall.

From that small, now bare spot, a bright light radiated. So bright that Kibo couldn't even look at it without being immediately blinded. Yet he did not let that stop him.

Kibo covered his eyes with one arm and slowly crept toward the wall up until he had reached the source of that light.

It felt...soft. Almost liquid.

FWOOSH

Suddenly, hundreds of images and words flashed through his mind. A triangle glowing with a faint blue light. Three figures fighting against an unknown force. The same three fighting against each other. Kibo's head pounded. The triangle grew brighter. Three massive magic sigils. A gleaming fortress in the middle of the sea. A red flag burning. All of the images slowly melded into the background until all that was left was one giant triangle, the blue light radiating from it so intensely it felt as though it would destroy his mind.

As quickly as the images came, they disappeared. The triangle slowly faded into the black void of his thoughts. Kibo's knees gave in as he fell against the door, gasping for air.

"What was that—"

The door finally let Kibo's hand go. The ground trembled and dust fell from the ceiling as the vault started to creep open.

In front of him lay a pristine hallway, its walls and floor made of strange grey metal, lines of blue light running through them. Unlike the aged vault door, the hallway was meticulously clean. It was unlike anything Kibo had seen in his entire life. It was completely alien.

Kibo walked down the hall, his footsteps echoing throughout. Foreign runes and symbols were engraved along the walls, each slowly pulsing every few seconds.

"What the... these runes..." Kibo squinted at the runes across the wall; they reminded him of something, but he could not quite grasp what it was. Then it rushed to him. "Wait a second, these are the runes I saw in my—"

Kibo bumped into a wall, distracted by the symbols. He turned to see a huge circular mark at the center of the wall. Hundreds of symbols were scrawled around it, creating a bizarre tapestry lost to the slow passage of time until now.

"Seems like some kind of magical seal..." Kibo traced the lines with his fingers.

Click

As he pressed his hand against the symbols, he felt it sink in, pushing a small circular part into the wall. A blast of air sent Kibo tumbling back onto the cold metal floor

"Ow. Seems like everything in here either sends me face-first into the floor or tries to spook the crap out of me." Kibo grumbled as he looked up at the wall. He watched as the symbols etched across the seal slowly disappeared. The gray seal the last to fade away, and with its disappearance, the walls slowly retracted into the ground, revealing a sea of artifacts and ancient treasures inside.

He gazed around at the massive stockpiles of artifacts. Old blades and armor were scattered on the floor, with several strange runes glowing through the dust that covered them. He walked by many broken bits of stone, each with its own unique enchantments carved into them. A little further, Kibo saw weapons that had the general shape and appearance of that of a firearm, but they seemed so bizarre and advanced that they could not have been crafted by human beings.

At long last, Kibo made it to the very end of the hallway, standing before a small open entrance to a room. Kibo stopped before the entrance and took a look into the room.

"Let's hope the damn exit to this place is here."

At first, the room seemed no different than the hallway before it, containing the same piles of artifacts, ancient weaponry, and tools scattered about. That is, other than the giant mural etched across the far side of the room. Upon the mural were hundreds of carvings depicting several different events and figures across it. One displayed human fighting demons, and another showed an angel bestowing power to three figures. Then another of those same three figures fighting amongst themselves. Just like the figures from his vision.

It all made sense now.

Wait a second, this mural, that vision, it must be the three mages, the first magic users to ever exist. He glanced over at the part where the three fought—or rather, where one fought against the others. *And that must be the Arcane Schism, when Ignis fought against his companions.*

But for the bits of the mural he understood, there were many more images that he couldn't piece together. *But those demons, I don't remember ever reading anything about a war between them and mankind. And that angel, was he the teacher of the mages? God, what could this mean?*

All the carvings, these long-lost events and images, led to one giant carved symbol in the very center of the mural: a massive triangle.

Kibo just stared at it, bewildered. It was all so strange. He scanned the room for clues but saw nothing. The walls had no answers. The marks underneath each engraving were in the same incomprehensible scrawl from earlier. The ancient tablets and broken artifacts scattered around the floor were no different.

But then something else caught his eye.

An ancient sword, gleaming with blue light.

It stood atop a particularly massive pile of relics and rubble, its glowing blade engraved with strange runes, its hilt made of pure gold, encrusted with several bright jewels.

But the most noticeable part of the blade was the glowing blue triangle on the hilt, the same one he had seen on the massive mural and in his visions.

"This has to be it!"

Kibo clambered up the pile, the rubble under his feet falling as he got closer and closer to the blade. Its light grew brighter with each step he took up the mountain of relics. Kibo started to feel something he hadn't for a long time. Pure, unadulterated hope.

It had to be something powerful.

His thoughts ran wild. Those hours wasted training, humiliation at the hands of Siris. Finally, his days of being helpless were over. He could possess the power that fate had unjustly stolen from him.

Kibo grabbed the sword and, with all his might and vigor, ripped it from its resting place.

Crack

The blade broke in half. Its once-bright glow faded instantly. He had, perhaps, pulled it a little too mightily. Kibo stood there, face completely frozen, unable to comprehend what had just happened.

Then it all came crashing down on him.

"Shit, shit, *SHIT*!" Kibo frantically dug through the pile of artifacts, searching for some way to fix his mistake, to not let his one chance at a future slip away from him.

He dug deeper but found only shattered relics and rusted artifacts. The deeper he went, the heavier his heart became. There was no way to fix it. His golden opportunity was taken from him.

"Just a little bit more. Please..."

His hand brushed against something strange. It was not like the other relics. They all felt dead, rusted, drained of all power and life from the passage of time. But this relic? It felt warm and alive, beating rhythmic like a robotic heart. Kibo's eyes widened.

Like a blood-starved tick, the object quickly latched onto Kibo, digging itself into the palm of his hand. Kibo staggered back in pain, opening his mouth to scream, but couldn't make a single sound. His entire body started to slowly shut down, and he lost all sense of control as visions flashed before him yet again.

He saw a strange being forging a machine. Then a different figure standing atop the massive fortress in the middle of the sea. Three large rooms, filled with runes and machinery. As these images flashed through his mind, Kibo saw a small object growing ever so slightly in the center of all this commotion. It was the same symbol he saw all over the vault: a bright blue triangle. It grew larger and larger and larger until it had eclipsed everything in its blinding light as it shone with the might of a star.

Then, it vanished, fading into the deepest recesses of his mind, taking with it Kibo's consciousness.

CHAPTER 2

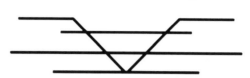

"Ugh, my head..."

"Sorry, master, my calculations underestimated the shock the integration process would have on you."

"Huh?" Kibo shook his head. What was that?

He looked around, searching for the source of the voice. But he saw nothing, not a single soul.

"Must've been my imagination." Kibo patted himself down before feeling something weird in his right hand. Something had nested itself into his skin, pulsing every few seconds. He slowly turned his hand and saw a small blue triangle, right in the middle of his palm.

"What the hell?" Kibo reached for the strange device. Its edges were made of a polished metal that was incredibly smooth and warm. A small, blue triangle glowed softly at its center. As Kibo yanked at it, a sharp spike of pain pierced his body, sending him crumbling to the ground in agony.

"ARGHHH!"

"I have become a part of your body, master. You can't pull me out, as the process would deliver a lethal amount of shock and would lead to your carbon-based body disintegrating into ash."

Kibo looked at the triangle, eyes widening as the situation slowly washed over him. "Wait a minute, are you speaking to me?"

"Affirmative, I am communicating to you through your mind, as I have become integrated with your body."

"Huh, so what exactly are you? Like do you have a name?" Kibo asked him, trying his best to understand the triangle.

"Yes, I do. My designation from my creator was 'Arcanus.' I am a combat analysis and assistant Artificial Intelligence."

"Wait, wait, wait. You're a *what*?" Kibo asked, still utterly confused. He expected some overly complex and confusing answers but instead heard a long, drawn-out sigh.

"Well, there goes my first impression. Okay, how can I explain this to a simple fleshy being like you?" Arcanus paused, trying to simplify his explanation. *"Are you familiar with what a robot or golem is?"*

Kibo stood quietly for a moment, surprised by Arcanus' sudden shift in tone. "Yeah... I've seen a few golems in the city from time to time," Kibo exclaimed. The same look of confusion washed over his face yet again. "But what does that have to do with you? I mean, you don't have any sort of body or shape. And you've dug yourself into my body, leeching off of me like a parasite if I'm going to be—"

ZAP

"OW! What was that?"

"I decided to administer a little shock to your system."

"A little? Felt like I got hit by a bolt of—"

ZAP

"OW, OW, OW! Okay, I'll shut up!" Kibo relented.

"I'm simply the frame, nothing more than the computational components and inner machinations of a robot. I mean, other than my occasional 'discipline,' I can't do jack," the blue triangle replied. *"But, with your help, the two of us can work together and truly become something great."*

"And how exactly are you going to do that? By turning me into a golem?" Kibo asked the machine.

"No. It is a bit more complicated than that." Arcanus paused yet again. *"You will understand better once you press this part of me."* The blue triangle started to glow fiercely, blinding Kibo.

"AH! What are you trying to do, leave me blind or something?" Kibo exclaimed, blocking the massive flash of light irradiating from his right hand.

"No. I was indicating that you should press my core." Arcanus then whispered, *"Now, if you press my core, there is a probability that it will activate my combat mode."*

"A probability?" Kibo asked, somewhat skeptical of Arcanus.

"Well, there is a probability that combat mode might not activate or malfunction, leading to the disintegration of the user. But don't worry, there's only a ten, maybe twelve percent chance of that happening."

Kibo broke out into a cold sweat as he looked down at the triangle in his right hand, a strange mixture of anxiety and relief filled him.

"You're telling me that just touching this thing can kill me? What's the point of making something for combat if you can die just by trying to use it? Only a complete idiot would use something like this, you stupid AI, robot thing!"

"Look, I tried my best to remain professional, but all you've done since you woke me up is complain and yell at me." Arcanus sighed.

"Wait, that was you being professional?"

If Arcanus had eyes, it would certainly be rolling them. *"This cave system has no food, a meager amount of water. I'd give you about a month before you suffer a horrible death from starvation. I bet having a chance of dying a quick and painless death would be easier than a slow and agonizing one, wouldn't it?"*

"Well, if it means being stuck with an annoying little robot for the rest of my life..."

"You know, I can read your thoughts, you stupid flesh golem!" Arcanus flashed intensely, sending another powerful shock through Kibo's body.

"Ow! You've made your point, I guess." Kibo sat up. "Just let me think about it."

Arcanus seemed relieved, glowing more softly. *"Take your time."*

"Hmm, pros and cons, pros and cons..." Kibo scratched his chin. "Pros: I get super cool powers and you can help me get out of here. Pretty good. The cons are... I have a chance of dying no matter what I do." Kibo kicked the dirt and watched the dust settle. He looked at Arcanus' core, furrowing his brow. "Fate gave this to me, another chance to overcome my weakness and become something great—without even using magic. More importantly, think of all the money, fame, and power I would get!"

"Yeah! It'll be pretty damn cool, won't it?" Arcanus exclaimed.

"Yeah, yeah, it would be pretty cool," Kibo said, trailing off back into his thoughts. *But all I can think about is father.*

"That doesn't seem to be what you care about. Am I right, kid?"

Kibo looked down at Arcanus for a moment and sighed. "There's someone I used to look up to all the time as a kid. He used to tell me every day, 'Don't worry, Kibo, one day you'll be the greatest mage out there, no matter how tough it looks now. You'll always make it through,'" Kibo recited, holding out his fist in triumph with a little chuckle. "He would always do that too, kind of to pump me up as well."

"What happened?"

"He disappeared." Kibo let out a shaky sigh. "Everyone keeps telling me that he's gone or that he died, god knows where. But I know that he's still out there, god damnit!" Kibo leaped to his feet. "And I promised myself that I would find him, even if I had to turn over every stone to find him!"

"That's the spirit, kid! Now let's get out of here and find him."

"Yeah, you're right! You know what?" Kibo looked down at Arcanus' core and smiled. "If I'm gonna die here anyway, I might as well take some risk." Kibo slammed his feet into the earth and stuck his hand in the air. Finally, he would call upon the power which he had lacked for so many years. He would achieve what he had strived for.

"Arcanus, come forth!"

Nothing happened.

"Um, I can't just transform on command, Kibo. You have to press my core to activate me." Arcanus sighed. *"And stop with that goofy pose. Thank god you did it here at least."*

Kibo blushed. "Oh, um, sorry about that. It's something I remember hearing about on a radio show as a kid and wanted to give it a try for fun. Thought it'd be funny but, uh, I'll just press it now. Here goes nothing." He pushed the core with a satisfying *click.*

A sudden burst of heat flowed through his body; it was like the playful shock from earlier, only subtler and gentler. Something slowly formed around his hand. As it did, however, the energy seemed to grow more intense. Kibo felt as though his body was about to explode.

Fwoosh.

The energy coursing through him faded and everything around him was silent once again. Everything seemed more or less normal. Kibo opened his eyes and looked at himself. His head was normal, legs were normal. Left hand normal, right hand...not so much.

Covering it was a strange metal gauntlet made of polished gray metal similar to the vault, but segmented and free of the symbols and runes that littered the walls and floors. From within the segments, a faint blue light glowed. Kibo turned his hand ever so slightly, taking in every single bit of detail. It seemed so intricate, beautiful in its alien way.

"Whoa, this thing is so freaking cool!" Kibo made a firm fist with his gauntlet and threw out a few punches. "What can I do with this thing? Can I use magic spells? Shoot laser beams? Oh, does it transform into a blade or some kind of weapon?"

"You can punch hard," Arcanus said in the most indifferent tone possible.

"You're telling me about an *alien* machine like you can only create a gauntlet that can punch hard?" Kibo sighed and sat down on the floor shaking his head. "What's the point? How could I get out of this damn death trap with just a metal glove?"

The gauntlet glowed intensely. *"Let me explain to an ungrateful little shit like you that I have been inactive for thousands of years. It takes time to recalibrate myself and bring out my full form."* Arcanus fumed, done with Kibo's complaints. *"The best way for me to gather the data—and the only way to do that—is by training with you. Besides, did you think you were gonna get out of here with any of this?"* Arcanus pointed out.

Kibo looked down at the mess of broken relics, weapons, and rusted parts.

"Huh, I guess you're right." Kibo looked down at the pile of broken equipment sheepishly. "So, the only way you can reach your full form or whatever is by constantly using you?"

"Yes," Arcanus replied. *"The more pressure you are under, the better. It is a simple sample and data gathering procedure."*

"Guess I'm gonna have to earn this, huh?" Kibo looked down at the gauntlet and shook his head. "Okay fine, just tell me how to get out of here already."

"All right." Arcanus said. *"I'm guessing you have the key ready for the door."*

"Uh, what key?"

"You know, the sword-looking relic with the glowing symbol on the hilt?"

"Oh." Kibo scratched his head nervously. "About that..."

"Don't tell me you broke the damn thing."

"It was an accident! I didn't think it would break so easily."

"Why, you little shit! Do you know what the hell you've done? Now you can't unlock the vault and get out!"

Kibo winced and expected another shock. Thankfully, it didn't materialize. He gulped and asked, "Is there another way out? There's gotta be. If whoever made this place can make a snarky robot, then I'm sure they can make a second exit or two."

"I am very close to jolting you, kid. Very. Close," Arcanus growled. Fortunately for Kibo, its tone changed to a chirp of pride. *"Lucky for you, reconnaissance and assistance are my fields of expertise, so finding the exit to this place is no sweat for an advanced AI like me."*

The symbol gleamed brightly and let out a loud ping. Within a few seconds, to Kibo's surprise, Arcanus suddenly spoke in a booming voice.

"About 300 meters to your left, you will find a small crack that will lead you to the surface." Arcanus paused for a moment, before stating in the smuggest tone possible, *"But, what'd you expect from the world's greatest AI?"*

"Wow, that was fast!"

"Kibo, you're a fleshy animal who couldn't comprehend even one percent of the simplest of calculations I do, and frankly, I think it'd be better for the two of us if you just listen to what I'm saying and get on with it."

Kibo rolled his eyes and started to walk toward the left. After passing several more piles of rubble and broken artifacts, he found himself in front of the largest pile yet.

"So where do I go now?"

"It is right ahead of you."

"Right ahead of me? But there's just a giant pile of junk in front of me." Kibo stared at the ancient artifacts closely, attempting to see what exactly he was missing. While at first, it looked rather unassuming, Kibo suddenly noticed what Arcanus was alluding to. "This mound of junk is inside the wall!" Kibo looked at the top of the rubble, where a tiny sliver indicated the entrance to another room. "I'm guessing you want me to scale up this thing?"

"*Correct.*"

Kibo examined the pile for footholds as he carefully scaled it. He heard the crunch and crinkling of broken objects beneath his feet as he got closer and closer to the gap, eventually reaching the small opening that was at the very top of the mound of rubble. He crawled through, then slid down the other side until he reached the bottom, ready to move forward once again.

However, Kibo hesitated for a moment, rooted in place. He felt a slight pang of fear as he looked at the place Arcanus brought him. It was abandoned and rusted over, far from the immaculate and well-kept rooms from before. The only reason he was able to see the extent of wear and tear was because of the faint flickering lights that lined the walls, constantly sputtering on and off, as if they were moments away from dying.

"*What's wrong?*"

Kibo suddenly snapped back to reality as Arcanus spoke up.

"Oh, uh, it's nothing," Kibo stuttered, heading off into the decrepit, ruined hallway.

As he walked through the abandoned hall, Kibo looked up and down the wall they were passing by, wondering, "*Man, who made all of this?*"

"*My creator.*"

"Wait, what? You mean you know the guy who made all this?" Kibo looked down at the glowing triangle.

"*Yeah, that bastard created this underground prison, then thought it'd be a fantastic idea if he left me buried here,*" Arcanus grumbled.

"Doesn't sound like you like him that much."

"*Oh yeah, I'll just be smitten with the guy who dropped me into a sealed vault for who knows how long,*" Arcanus said sarcastically.

"I couldn't stand being here for longer than a moment. Can't imagine being stuck here for however long you've been here." Kibo chuckled for a little bit, before turning back to his initial question,

"But do you remember who exactly made all this?"

"*Of course I do!*" Arcanus replied smugly. "*It was...*" Arcanus paused for a moment. "*Wait a moment, it's on the tip of my damn tongue. I know who it was, I remembered it like yesterday. I-I...*" The bright blue glow from the triangle slowly faded as Arcanus abruptly disappeared, leaving Kibo alone with his thoughts, waiting for Arcanus to return with his answer.

A minute passed.

Nothing.

Then five.

Nothing.

"Uh, Arcanus? You—"

"*I can't! I-I...*" Arcanus yelled, a clear frustration in his voice. "*I can't remember.*"

"Wait, you forgot who made you?" Kibo said, perplexed.

"*No, it's not that. I-it's like I can't access it.*" Arcanus trailed off for a moment. "*No, that's not it, I can't access anything!*" Arcanus started to flicker on and off rapidly, in what seemed to be his way of panicking. "*No, no, no! This can't be happening. How is this possible? Historical archives: corrupted. Schematics and blueprints: corrupted. Advanced computing systems: inaccessible?*" Kibo could hear the sheer panic in Arcanus' voice. "*What am I? What am I—*"

Kibo needed to do something. "Calm down, Arcanus," he said, doing his best to make his voice as still and calm as he could make it.

"*What do you mean, calm down? I can't access more than seventy-eight percent of my basic functions. How could I possibly be calm when almost all of my systems have been corrupted in some kind of way?*" Arcanus asked.

Kibo paused for a moment, thinking about what exactly he could say to soothe Arcanus' panic. "Listen, I know that you're panicking really badly right now because you can't access your memories. But right now the two of us have bigger things to worry about, such as getting out of here." After another short pause, he added, "And I promise you as you promised me, I'll do my best to help fix you." Kibo looked down at Arcanus, hoping that his words had calmed down the machine.

Arcanus did not respond, only glowed faintly in the dimly lit hallway, as if he were mulling over what Kibo had told him.

"So, what do you say, huh?"

"*Oh, all right, kid. I'll calm down. But, I am holding you to your word,*" Arcanus grumbled, to which Kibo laughed.

"Don't worry. Once we're out of here, I'll get you back in tip-top shape."

"All righty then, what are ya waiting for? Let's get the hell out of this damn prison." Arcanus' voice was full of excitement and energy, ready to finally escape the vault that held him for over a millennium.

Kibo smiled and turned towards their escape route. He sprinted with all his might, pushing his muscles to the point where they were on fire. He felt a rush of excitement, and more importantly hope, flowed through him.

Hope that he would not be held back by his inability to utilize magic, that he could finally match those who were ready to serve for the good of humanity. What seemed to him like a pipe dream was now a possibility, something that was now tangible. He had to only reach and—

It was a dead end. A large cavern wall with no exit in sight. "Wait, I thought you told me this was the exit, not a dead end."

"What do you mean, dead end? The exit's right in front of us," Arcanus exclaimed.

"Huh? Wha— Oh."

A thin crack ran straight through the far-left side of the wall, with an even thinner beam of light streaming from it. There was no way he could fit through it.

And he tried, to no avail. No matter how much pressure he applied, it was nigh impossible for him to push through.

"Damn it!" Kibo let out a frustrated sigh. The beam of light seemed to taunt him, to show just how close he was to breaking through, only to cut him completely off from freedom.

Then Kibo noticed something interesting about the wall. Could it be? "Wait a second..." Kibo got up close to the wall and gave it a few small taps.

Tap, tap, tap.

It sounded incredibly thin, almost hollow in fact. Kibo gazed up and down the wall and then back down at his fist. He knew what to do.

"Think you could break through this wall, Arcanus?" Kibo asked the machine.

"Of course! This gauntlet is made of the purest Sanoium in the world. It'll break through anything, no sweat."

"Well then, here goes nothing."

Kibo took a deep breath and stepped back. He drew back his armored hand and felt a sudden surge of power rush through his arm as he launched forward, smashing the cracked wall in one swift swing. The wall exploded into several tiny bits with a resounding boom.

"Whoa..." Kibo stared in awe at the massive gaping hole he had created, then back down at his armored fist. "Damn, this thing is something else, huh?"

"What do you expect? A few paper-thin walls are nothing compared to my superior design."

"Heh, guess you're right," Kibo said with a slight smile, staring out into the light that came flooding in from the hole.

"Are you ready to get out of here?"

"You bet I am!" Kibo stepped out into the light.

It took him a moment to adjust to the sudden beam of light blasting in from above. He was at the bottom of an old well. It appeared to be abandoned for decades. Kibo drifted his hand across the moss-ridden walls, weaving his fingers through the cracks on the stone. Beneath his feet was a murky and dreary puddle, dwelling miserably in the ruins of its once pristine well. Finally, after what felt like an eternity, Kibo looked up and saw it—a circle of beautiful blue sky.

"Heh, I can already tell what I gotta do to get myself out of this mess. Looks like this is gonna take a while." Kibo grunted as he did a few small arm stretches. He took one long look at the vast walls of the well, trying to come up with the best route to climb up.

"I recommend taking the path up to your right." Kibo heard Arcanus in his head. He turned to look to his right and saw exactly what Arcanus meant. Nearly the entire right side of the well was covered in large, deep cracks that went all the way to the very top of the well.

"It's pretty nice having a guide around, even if they can be a bit annoy—"

ZAP

"Ow! Okay, okay, I'll get on with it." Kibo looked begrudgingly at the triangle in his hand, which was glowing quite fiercely. And it would not take a genius to realize that probably was not something pleasant.

After taking one deep breath, Kibo burrowed his hand into the large crack in the wall and started to slowly climb his way up. Slipping his feet and left hand into the large cracks, he would use his right hand to widen or create larger cracks with the gauntlet. With every step he took higher, Kibo felt more and more anxious, his body heavier with every step.

Upon climbing halfway through the well, however, Kibo's right foot landed on something wet and weak. Although it felt stable at first, the crack in which he had shoved his foot broke apart, almost sending Kibo falling to the bottom of the pit.

"Whoa, whoa, whoa, kid. Watch where you're climbing. You gotta be calm and cautious. One mistake and you'll be rubbing your butt sorely in five seconds flat," Arcanus warned him.

"I know, I know," Kibo snapped back. His entire body was drenched in sweat, his heart pounding against his ribcage from the sheer amount of dread that had built up in his body.

Letting out one panicked sigh, Kibo put his foot back in place and started to climb once again. He grit his teeth, his limbs straining as his body burned like it was on fire. But he could not stop now, not when he was this close.

He kept telling himself, that only a few more steps and he'd be out, if he just went slow and steady, he'd be there. But those thoughts slowly disappeared into the back of his head as he stood just centimeters away from the top. Seeing his freedom so tantalizingly close, Kibo abandoned reason and caution for just a single moment as he thrust his entire gauntlet into the wall, trying to launch himself out in one reckless move.

CRACK

A massive chunk of the wall suddenly collapsed, sending Kibo back towards the earth. As he fell, Kibo watched in horror as the comforting blue circle grew smaller. He was centimeters away from freedom and he blew it.

"God damn it!" Kibo rubbed his head. His entire body ached; his legs, in particular, felt as if they were screaming from the pain. Yet despite all the pain, none of it compared to the sheer anger he felt.

"You dumbass! What did I tell you? You had to take it slow or stupid shit like this would happen. God, how the hell did I get stuck with an impatient brat like you." Arcanus flared up, yelling at Kibo.

Yet, Kibo did not even look down at Arcanus, only staring up at the wall, a look of pure determination and anger burning in his eyes.

"I won't forsake this chance you've given me," Kibo stated in a grave tone, as though nothing else mattered to him. "And I sure as hell don't plan on dying in this ditch, not while I've been given a miracle like this." Kibo turned down his gaze back to Arcanus and tightened his fist. "I ain't gonna rot away as some nobody."

Kibo brought up his right hand and burrowed it into the wall as securely as he could, starting the climb up the well once again. With Arcanus just watching him, dumbstruck.

Kibo seemed like nothing more than an average juvenile human male, simple and timid. But that look of sheer determination was unlike anything Arcanus had ever encountered. It made Arcanus think.

"Hey, kid."

"What," Kibo said bluntly, not even glancing at Arcanus, his focus still squarely on the long and cracked wall before him.

"About the stuff, I said before about you being an impatient brat and all that—"

"You didn't mean it?"

"Oh, uh, well yeah," Arcanus said awkwardly.

"Yeah, I know," Kibo said. "We all get a bit angry sometimes, even advanced, powerful machines like you," Kibo added with a little devilish smirk. "But we don't always mean the things we say." He paused for a moment to think. "Hell, what you said isn't even close to half the shit that people say to me sometimes."

"That's good to hear," Arcanus said, flickering softly. *"You should probably focus on climbing out of- Wait! Watch out for that brick!"* a giant rotted brick fell out of the wall, narrowly missing Kibo.

"Whoa, that was a close one, thanks!"

"Yeah, no problem."

For a while, the two of them stayed quiet, climbing closer and closer to the top of the well. Despite his sense of determination from earlier, Kibo felt himself getting anxious like before. But this time, he was determined to reach the top. With each foothold he managed to clear, he became ever more focused on his goal. Eventually, the edge of the well was just a few centimeters above him, and he reached up without hesitation.

But in that moment of carelessness, Kibo committed the same tragic mistake.

"JESUS!" Kibo yelled, digging further into the wall with his gauntlet. He grabbed another weakened section of the wall, and it all just fell apart. Both of his legs and right hand were now just dangling in the air, Kibo barely able to cling on with his gauntlet.

"*Why did you rush like that again? Now look what you—*"

"I know what I did! I don't need you telling me about it again," Kibo snapped. The anger and shame Kibo felt were not for Arcanus, but for himself. How could he say all that and then just go and do the same thing again?

But he was not going to give up. He was an inch away from freedom, and he sure as hell was not going to let go.

"I've climbed all this damn way, and I'm not gonna fall back to the bottom again." Kibo felt a surge of adrenaline rush through his veins. He raised his left hand and looked around until he found another crack in his range. And then, with all his might, he dug deep into the stone wall, launching a thick cloud of dust into the air that sent him into one major coughing fit.

"What the..."

As the dust settled, he saw a faint blue light flickered through.

Another brilliant metallic gauntlet formed around Kibo's hand, glowing fiercely through the cloud of dust.

Before Kibo could even process what was happening, Arcanus started to flicker rapidly. "*It's happening already.*"

"What is?"

"*Just now, you were at your limit, emotionally speaking, giving me a boost of strength that allowed me to form another portion of my full power,*" Arcanus exclaimed. "*I'm amazed that you had enough strength to release another part of me, and just a few hours after merging with me, too.*" The gauntlets flashed brightly. "*Color me impressed, kid.*"

"Really?" Kibo exclaimed. But rather than dwell on it any longer, Kibo decided to get out of the well before he fell for good this time.

Kibo clambered toward the top once again, this time making sure he grabbed onto a stable handhold and, for the final time, pulled himself forward.

He landed face-first in the cold dirt, having underestimated his strength. But despite planting his face right into the ground, he started laughing. Watching the rising morning sun and breathing in the clean, fresh air, he felt so liberated. Just looking up at the bright blue sky, he could not help but admire how pretty it was.

He was free, in more ways than one.

"Well, what now, kid?" Arcanus asked.

With a big goofy smile plastered across his face, Kibo answered the machine, "To become legends."

"Man, you are embarrassing."

CHAPTER 3

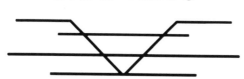

July 20th, 1966, Today was the day: the entrance exam. He sat up, thoughts rushing through his head about the crazy stuff that happened before and what was going to happen today. Arcanus, exam day, Siris, his dreams. Kibo slammed his head into the pillow and sighed. Today was the day.

Kibo heard familiar humming and looked at the sigil in his hand. *"Look, I know you're excited and all, but your sorry ass is going to be late for the exam."* Arcanus said.

His heart pounded as he jumped up from his bed, rushing towards the bathroom. Quickly, he washed his hair and face and scrambled into his clothes. From the kitchen, the smell of food warmed up his soul and stomach.

Hearing his footsteps, his mother smiled warmly. "How's my wonderful boy doing? I see you can hardly hold in your excitement for today. Here, eat up your breakfast before you set off."

Kibo looked at his mom's kind smile and the steaming, yellow omelet in front of him and grinned. He quickly reached for his seat and began wolfing down his breakfast.

His mother chuckled. He looked like a stray dog dumpster diving. She soon joined him in eating. Although no words were traded during breakfast, there was that familiar, comfortable feeling. But that feeling slowly eroded as she eyed the sigil on Kibo's hand. It was suspicious how he suddenly had gained such power, but having married a mage, she'd come to accept the absurdity of magic.

"When life gives you lemons, right?" she thought. *"Still..."*

It had been nearly two days since she had seen him. She'd asked everyone if they knew where her boy was, yet no one—not even that stuck-up noble girl—knew where he could have been. She could feel her anxiety grow with each passing hour, worrying about what could have possibly happened to her son.

Where had her Kibo gone? It was far too unusual for him to have just gone somewhere without telling her.

She could wait no longer. At around nine in the morning, she rushed towards the phone in the living room to phone the police, past their faded blue couches and coffee table towards the desk in the corner.

But, before she could even pick up the phone, she heard a loud *bang* come from the front door. She turned around and stared at who had just entered with a look of both relief and shock.

It was the ragged form of her son, holding onto the door, gasping for air. His clothes were covered in muck and holes. There were bruises and cuts wherever his skin was visible. It seemed like he had gone through a war and back.

"Kibo! My sweet, sweet boy." She rushed towards her son, grabbing a hold of him with all her might. "You made your poor mother sick. Oh my god, look at your clothes. They're a complete mess. Where have you been?"

"I'm all right, mom! There's nothing you have to worry about." Kibo slid out of his mother's grasp. "Everything is going to be much better for us."

"Better? What do you mean? What happened?"

"Because of this thing right here." Kibo lifted his palm and showed her what exactly he was referring to. Dug deep into his palm was a brilliant blue triangle, glowing brightly in the darkness of the room.

"What is that thing?" she asked, taken back from the alien thing embedded into her son's hand, like a parasite feeding off its host.

"It-it's complicated." Kibo paced back and forth in the living room. "But I'm finally going to be like all other kids. I can finally follow dad's footsteps and become a great mage," Kibo said, barely able to contain his excitement. "I can't wait for the test next month."

Yet, she did not hear a single word coming from Kibo's mouth. All she could see was the deranged, almost primal look on her son's face. And the most unnerving part? The crazed smile stretching his lips.

"Well, I'm heading off to my room." She snapped back to reality as Kibo started toward his room.

"Wait, Kibo." She ran after him. "I know you must be exhausted right now, but at least clean off all that muck on your body first. And your clothes, oh, that shirt was a gift from your grandmother."

Eventually, she managed to get Kibo to take a shower and throw out all of his dirty clothes. But one thing remained seared into her mind during all that time. That glowing triangle.

It wasn't long before every last morsel of breakfast was finished and the two started to head out. Kibo got up from the table and grabbed a small bag holding the supplies for his test, while his mother grabbed her car keys. The two got into their old sedan, driving towards the testing center, located by a nearby Bastion headquarters.

I would head there all the time. Never thought I would be heading to the exam facility for real this time, Kibo thought to himself. *To think I was lucky enough to have the exam this year be located in not only Russia but also be this close to my home.* Looking up at the highway sign, only five miles away now, he listened to the calming tunes playing on the radio and his mind started to wander.

As such, it wasn't long before his mind drifted towards the extremes, swarmed with possibilities of what could happen today. What if he failed? What if Siris was there? What if Siris made him fail? He gripped the edge of his seat hard enough that his fingers dug into the leather seat. The highway ahead appeared more and more sinister with every passing minute.

Fortunately, his mother noticed his unease. "You remember Old Man Sergei?"

"Sergei?" Kibo asked, shaking his head. "What crazy adventure has he got himself into this time?"

They both chuckled.

"Well, he was arrested for the fourth time this month for drinking and driving."

"That's not surprising. Shouldn't he be in jail by now?"

"True, if he wasn't the *dedushka* of the local chief of police. But that's not the funny part," she said, smiling. "He started to kick the policeman—you know Mikael, right—in the groin. The poor man was on his knees crying. Even the police chief had to reprimand Sergei!"

"That's horrible!" The two broke out into a laughing fit for at least a minute. Kibo swore that he heard Arcanus snicker too.

Old Man Sergei was a local legend thanks to his shenanigans. It seemed as if he was doing something crazy or unimaginable every other day.

Their laughter eventually died down into a comfortable silence save for the faint classical radio. Kibo glanced down and brushed the sigil on his palm. Even though he had looked at it hundreds of times, he still was in awe of its immaculate design. It seemed so elegant and beautiful, the soft glow radiating from its center both soothing and calming to watch.

His mother suddenly broke the silence. "The test is all that people are talking about, you know. Even a town drunkard like Sergei was talking about the exam."

"That's saying something, huh?" Kibo chuckled nervously.

"Indeed. No pressure, but the spotlight is on you." She tried not to frown but failed. "And a lot of other people. The government and even the global news reported record numbers of recruitment. This could be very competitive and dangerous, you know?"

Kibo looked back at his mother and beamed. "I know. I'm ready to tackle this thing," he said with full confidence, slamming his fist into his palm.

She felt her heart beat faster. *That pure idealism.* She couldn't hold herself back any longer.

"Kibo, I have to tell you something."

"What?" Kibo raised an eyebrow.

"I will always let you follow your dreams, no matter what." She tried to keep her focus on the road. "But every time I saw you work harder and harder at magic and fail, I would..." She stopped herself, almost unable to say what was on her mind. "Oh, I can't believe I'm saying this, but I would feel relieved." Her voice cracked slightly. She felt tears starting to well up in her eyes as she continued. "I-I know this sounds very selfish of me, but I don't want the same thing that happened to your father to happen to you." She braked and swerved to the shoulder of the road. She lay against the steering wheel, her tears flowing down the wheel. "I don't want to lose the most precious thing in my life. Please don't leave me. I don't want to lose you. I don't—"

"I won't."

She turned her head upwards towards him. "What?"

Kibo looked into his mother's sorrow-filled eyes and his heart tensed up. Tears came into his own eyes too. It was hard watching his mother cry, but he knew he had to do it.

"I promise you that I'll come back here. Not as a stronger person," Kibo smiled and held his mother's hand, "but with father. You and I know that he wouldn't die so easily, not my father. I can swear that on my heart."

Kibo's mother saw the look of determination in her son's eyes. "You have that same fire as your father. I don't know why I even tried, because I know that nothing will stop that stubborn side of you from reaching your goal," she whispered to him. "Just like your father."

"I love you, son," she whispered, hugging Kibo tightly.

"I-I love you, too." Kibo felt tears stream down his cheeks. It was the last time he would be with his mother for a long time.

Kibo rushed towards the Bastion facility, pumped up with excitement. The massive fortress stood out next to the comparatively small Bastion office that had been there beforehand, despite its construction having begun only a few months prior. Its high walls were made of glossy, white concrete that gleamed in the sun. Its enormous black gates looked as though they could take a wave of artillery before being even slightly dented. Its symbol, a silver heater shield, hung right above the gate. A huge crowd of examinees, onlookers, and some reporters crowded the entrance, barely held back by a platoon of Bastion soldiers. It took a few minutes for Kibo to squeeze through the huge mob to the entry stand.

"Name, ID, and papers, please," the entry guard stated bluntly, holding out his hand for Kibo's documents.

"Kibo Kozlov, age 18." he stated bluntly as he presented his ID and papers. The guard went over his ID and papers, looking over and checking every detail he could, taking occasional glances from the ID to Kibo's face to confirm his identity.

"Kibo, huh? That is a strange name you've got here."

"Oh, I was named after one of my dad's friends, they were in the same squadron in Bastion," Kibo responded quickly, caught off guard by the question.

"I see. Like father, like son, go figure." The guard nodded before folding all of Kibo's papers and ID. "Here you go. Welcome to Bastion, kid. Be sure to check your paper for which testing room you'll be heading off to."

"Wait, I can go in?" Kibo asked as if he couldn't believe the words that came out of the guard's mouth.

"Yes. Now head on in before you hold the line any longer," the guard barked, to which Kibo obliged gleefully.

As he stepped into the faculty's courtyard, he looked around with a goofy little smile and let out one big, long sigh.

He was finally here.

The other recruits were just like him: young, vigorous, and eager to prove their worth to the world. It was a strangely comforting scene, one where he and the others all shared something in common.

But he also felt isolated. He saw no familiar faces, no one to ask or talk to about the upcoming exam. He was surrounded on all fronts by a horde of examinees rushing past him like he was not even there. Despite being among so many people, he still felt the same as he always did, alone.

Smack!

A hand slapped down on his shoulders, violently snapping Kibo out from his trance. "Ow! What was that for?" He turned around to see who the culprit was and found himself face to face with a smug-looking boy. He looked to be about the same age as Kibo, only slightly shorter. He had dark, unkempt hair. He wore casual, if worn-out, clothes: slim jeans, a chore jacket, and a beaten pair of Chucks. Most curious of all was his rapid-fire voice.

"Hey man, ya were in a little daydream, so I decided to give ya a wake-up call. Nothing else to it." he said, a smug, annoying grin on his face. "Ya wouldn't want to miss the test 'cause you were too busy staring at nothing." Then he leaned in closer and whispered casually, "But, to be fair, I can't blame yah. The gals here are pretty hot, y'know?"

"Gals? I wouldn't do something like *that*." Kibo said sheepishly, his face bright red.

"Hey, hey, I'm just joking, man!" He smacked Kibo's shoulder again. "Let's go before we're late for this test!"

The boy waved over to him. Though slightly annoyed by his antics, Kibo followed him anyway, rushing toward the central Bastion building.

On their way there, the boy asked him, "By the way, dude, what's your name? Don't always wanna end up calling you 'dude.' That would be sort of weird."

"Oh, my name's Kibo. What's yours?" Kibo asked, relieved by the simple question.

He pointed at himself with his thumb and smirked. "The name's Rex. Ya can just call me Rex."

Kibo just rolled his eyes and continued with him towards the entrance. However, he was a bit more curious about his companion. "Rex, huh. Where exactly are you from?"

"Me? I'm from Italia! How about ya?"

"Italia? Don't they speak a completely different language from ya?" Arcanus asked Kibo.

Yeah, he does. Must be some sort of magic over this place. Probably some kind of translation magic that lets us talk to each other, Kibo replied, before turning back to Rex.

"Oh, I'm actually from nearby. Russian from the day I was born."

They eventually reached the front door of the building. Two Bastion guards stood silently at either side of the gate, keeping guard over the door. This was the real deal. Rex quickly rushed through the doors without a second thought, leaving Kibo in the dust.

"Hey, wait up," Kibo muttered under his breath. *This guy...*

All right, Kibo, you're finally here. Kibo reached for the door and gripped it tightly, then he let out a quiet exhale. Despite being so much smaller than the entrance to the facility, they seemed to stand far taller than the gates behind him.

"Well, what are you waiting for? Head on already," Arcanus exclaimed. Kibo chuckled, letting out one last breath before opening the door and stepping forward into the unknown.

He stood in a massive hall, its walls covered in pure, white marble, with dozens of massive gold pillars supporting the arched ceiling. Hundreds of applicants rushed towards their respective testing rooms, which were labeled with giant letters.

Kibo looked around for Rex, but he was nowhere to be found, as if he had been swallowed by the massive horde.

"Might as well go on without him. Let me check, which room was I going to again?" Kibo muttered as he pulled out the crumpled entrance paper he had stowed away in his small bag.

He read down the paper until he spotted it written in big bold letters: *Room F. Desk 34.*

Kibo looked at the giant buzzing swarm of examinees, wondering how he was going to cut through the crowd. There must have been at least a few hundred people rushing toward their exam room. They all seemed to have come from not only across the country, but from across the globe.

"All of these people are traveling thousands of kilometers to make it to this test facility, all while you live just a drive away," Arcanus mumbled to himself.

Yeah, what about it? My dad needed to be near some sort of Bastion facility to make easy contact with Bastion, so we kind of had to, Kibo snapped at Arcanus.

"Hey, I didn't mean to offend. Just kind of in awe of this place," Arcanus said. *"I didn't think you humans could progress so fast—from a bunch of stone huts to this."*

"We can talk about this stuff after I get through the test," Kibo said as he squeezed into the crowd and down the hall towards his exam room until he finally caught a glimpse of room F.

Kibo managed to reach the exam room just in time. "Ah, I was wondering where the last examinee was. We're just about to start," the proctor said as Kibo entered. "Please take a seat at your desk and get ready for the exam."

Kibo took a look around the exam room. It was full of other young applicants who were just like him: anxious and excited. Many of them were chatting about important topics and ideas, while others were reviewing their notes and papers as a last-second review. As Kibo took his seat, his thoughts flashed over all the test material in his head.

The proctor cleared his throat. "Remember to read everything and go over it carefully. Any form of cheating or talking with one another will lead to automatic disqualification. Those who pass this test will then be allowed to take the second part of the exam," the proctor said in the bored tone of someone who had repeated this speech several times. "Remember to fully

answer and complete as many problems during the time limit."
She held up a watch and waited for the class to fall completely
silent before saying. "Begin."

A massive flurry of papers and frenzied scribbling erupted in
the room. Kibo opened his exam booklet and took a quick look
at all of the questions. His eyes scanned the paper and his heart
sink as he went further and further down the questions.

He could not remember a single thing.

Crap, crap crap. I can't think!

*"Kid, calm down. Did you forget about me? You've got a
goddamn computer embedded in your body. I can answer any
questions you got,"* Arcanus smugly said to Kibo.

Kibo exhaled. Of course, he had Arcanus by his side. How
could he forget that? With him, this test was gonna be a piece of
cake.

Okay, so what's the answer to question 1? Kibo asked,
looking down at the exam with a cocky grin.

*"Uh yeah, I think I may have gotten a little overconfident
there,"* Arcanus said sheepishly. *"How should I say this?"*

"Your memory's still corrupted?

"My memory's still corrupted."

Kibo slowly laid his head on the table and rolled his eyes.
Why did I even think you'd be any help?

"Hey, I mean, I did get us out of that cave," Arcanus
retorted. *"And I don't think you're gonna need my help
anyway."*

Kibo looked perplexed for a moment at what Arcanus said,
mulling over what he had just told him.

And he laid there, thinking over it some more.

And some more.

And more.

"Hey, uh, kid. You know that you're in the middle of a—"

Kibo sat up in his seat, opened his eyes, and picked up his
pencil, filled with a renewed focus.

He looked at the first question and reread it. It was, as with
many starting questions, simple: *What are magical affinities?*

Kibo, now cleared of his anxiety and doubt, reread the
question and wrote: *Magical affinities, magical affinities.*
Kibo's mind started to drift, thinking back to a time when he
was far younger...

"Would anyone in the class like to answer?" a man asked several young children, pointing at a blackboard behind him. They all sat before him at small wooden desks, with most of them not much older than eight or nine years old. They all looked at the board behind the man, at the question scribbled into the board: *What are magical affinities?*

Many of the children stared at the question blankly while others fuddled with their notebooks and pencils, confused as to what the question even was. Some raised a hand but brought them down as quickly as they raised. Eventually, it seemed that only one child in the room knew the answer. It was a boy in the front, sitting just an arm's length from the board, his hand raised straight up in the air, with a bright smile that showed not a lick of doubt.

"Ah, looks like Kibo has the answer to this as well?" the man said with a playful smirk, almost as if he had already anticipated it.

"A-A magical affinity is the certain magic a person can use the best. And it can come from either their mom and dad or be completely random!"

"Correct again!"

There we go! That should be it! Kibo quickly jotted down his answer from memory.

"*That's it, kid. Come on, let's hit the next question.*" Arcanus encouraged Kibo, who eagerly flipped to the next.

Who was the first to wield magic?

"Gelus, the ice sage, Tonitrus, the thunder fist, and Ignis, the fire blade," Kibo answered eagerly, sitting at the very edge of his seat.

"Correct again, Kibo. Good work." his teacher said proudly. "You all could learn a thing or two from your friend Kibo here."

One of the kids, however, just rolled his eyes and smirked. "Yeah, like I'd wanna learn from a kid who can't even use magic," he whispered to the person next to him, snickering quietly. Kibo had also heard him loud and clear.

There we go. Kibo wrote down the answer, shaking away the unpleasant bit that came with that memory. He flipped to the next page, dredging through more questions.

Time ticked by as Kibo slogged through the test. They seemed to be random in terms of difficulty. He breezed through most of the easy questions before tackling the harder ones.

...is the force which allows us to manipulate the elements, nature, and even space itself. To do so, one requires mana, which is the mental and spiritual energy that resides in one's body. Kibo turned the page and sighed. *What are magic and mana, and their relation to each other?* Easy pickings compared to that last question of magic-infused nuclear fission.

"Five minutes remaining," the proctor announced, her voice echoing throughout the quiet room. Other test-takers shuffled in a panic to quickly finish up; Kibo was no different. He had barely finished half the questions on the test, and only God knows how many he answered correctly. Kibo rushed through the pages on the test, looking for a simple question he could complete before time eventually ran out. He didn't want to be stopped at the very first roadblock of his dream. Kibo's eye was caught by one particular question: *What is Bastion?*

Well, that's pretty obvious. It's a peace-keeping force that maintains peace across the globe, Kibo thought at first, but the more he thought about it, the more doubt started to churn in his gut. *Why would they ask such a straightforward question as the last one? Unless...* Kibo scratched his head, becoming more and more conflicted the more he looked at the question.

What is Bastion? That's all there was to that question, just three words. Yet, it was also a question that could be answered in so many different ways.

What *is* Bastion?

Kibo's head started to spin the longer he dwelled on the topic. He laid his head on the table to rest and clear his mind, not wanting to have some existential crisis while in the middle of a test. Kibo closed his eyes and started to think. *What is Bastion?*

Kibo sat at the entrance of his house. It wasn't anything big, a simple two-story wooden home with a flat roof and a pair of cracked, concrete stairs at the front. Kibo tracked his hands across one of the cracks in the stairs, waiting for someone. Despite the warm and cheery spring weather, Kibo's heart sank to the bottom of his chest.

At last, he heard the doors behind him slowly open. "Ah, there you are." Kibo's father sat down next to him on the stairs. "How are you feeling?" He was almost identical in appearance to Kibo, except far older, with a scruffy beard across his face.

"Good," Kibo responded bluntly, with an equally sullen expression on his face, staring at the moss-covered steps beneath him.

"Come on, Kibo. I'm your father. No need to be shy." His father looked down at him with a warm smile. Kibo stood silent for a bit, watching a tiny ant crawl out of the crack in the stair. At last, he turned towards his father and sighed.

"Someone said something mean to me," Kibo mumbled.

"And what exactly did they say?" he asked Kibo.

"That I can't use any magic."

"Ah, is that what got you upset?" he asked Kibo.

"Yes."

His father looked at him before stooping down a bit closer. "And why did that upset you?"

"Because if I can't use magic, how can I help people?" Kibo said, a sense of desperation in his voice.

"Well, do you need magic to help people?" Kibo was taken aback by the question, not knowing what to say. His father got up and grabbed both of Kibo's hands in a tight fist.

"Kibo, I know how much you want to be a mage like me, to join Bastion and help the world. But life doesn't always give us what we want." He paused for a moment. "Yet, I know that if you truly want something, if you put your mind to it, you can achieve it." He let go of Kibo's hands and chuckled.

"So, don't ever let anyone or anything make you doubt yourself, my son. Because I know in the end, whatever you do to reach your goal, you will do the right thing."

Kibo opened his eyes and let out a deep breath, drawing his pen one final time, ready to answer the question.

Bastion is not an organization, but a symbol, one which is forged by not one, but all those who reside in this world. It is what the people desire it to be, and mold it to their ideals. It is upheld and supported by many nations across the world, who believe that Bastion will bring hope in times of depression and war, relief during famine and disaster, and justice to those who commit injustice. Bastion stands for the unity and good within humanity, and that is what Bastion is.

"Time's up! Drop your pencils and pens, and be prepared to have your papers collected." Kibo had managed to finish answering the last question just as the proctor spoke up. He turned to see her smiling as if this was her favorite part. "Oh, and don't bother to sneak in some last-second writing."

As she finished that sentence, all the test papers vanished from their desks. The examinees were taken aback by the sudden disappearance of their exams, with some looking about to see where the tests could have gone. Slowly, they started to talk and bicker amongst themselves.

"Ahem." The room fell silent as the proctor cleared her throat. "Your papers have been graded and posted in the main hall. Once again, I will remind you that passing the written test will let you take the physical portion of the exam."

The room looked at the proctor, dumbstruck, not able to comprehend what she had just uttered. How could they already be done?

Eventually, the confused silence was broken by one of the examinees in the room. "Wait, you're kidding, right? There is no way you could have checked and graded every single test in here that fast, right?"

She stared at the examinee blankly. "Does it *look* like I'm lying? Go on and check for yourself."

After taking a single moment to process what she had just told all of them, the examinees rushed towards the door.

"Whoa, wait up!" Kibo rushed after the stampede of examinees and made a beeline to the main hall. As he got closer to the crowd at the end of the hall, he saw a massive blackboard, covered in hundreds of tiny scribbles too small to be seen from afar. But that didn't matter, because Kibo already knew what those unintelligible scribbles stood for. With every step toward the crowd, Kibo prayed that he would see his name on the list of those who passed.

"How the hell am I gonna find my name?" Kibo muttered to himself. He scratched his head as he squinted at the hundreds of names on the board.

Yet as he stared at the far away board, Kibo's eyes started to focus further, turning the once incoherent scribbles into clear and defined words. Kibo was taken aback by the sudden clarity of his vision.

"You can thank me for that." Arcanus beamed. *"One of the minor enhancements I made to this fragile, fleshy body of yours was to augment your eyes. You can now magnify anything up to four times larger than your previous, inferior biological receptive motors."*

"Wow, uh thanks," Kibo replied, not sure how to respond to Arcanus. He had something more important to focus on, such as the board.

Relieved to be finally able to see the thing in the first place, Kibo started to scan down the massive list of names from the beginning. Thankfully, all of the names were ordered alphabetically, allowing him to move quickly to the list of names that started with K.

Karen, Katia, Kazimer, Kartion. Sweat dripped down his brow as he slowly came closer and closer to the end of the section. His heart beat faster with each passing name.

Kibo Kozlov.

"Yes!" He let out one long exhale. It felt as though he had lifted an entire mountain off his back. He had cleared the first trial.

He was one step closer to his goal.

"I don't know why you're so surprised. It'd be pretty boring if the story ended here," Arcanus mumbled.

"Wait, what?"

"Never mind, just focus on the next test."

Kibo looked around himself to see how others were reacting. Many were dejected or frustrated. One applicant even fainted on the spot. On the other hand, some were overjoyed, screaming at the top of their lungs or crying. A few smirked confidently, while others fidgeted nervously at the other exams to come.

The buzz of noise was suddenly silenced by the boom of a voice from above.

"Those who have passed the test may enter the secondary testing facility located at the left of the hall. Those who had failed the test are now required to exit the building and may attempt the Bastion entrance exam again next year." The PA system crackled off.

Those who failed were escorted out of the room. Kibo heard a few examinees, unable to accept that they failed, shout and fight as they were forcefully removed by guards. Kibo and the lucky few who had passed were directed towards the left part of the hall, slowly merging with a small herd of the examinees who passed. Above the entrance was a sign reading: *Physical Test Facility*.

The room was a strange one. It had many small white doors, each labeled with a specific number, lined up across the left and right sides of the room. While in the center of the room was a small wooden platform with a small stand atop it, most likely used by the instructor for this next test. As Kibo looked around the odd room, someone tapped him on his left shoulder. He glanced back to see no one there, only to hear a recognizable voice on his right side.

"Haha, gotcha."

Kibo turned toward Rex, laughing at the little trick he pulled off.

Jeez, not this guy again. Kibo sighed, doing his best to hide any displeasure he may have had. "Hey, Rex."

"Hey, man, you passed that test, too? Didn't expect anything else from ya! I mean, anyone can pass a test with a few hidden slips of paper and cash," Rex said cockily.

Kibo looked at him in complete shock. "You did what?"

"What, you don't do that?" Rex scratched his head and looked at Kibo in genuine confusion. "I mean, it's easier than guessing on a test, right?"

Kibo nearly exploded into a full-blown lecture about the ethics of academic dishonesty, before remembering that he had tried to do the same thing in the exam. Deciding it was better to stay quiet, he sheepishly stood there. Everyone else in the room had gone silent and Kibo looked about to see exactly why.

A man sauntered to the front of the room, looking at all of the examinees before him. He was dressed in an expensive-looking black suit with the Bastion pin on the lapel. His face was covered in several scars, no doubt from the years of conflict he must have been through. The man watched as the last of the examinees who passed the written exam walked in and cleared his throat.

"To those of you here, I congratulate your success in passing the first test," he said warmly, clasping his hands together. "But as much as you all must feel happy for getting to pass such a difficult test, this is still not the end of your exam as many of you probably know." He pulled out a strange compass-like object from his pocket. It had a black screen with a green grid, along with three small slots above the screen.

"All of you still have much to face before you are allowed to enter Bastion. You will now be taking the first part of the physical exam, which is split in two. The first part of the test will take place in the environmental adaptation, cooperation, and navigation facility. You will be placed in groups of three, designated by the cards handed out to you by our fellow staff members. With your group, you will work together in various environments to collect three different gems. You will each be given a radar, like the one I am holding, which will lead you to all three gems. You may choose how you will extract these gems.

"Upon retrieving all three gems, you must return to the center of the physical test facility to pass on to the second part of the physical exam." He paused for a second and glanced down at his clipboard. "Only the first ten teams to successfully pass this portion of the test will be allowed to move on to the next part of the test."

He said it quickly as if this were an insignificant detail, but that one small detail immediately raised the stakes of the next exam by an insane margin. Kibo looked around. Many were gasping or muttering. A few were already discussing with each other different strategies as several staff members walked around the room, handing out cards to the examinees.

"Thank you," Kibo replied when he received a card from one of the staff. His had the number 3 on it. As he was thinking about his potential teammates, a familiar hand slammed onto his shoulder.

"Hey, would you look at that. Number buddies. What a coincidence," Rex exclaimed and again playfully nudged (that is, harshly pushed) Kibo's shoulder.

Kibo rubbed his shoulder and pouted. "Two things: First, please don't sneak up on me again. And second, isn't it a little strange for you to get the same number as me, while you're standing right next to me?"

Rex looked utterly confused. "I guess it's convenient. What do you mean?"

"What do I— You know what? I'm not even going to try. Let's just head over to our gate." Kibo rubbed his temple.

"Okay then, come on. Let's find this place we gotta hit up," Rex exclaimed, running ahead while signaling for Kibo to follow him.

Kibo used his modified eyes to scan for the gate, but it didn't make finding the gate any easier. The whirling crowd of examinees and staff made it impossible for him to see anything in front of him.

Then someone caught his eye.

Siris.

He quickly looked away and grabbed Rex's arm, pulling him behind a pillar.

"Whoa, dude! What's the big idea?" Rex asked as he pulled his arm away from Kibo's grip.

"There's someone who I don't wanna see right—"

"Well, well, well. Look who we have here."

Kibo froze, he did not need to turn to know who was behind him.

"I'm quite surprised that you made it this far. Though I don't suspect you'll get any further than this. I mean, what could a powerless farm boy like you do?"

Kibo turned to see Siris staring right at him, with that same malicious smile etched on her face, and that familiar glint of superiority.

Not this again, please not again. Kibo gulped. "I—"

"Ya better watch that tongue of yours, stronza." Rex suddenly stepped in between Siris and Kibo, staring down the frost mage. Rex's laid-back persona was instantly replaced with a defensive one. "I don't know what kind of history you two got, but I don't need to be a genius to tell that you're one stuck-up asshole."

Siris chuckled. "Oh, it seems like you've finally gotten yourself a friend. Guess you can find other worthless rejects like yourself."

"*Acquaintances.* We just met, actually," Kibo said, trying to defuse the situation. But Rex already tightened both of his hands into a fist. His eyes glowed blue.

"I don't know what the hell you're going on about, but I think ya probably know what is about to happen."

"Of course." Sirius smiled, cracking her knuckles and pulling both of her hands up in front of her, eyes glowing an icy blue. "I'll be leaving you as a pile of ice on the floor."

The two stared at each other, waiting for the other to make a move. The tension slowly built around them as other examinees came to see what the commotion was. Hell was about to break loose.

"*Kibo,*" Arcanus whispered. "*Do something.*"

Kibo snapped out of his trance, realizing how bad this could turn out. Quickly, he dove in front of Rex, putting himself between the two. "Rex, it's fine, you don't have to get yourself involved in my problems." He pushed him back. "I think I'm capable of handling them myself."

Arcanus groaned. "*That's not what I meant. This could be pretty bad.*"

Kibo ignored it. He had to stand his ground this time, subconsciously rubbing the sigil on his hand.

Siris smiled. "Seems the dog is finally trying to bite back."

Kibo winced a little, looking into her piercing eyes. But he stared back at her and refused to back down. "Siris, you've called me a powerless farm boy and other shit, and I'm going to be honest. You're right," Kibo said, much to the surprise of Siris. "But I finally attained something far greater than either you or I can imagine. And with every passing day I'm getting stronger." Kibo glanced down at the sigil embedded in his hand. "And you bet I'm going to make sure that you see how strong I've gotten. Just you wait." He snapped his gaze back at Siris, raw determination in his eyes.

Siris was taken aback by Kibo's newfound confidence, but maintained her posture. "While I'd like to see what 'powers' you attained, I highly doubt it's anything special." Siris casually flung her hair over her shoulder and walked towards her gate. "*Dasvidaniya*, mutt."

The disappointed crowd dispersed, seeing that there would be no fight. Kibo and Rex started to slowly walk to their gate again, a veil of awkwardness over them. Eventually, Kibo broke the silence.

"Hey, thanks for standing up for me." Kibo turned to Rex.

"Don't mention it. Really." Rex's voice had returned to its normal relaxed tone again. "Who is she, anyway?"

"Oh, she's Siris Vasilyev. She's part of the Vasilyev family, one of the magical houses in the White Assembly. They've been around for god knows how many hundreds of years. And of course, she's a prodigy of magic, like the rest of her family."

"Yeah? All I saw was a goddamn asshole," Rex said.

"Yeah, you got that right." Kibo shuddered. All the memories started coming back to him. "One time, she froze me from the knee down just for bumping into her. And because her father is a high-ranking official, she grew up as a spoiled brat who didn't care about anyone except herself. Her magical aptitude too—all that power to help people with, and she just uses it to toy with me."

Rex nodded sympathetically. "Guess I nearly just picked a fight with Vasilyev, huh? Don't know whether to feel proud or scared shitless."

"Me too. Trust me."

The two laughed. Kibo let out a small sigh. At least she wasn't around for now.

Soon, they stood before their gate. It was a simple but large metal door with the number three labeled above it. To their luck, their other group member had already arrived.

He was rather muscular and tall, with slick black hair. He dressed similar to those western greasers: leather jacket, denim, boots, and slick, combed-back hair. A leather pouch was strapped across his thigh. The young man was staring blankly at the ceiling, eyes squinted and eyebrows furrowed. However, his most notable feature was his eyes, which were a murky gray color.

Rex, wanting to snap him out of his brooding, decided that the most logical way to do this is to slam down on his shoulder.

"Hey, man. You seem to be sleeping in broad—"

Bam.

"AH! OW!"

The brooding kid grabbed Rex's arm so quickly that it seemed like a blur, turning down his eyes towards him fiercely.

"Um, uh... You're gonna let go—" Rex started.

"I suggest backing off if you know what is good for you." He scowled before letting Rex slip from his iron grip.

Rex quickly pulled his arm away and gave back a sharp look. "Jeez, another one? Everyone woke up on the wrong side of the bed today. He almost broke my damn arm," he whispered to Kibo.

"You know what? He's not completely wrong," Arcanus mused. *"But I think it'd be nice to give him a better first impression of us."*

- 44 -

Kibo looked down at Arcanus before he stepped forward per Arcanus' advice.

"Hey, sorry about my friend. He can be a little pushy at times." He extended his hand. "My name's Kibo Kozlov, and the guy next to me is Rex Ricci. Nice to meet you."

He stared at Kibo for a second, before swiftly grabbing Kibo's hand in an iron grip. "The name's Akira Kaze. Good to see at least someone has some courtesy."

"Oh, *ow*. Nice to meet you, Kaze." Kibo tried his best to hold in the pain from Kaze's crushing grip.

"Your name sounds familiar. Where are you from?"

"I was named after my dad's closest friend. He and my dad both served in Bastion during the—"

A voice suddenly boomed from the ceiling of the giant room repeating the same message over and over.

"Part one of the physical exam will begin shortly! Make sure your entire group is ready and at your designated gate! Part one of the exam is will begin shortly!"

The three turned to see their gate slowly creak open, revealing a pitch-black void, sucking the three cards in their hands. All three of them looked at the dark void in both awe and fear. None of them seemed willing to move.

That is, until Rex bolted towards the gate.

"We ain't gonna get anywhere if we just stand around. I better see your asses on the other side," Rex hollered as he slipped into the void.

"Rex!" Kibo tried to reach out for him, but he had already disappeared.

Kaze rolled his eyes. "Guess there's only one thing to do. Are you ready?"

"I don't have any other choice."

Kaze took this as his cue and nodded. "Remember, no matter where we end up, we have to find each other and group up as quickly as we can if we want to get past this part," Kaze stated as he dashed into the void. "I'll see you on the other side!" Kaze did a quick salute as he disappeared into the darkness.

Kibo took one last look at Arcanus, and the gate then took a step forward. Until he stood just short of the edge, looking off into the deep murky nothingness.

Arcanus glimmered. *"Hey, kid. Are you all right?"*

"Oh, yeah. It's just..." Kibo trailed off. He looked off into the void. It seemed so terrifying and otherworldly. Like it would swallow him and leave him to suffer in some dark, endless prison. He would never know for sure until he went through.

"God damn it, I ain't letting some creepy door stop me." Kibo stared gravely into the void one last time. It was not or never. Kibo jumped in and let himself fade away into the darkness.

CHAPTER 4

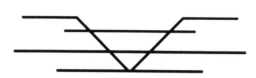

"What the..." Kibo rubbed his face slowly as he got up off the floor, trying to get his bearings. "Where am I?"

"Well, I wonder. Where else could we be?" Arcanus asked sarcastically.

"Yeah, yeah, very funny," Kibo responded as he looked around. They were in the middle of a large forest, surrounded by rows of evergreen trees and tall, dark green grass.

Before he could get onto his feet, he felt a sudden force pull him back down.

"Ow! What was that?" Kibo snapped around to see that it was none other than Kaze.

"Kibo, stay down. There's this thing going around," Kaze growled. "And I'm not talking about this guy."

"Wait, who? Ah. I see." Kibo turned to see Rex, who was restlessly trying to rip out of Kaze's grip. "Stay down. God damn it, are you trying to kill us? Did you see how big that thing was?" Kaze snapped at him. "Listen, I don't know what the hell we've stepped into, but we gotta get out of here," Kaze said as he looked over the grass.

Something groaned in the distance. The three of them froze instantly. Its limbs creaked with every step, each one sounding closer than the last.

"Get down," Kaze exclaimed.

As if by instinct, both Kaze and Kibo dove for the tall grass, with Kaze dragging Rex down in between him and Kibo.

"Just let me land a few hits on that thing and it'll be over," Rex complained.

"Have you lost your mind? Do you know what that thing would do to the three of—"

They were interrupted by another groan. The three of them, in complete and utter fear, turned to see a massive creature standing just a few meters from them.

The creature seemed to be completely alien, as if it had been brought from another world for the exam. Its hide was a dark blue, covered in several wrinkles and void of any form of hair or fur. The beast's hind legs were short and stumpy, its feet flat and tough like that of a rhino. Its arms, by contrast, were so abnormally gigantic and weighty that it had to walk on all fours just to maintain its balance. However, none of this was as unsettling or strange as its head, which was minuscule in comparison to the massive shoulders that surrounded it. Its neck was incredibly long, allowing it to scan for prey in every possible direction. The most frightening part of its head was the mouth, which consisted of a single gaping hole filled with serrated teeth like a leech or lamprey. Finally, the last bit of its odd anatomy was located right above its mouth—its large green eye surveyed the surroundings with a primal gaze of hunger.

"*Oh, crap.*" Kibo's heart dropped.

The beast came to a complete halt just a few centimeters from them and looked down at the spot where Kibo lay, staring directly at him with its singular green eye. Its gaze pierced the deepest recesses of Kibo's soul. He was done for.

But then, the creature suddenly turned its gaze from him and stepped away.

"*What the...* What just happened?" Kibo asked.

"I have no clue. I thought for sure it was going to trample us to death." Kaze gulped. "I think we'd better get the hell out of here while that thing's distracted."

The three of them dashed across the woods, stopping every so often to check if the coast was clear.

However, just as they went to hide behind some shrubs, they saw another group of three, just like them, walking into the middle of a small clearing.

"Ah, there's another group, we should go—whoa!" Kaze stopped Kibo dead in his tracks.

"Remember what the man said before the test. Only the first ten groups can pass. We can't trust anyone else, no matter who they are." Kaze scowled. "In their eyes, we are another obstacle. They could easily try to sabotage us."

They continued to observe the other group, who seemed to be just chatting amongst themselves. Kaze and Kibo were barely able to make out what they were discussing. The one that seemed to be the leader stood in front, clearly holding something in his hand. They were pretty quiet for the most part, but one of them let out a sudden scream.

"Ugh! What is this?" one of them suddenly exclaimed. Kibo and Kaze looked down to see that she had stepped into some strange, purple-glowing liquid, and was frantically trying to wipe it off her boots.

"No idea, but how did you step into it? It's not exactly hard to miss." one of the teammates laughed.

"It wasn't glowing at first," she yelled at him, her face beet red.

"Knock off you two," the leader barked at the other two, who begrudgingly quieted down. He furrowed his brow and stared at something in his palm. "Which way is this tracker pointing? If we're gonna find this stuff, we gotta move fast."

Kibo and Kaze looked at each other in confusion. What tracker? They both quickly turned out their pockets and looked around their clothes to find nothing. They both then turned their heads back at Rex.

"Uh, what's wrong?"

"Rex, did you get anything before you headed through the gate?"

"Nah, I don't think so." Rex patted himself down. "Wait a sec!"

Rex reached down his pockets, and sure enough, found a tracker in his back pocket. Kaze looked over Rex's shoulder and motioned Kibo to come closer. Kibo and Kaze gazed down at the tracker and could see just how complex the device was from up close compared to when the instructor showed it to them. It seemed to be a radar of some sort, made of gold with three odd slots on the top. The black screen pulsed rhythmically, displaying different dots relative to the green guidelines. Three were present: red, orange, and green. But something seemed off.

"Is it me, or does that green dot look like it's getting closer?" Kibo squinted at the radar. "Huh, yeah it is. It's getting— WHOA!"

The three of them suddenly lost their footing as they felt the ground beneath them tremble, with the sound of something rushing towards them with a thundering *boom*.

"What's going on?" Kibo said, grabbing the tree next to him for support.

"It's here." Kibo turned to see Kaze, looking out into the clearing with a look of sheer terror in his eyes. "That thing is here."

Roar!

The strange creature from before crashed into the clearing, violently tearing through the dense thicket of bushes and trees. Its terrifying gaze was fixated on the other team.

"Oh, shit!"

The leader of the group was sent flying into a tree by the beast's massive forearm. The other two launched off a mixture of fiery and icy bolts towards the creature. But the beast easily shrugged off the magic like they were nothing more than a few annoying fleas, before letting out another unnerving roar.

The creature slammed into the boy and grabbed the girl. It threw her into another tree, instantly knocking the living daylights out of her. The surviving team member managed to break free of his daze, trying to charge up another frost bolt, only to be slammed down again.

Kibo and his team stared at the beast, unable to utter a single word in shock, The entire group demolished in less than a minute.

When the beast turned down to savor its spoils, all three of them had vanished.

Kibo's gulped. This nightmarish thing was, without a doubt, extremely dangerous. They had to get away from that thing, and now.

"What are we waiting for? Let's get out of here!" Kibo frantically whispered to Kaze. Yet, when he turned over to Kaze, Kibo just saw him standing there, frozen in place like a statue. The only part of his body that moved was his pale face, which looked back and forth between the tracker—now in his hand—and the creature.

"What's wrong?"

"It looks like our target is...that thing." Kaze trembled. Despite all his effort to mask it, Kibo could hear the fear in his voice.

"Are you crazy? That other team got demolished," Kibo exclaimed.

Arcanus chirped up, *"You'll be fine. You got me by your side, remember? I can give you moral support."*

Kibo looked down at Arcanus and raised his eyebrow. *"Really?"*

"Oh, and I can gather some tactical data about that thing to give you an idea of how to take it down."

What? Why wasn't that the first thing you said? Kibo replied telepathically in disbelief.

"Eh, I wanted to see how you'd react." Kibo's face-palmed, letting out a sigh of frustration.

Okay so, what data can you give me?

"Well, I need some time. This thing is alien to every single animal I've seen through your eyes so far, so it's gonna take me a while to dissect it. I'd suggest getting together some kind of plan to deal with that thing while I figure out its weak point."

All right then, Kibo said as he turned to Kaze. "So, what's our battle plan? How the hell do we take down this thing?"

Kaze stared at the beast for a while before finally speaking up. "Well, first we need to get this thing somewhere cramped. It'll be harder for it to move around and smash us with its huge arms. A tight grove of trees or some boulders would work. Then, we could try to engage it from a distance, since well, I don't think I need to explain why."

"Thankfully, I can do that with this." Kaze snapped his fingers, generating a gust of magical wind energy, pulling out what appeared to be a rifle round from a small pouch with a flick of his wrist. "A 7.62 ought to do it if I can land a good hit." He turned toward Kibo and asked, "What do you have?"

"I got some simple magical equipment I can fight up close with," Kibo stated.

"Keeping us vague and simple so as not to draw attention, I see," Arcanus said in approval. *"Nice. Just like we planned."*

"You do you, just make sure not to block my line of sight," Kaze said as he looked at Kibo and shrugged. "Finally, we have to make sure we keep that spaz safe since he'd rush down that thing the first chance he gets. At least I got the radar from him before he broke it." Kaze pointed at Rex.

Kibo glanced where Kaze was pointing and froze up. "Uh, we have a problem."

"What do you mean? Oh." The wind mage looked behind him. Rex was gone. "Oh god, where did he go?"

Suddenly, the creature roared.

"Come at me, ya shit! I'll take ya head on," Rex shouted as he charged the hulking creature.

The hulking brute rushed towards him, flailing its bulky arms at Rex. The monster pounced forward, ready to crush him. The two collided, creating a thick cloud of smoke and dust. Kibo looked away, unable to bear the sight of Rex getting pummeled. A sinking feeling of anxiety built up inside him at the sound of the creature pounding what was probably Rex's remains. They needed to do something. "We gotta go help him. He's gonna get turned into a pile of mush if we don't help him right now."

Kaze smirked. "That damn bastard. I think he'll be fine without us."

"Huh, what do you mean?" Kibo was dumbstruck by what he saw. The creature was furiously pounding the earth, left and right, with all its might.

Yet, Rex gracefully dodged every swing. It seemed as though he was somewhat bored.

"Damn, those guys got knocked out by you?" he said, casually dodging another strike. "They must have been terrible then!"

The creature, frustrated by his speed, quickly roared and swung even faster. Even then, the smug warrior continued to evade every attack.

"Those kids should've known being strong can't win ya fights," Rex said as he leaped backward. He took a stance and crossed his arms. "Let me show you how a real man deals with his problems." He glanced at his side and winked at Kaze and Kibo.

In one fluid motion, he snapped both his arms back to his side, small sparks flying off his hands. At first, they fizzled for a few moments, growing quieter with each passing moment. Then it all came at once.

An explosion of electrical energy burst from Rex's arms, covering both of them as he molded both of his limbs in the shape of a cobra.

"I think it's time I gave you an ass-whooping," Rex roared, lunging at the eldritch creature. "Come here, yah meathead!"

Dodging a right hook, he countered by piercing the beast's abdomen with all his might. The bolts of electricity zapped over to the beast, eliciting a cry of pain as its body violently spasmed and shook. The massive creature tried to swing its arms for some sort of counter, but its hulking fists fell limp to the ground.

"Didn't think it'd be so easy to make ya go limp." Rex smirked as he brought back both his arms. "How about we finish this?"

Rex decimated the creature with incredible precision and power. It was unlike anything Kibo had seen. The immense speed and power behind Rex's fists far beyond anything he could muster. Rex slammed his fist into the creature's head, sinking deep into its face. The creature let out one last painful groan as it staggered backward and, with a small whimper, fell to the ground.

Both Kibo and Kaze watched the limp body in stunned silence. The beast that had single-handedly wiped out an entire group within mere seconds lay defeated, its particularly smug opponent standing above it in triumph, his arms held out in the air like a victorious boxer. Kaze got up out of the bushes and cautiously stood before Rex and the subdued creature, his eyes darting back and forth between the two.

"Well, good job on taking that thing out, Rex," Kaze begrudgingly congratulated him. "But you almost risked all of our lives right then and there. If that thing had hit you a single time..."

Rex rolled his eyes as he walked over to Kaze. "Oh c'mon, man! I beat the shit out of that thing. All that matters now is that I took down the beast and that's the end of it. No need to dwell on the past, am I right?" Rex pointed back at the beast. "What's it gonna do? Come back from the dead?"

The group felt the ground shake as a massive roar erupted from the beast. Rex and Kaze snapped their heads towards the source, only to catch a sudden blur. The only thing Rex saw before the impact was the beast's singular green eye, staring down at him with unbridled fury.

The beast slammed into Rex with its full strength, hurling him into a tree. "*Oh, shit,*" Rex rasped. His entire body was on fire. Yet, despite his battered state, he propped himself up against a tree and looked up at the beast.

The beast let out a guttural groan, taunting Rex.

Rex tried to stand up and form a fighting stance, gritting his teeth. "*Damn it! That bastard took me by surprise.*"

Rex beat his chest and shouted, "Come on! What's the worst thing you can do?" As if he had flicked some sort of switch, the beast suddenly let out a fierce roar and charged toward Rex. But he couldn't, Rex simply could not move; not a single fiber in his body would listen to him. The beast drew closer. "Didn't think I'd get my ass handed to me by that thing." Rex chuckled.

The stomps were getting louder and louder.

"Heh, guess this is the end of the line for me." Rex closed his eyes and waited for the impact. It was over for him.

And then, in a blur, Rex was gone.

The beast landed on its four limbs with an explosive boom, but something was off. Its eyes widened when it saw that it had missed its prey.

"What the?" Rex slowly opened his eyes.

"You all right?" Kibo asked him, glancing back and forth from Rex to the beast, which had gone into full-blown rage, searching all over the place for Rex.

"Yeah, I'm all right." A massive burst of pain shot through Rex's arm. Fortunately, Kibo muffled his screams with his hand, all while trying to stay focused on keeping a lookout.

Rex looked at Kibo's hand in bewilderment. It was covered in a strange metallic gauntlet, far more advanced than any piece of equipment that Rex had seen. But he didn't have much time to examine the glove as it was smothering his entire face. Rex started to smack Kibo's arm with all his remaining strength, trying to grab Kibo's attention before his face got caved in.

"Wait, you have to quiet—oh."

Kibo snapped his arms away from Rex, his face turning a bright red from embarrassment. "Sorry about that, Rex. I'm not used to these things yet."

"Jesus man. You almost killed me," he whispered back harshly. "Where the hell you get stuff like that?"

A small gust of wind passed right above them. There was something strange about this particular breeze. As if it was saying something.

"Kibo...Rex... I have A plan."

Both of them looked at each other, confused. The breeze sounded just like Kaze. Another breeze passed by them, carrying another curious message.

"I need you two... to lure the beast... In my direction. I can...take It out."

Kibo peered through the grass. Sure enough, he caught a glimpse of Kaze's head across the clearing. Their eyes met, and the wind mage motioned him over.

"I gotta help you guys," Rex said, attempting to stand up. He let out a sharp grunt of pain as he fell back to the ground.

"*He's hurt badly, Kibo. Anymore and it'll be serious,*" Arcanus stated gravely.

Kibo nodded. "Rex, you've done all you can. Rest for now. It's our turn now to deal with the beast."

Rex thought about it for a moment, before letting out a conceited sigh and muttering, "Heh, guess you can say that the spirit's willing but the body just ain't, huh?"

"I don't think that's the right saying," Kibo said, but Rex was already unconscious, his ragged breathing the only sign of life left within him.

"*Damnit, we gotta get rid of this thing before something really bad happens to Rex,*" Arcanus growled. "*Come on, let's get moving.*"

"Right," Kibo exclaimed, turning in Kaze's direction.

Kibo crawled through the underbrush to Kaze, doing his best to hide from the beast. It seemed over its tantrum and was instead slamming down the trees and ripping out the underbrush around the clearing, searching around for the three of them. Occasionally, it would stop, and spit out something strange from its mouth. Kibo had to get started before it got to Rex.

"What is that thing doing?"

"*Hmm, it must be that strange liquid that the girl from before stepped in,*" Arcanus said. "*And it's clear, like the girl said; it seems to only turn purple when it comes into contact with other animals like yourself.*"

"Could you please not refer to me as an animal?" Kibo grumbled.

"*Yeah, yeah. Look, what is important is that we get to that other kid over there and hear out what kind of plan he's come up with. Considering the rate that thing is tearing through here, I'd suggest you speed up and get to Kaze before he tears us all apart. And make sure to avoid that substance.*"

"Got it," Kibo replied

Deciding to take a faster, but riskier route, Kibo stepped into the clearing and moved as fast as he could while staying silent until he was just a few steps away from where he last saw Kaze.

Just a bit further and we're safe. Kibo froze as he felt his foot dig into something wet and slimy. His foot trapped in the same strange purple substance from before.

A familiar roar erupted behind Kibo.

"Shit, I told you to watch out for that thing's spit," Arcanus exclaimed. *"Get the hell out of here."*

"Arcanus!" Kibo bolted from the beast. "You should have told me earlier."

"I told you already—"

The stomps were getting louder. Kibo glanced back to the one-eyed beast, no more than an arm's reach away from him.

"Crap." Kibo barely managed to shield his body with his arms when the beast swung at him with its full might. "That hurt like..." But Kibo felt nothing more than a little sting in either of his arms as if the gauntlets had absorbed all the shock from the creature's blow. He tried to regain his footing as best as he could, but there was no time for him to recuperate as the beast reared for another blow. Kibo instinctively swerved to the side, barely dodging it.

"Heh, guess all that militia training wasn't for nothing," Arcanus said.

"I don't think now's the time for quips, Arc!"

The beast threw another powerful swing at Kibo, narrowly missing by mere centimeters. It swung at him again and again.

"Shit, what do we do, Arcanus?"

"Give me a second. If you didn't move so much, I'd have found its weak point by now."

"You'd better be close. I don't know how much longer I can dodge this thing's attacks," Kibo exclaimed, just barely twisting his way out of another one of the beast's enraged blows, hearing only the sound of its fist slamming into something with an earth-shattering *boom.*

"Jesus." Kibo turned around to see a tree behind him was completely obliterated, with only the broken remains of its branches and stump remaining from the strike. Kibo gulped and looked back at the beast.

Whatever your plan was, Kaze, I hope it was worth going through all this crap, Kibo thought as he frantically brought up both of his fists as the creature charged at him.

The beast slammed directly into him with its shoulder, sending Kibo flying across the clearing and into a tree with a deafening crack, crunching deep into the tree's bark.

Kibo coughed as he tried to get back up onto his feet. He winced as a spike of pain shot through his arms, the armor on both of the gauntlets scraped off by the beast. His last line of defense was shattered.

"Get a-movin'!" Arcanus panicked.

Kibo grit his teeth, the power surging through the remains of his gauntlets. "No, I'll take him on."

"God, you're crazy. There has to be a better way."

But Kibo wasn't listening to Arcanus anymore. The only thing he could think of was Rex's broken state, his limp, broken body pummeled by the beast in front of him. He had to fight it. If Rex could take a blow and survive, so could he. Kibo had to take it down.

He balled his fists as the beast started to charge yet again. It let out another trembling roar as it swung both its arms, ready to land another blow on Kibo. He brought his fist up as he waited for the beast to get closer. He watched as the beast got so close to him that he could see the disgusting ooze dripping from its gaping mouth. Finally, it was his turn to strike.

"This one's for Rex," Kibo yelled as he charged, screaming back at the beast.

"Wait, Kibo! You just gotta hit it in the—"

Ping!

A small blur streaked above him, followed by what sounded like a boil being popped and an ear-shattering roar.

Something had struck its terrible green eye directly. The beast instinctively scrambled to cover its eye with one grotesque hand and staggered back while swinging the other. Kibo brought back his fist and felt the adrenaline rush through his veins as he put every bit of vigor and power into this one strike.

A perfect hit.

Kibo roared as he slammed his gauntlet directly into the beast's face. His fist sunk deep into the beast's eye and caved in the rest of its face. The beast hit Kibo away with the last of its strength, but it was too late for the beast.

Letting out one final, whimpering shout, the beast crumpled to the ground as a slow disgusting puddle of odd fluids built up underneath it.

"Is it over?" Kibo panted. A sudden wave of exhaustion washed over him.

"*I'm not detecting any heartbeats or signs of movement,*" Arcanus replied. "*I'd check just to be sure, kid.*"

Keeping his guard up, Kibo edged toward the beast. As he drew closer to the beast's side, he expected another roar, even a spasm or two. But the creature laid completely still, not letting out even a whimper. It seemed that the beast was finally slain.

"He's totaled, all right. I made sure of that." Kibo turned back to see Kaze limping towards him, the entire left side of his body covered in bruises and cuts.

"Kaze! If you had told me you were this battered—"

"—you wouldn't have brought the beast towards me, I know." he suddenly groaned, clutching his arm. "Taking down the beast was our top priority. I got something in store, anyways." Kaze winced as he sat down near the beast.

Kibo knelt next to him. Kaze's left arm had to be broken. The span of bruising and cuts across it didn't do him any favors either. Yet, despite the sheer pain he was in, Kaze still had the strength to slowly reach into the leather pouch by his side and pull out a strange vial.

It was filled with a luminescent blue substance swirling within the vial. Slowly, Kaze raised it to Kibo. "I-I need you to unscrew this and inject it into my arm."

Kibo's eyes widened, but Kaze was dead serious. He had no reason to hesitate "All right." Kibo gently unscrewed the cap off the vial, revealing a needle poking out of the top. He turned over to Kaze, and with one deep breath, gingerly pressed the needle into Kaze's shoulder.

Kaze let out a relaxed sigh as he slowly injected the vial into his bloodstream. Then he stepped back for a moment and watched what happened next in awe.

"Whoa." The bruises and cuts across his left arm faded, sealing themselves back up as the purple and red bruises across his arm slowly dissipated. Kibo could hear Kaze's fractured bones lock back into place as they mended. The other injuries across Kaze's body were healing as well, albeit much slower. Eventually, if it weren't for the tears across his jacket and pants,

Kibo would never have even guessed that Kaze was injured in the first place.

"Guess that first aid training from the militia came in handy, huh?" Arcanus mused.

Yeah, yeah. Kibo brushed Arcanus off as he looked down at the now-empty vial in his hand. "What kind of miracle drug is this?"

Kaze reached down into his pouch with his right arm as he cautiously stretched his left. "It's concentrated sapphiron sap, from my homeland. It's quite effective at healing most injuries, but almost impossible to get your hands on just a single drop of this stuff." Kaze cleared his throat. "You won't believe the people I had to go through to get just two vials of this stuff."

Kibo glanced back at where Rex was unconscious.

"Well, looks like we're gonna have to use this last vial."

To his surprise, Kibo turned to see Kaze looking down at Rex with a small grin. "Even though he's the knucklehead who got us into this mess in the first place, he'd be a bigger liability injured," Kaze conceded, pulling out the second vial from the pouch.

"Damn straight," Arcanus said.

The two went over to the spot where Rex was and found him sitting up with his back against a tree. He was half-conscious, but breathing. He looked up at the two of them and smiled weakly. "Well, what are ya gonna do with me?"

"This." Kaze swiftly grabbed Rex's arm and injected the vial into it.

"Ow. What was that? Whoa...WHOA" Rex's eyes suddenly flew open as he felt a sudden rush of energy flood his battered body. Rex looked down in amazement as all the rips, bruises, and any other kind of injury across his body either disappeared or sealed themselves up. Eventually, like Kaze, it seemed as though nothing had happened to him.

"Hot damn, that was some crazy shit. Where can I get more of that?" Rex mused, to which Kaze just rolled his eyes.

Kibo turned his gaze back at the beast and the radar in Kaze's hand. It was still beeping. "Well, what do we do now? I mean. That man told us we needed some sort of gem from this thing. But I have no clue where they could have put it."

Kaze joined him and eyed the creature closely. He looked down at the tracker in his hands. "Radar's still pinging, so it has to be somewhere on or in it."

"Well, which do you think it is?"

Kaze furrowed his brow. "Probably inside."

The tracker's beeps become more rapid as Kaze edged closer to the creature's body. Eventually, the screen turned a dark red as Kaze hovered just a hair's length above the creature's body.

"Let's take a little look at this thing, shall we?" Kaze crouched down near the head, which it had grasped with its hand in its last painful moments. Kaze moved it and stared at its ravaged face. He had hit it squarely in its eye, and a dark green fluid oozed from the socket.

"Ugh, can't believe I'm going to do this." Kaze closed his eyes, before thrusting his arm into the beast's eye, crunching through various strange bits and organs inside it. With a grunt, he pulled something out, spewing the dark green fluid everywhere.

Kibo leaped back in disgust as he looked at Kaze covered in a mix of green guts and ooze. "Gross! Please tell me you did that for—"

"Yeah, for this." Kaze lifted his hand into the air to display a small green emerald in his hand. It shone in the sunlight, covering the ground in a brilliant mix of bright green shapes and light. "Looks like this is what we're hunting for."

Kaze placed the crystal near one of the slots on the tracker and felt it automatically click in, turning the screen back to the green grid it had from before. Except now, there were only two arrows left on the screen—their next two targets.

"One down. Two more to go."

CHAPTER 5

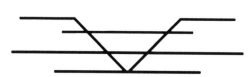

The subtle curves of snow-covered hills in the distance were its only visible landmarks.

In this frozen hell, three figures trudged through the thick snow. Two of them wavered in the merciless cold, holding onto their coats for dear life, preserving every last bit of warmth they could. However, one of them stood defiantly against the cold wind, not affected at all by the cold. She looked off into the distance, determined.

One of the figures, a tall boy in the back, collapsed onto his knees. "Siris! We *need* to rest and warm ourselves. The cold...it's too much."

The other, a girl wearing a balaclava, nodded her head in agreement. "If I'm going to die, it's not gonna be in the middle of some frozen wasteland."

Siris stopped and turned around slowly, staring down at them with a look of bitter contempt. "We are *not* stopping until we reach the waypoint," Siris snapped at them before turning back toward their destination. "Oh, and one more thing." Siris looked at the two of them over her shoulder. "If you dare to fail me, I will make sure to have you two displayed as statues in the Mikhailovsky Palace."

The two looked down at the ground, nodding reluctantly. She watched them get up with a slight smile, before that quickly faded. Seeing their submission only caused her to remember something unpleasant.

She had almost forgotten about *him.*

Kibo's mere presence at the exam bothered her greatly. It didn't make any bit of sense to her. How could someone like him be let into the exam?

What was that boy going on about? He disappears for a month, and the first time I see him, he goes on about attaining some new power? Hmm, did he finally figure out how to harness magic, or did he find some sort of weapon or tool to aid him? I'm probably just overreacting. How could a peasant boy without a magical affinity be able to keep up with the training and power of my family?

Her father told her how people like Kibo were nothing, those who should never even be given a chance to try and use magic. He was nothing more than a powerless commoner. He had no finesse, no innate ability to utilize magic. Yet, despite his constant failure, he kept trying over and over. He was a nobody, just an average commoner without power. So why did he keep going for that impossible goal, even when she tried to stop him?

She marched faster down the hill. She couldn't let herself be distracted by the local idiot. But try as she might, she couldn't rid her thoughts of that look of sheer confidence on his face as he talked back to her right before the physical portion of the exam was unlike anything she had seen.

Siris felt the tracker start to vibrate. They were getting closer. As she glanced back up from the tracker, she saw their destination: the entrance to a massive cavern.

She lit up in anticipation. Their target was sure to be in there. She snapped back to her followers, who both flinched by pure reflex. "Well, well, well. Looks like you two are finally going to be able to *rest*. Come on."

As they drew closer to the cave, the wind around them suddenly whipped itself into a frenzy, pulling the snow into a whirlwind of ice and frost.

"What's happening?" The girl in the back panicked.

"Could be some sort of elemental shift in the magic of this place," the boy shouted. The two of them watched in fear as the wind roared louder and louder, but Siris stood calmly in the snowstorm, unfazed. She was in her element.

"Hmph, just leave it to me." Siris smiled as she ran down the hill, the other two desperately trying to keep up. The storm grew stronger and fiercer by the second until it blasted them with its full might. They screamed and jumped onto Siris, holding on for dear life. "Didn't I tell you two cowards that there was nothing to worry about?" Siris said in annoyance as she pulled her teammates' trembling arms off of her.

"What the?" The two of them opened their eyes and stared in amazement. The blizzard that had been desperately trying to smother them in its frozen fury was blowing away from them in all directions, as though it was blocked by some invisible wall.

Siris grinned as she looked up at the blizzard and raised her arm.

"I think you two forgot where I'm from." With the snap of her fingers, the blizzard parted in front of Siris, laying out a clear path directly to the entrance of the cave.

"How-how did you do this?" the boy asked in amazement as Siris treated the massive blizzard like it was nothing more than a pesky breeze.

"This? Oh, I do this every time I go to class." Siris looked at him smugly. "Well then, what are we waiting for? Get a move on." Siris snapped the two of her teammates out of their trance.

Cutting through the blizzard, they finally managed to reach the mouth of the cave. It was quite something to behold.

"Whoa, this place is pretty huge," the girl in the back said as they walked in. Her voice echoed into the cave. Compared to when they looked at it from afar, the cave was much larger than they expected. Across its ceiling and floor, it was covered in a mix of stalactites and stalagmites made of both stone and ice. It almost felt as though they were walking deeper into the maw of some giant icy beast.

As they tread deeper into the cave, their surroundings became darker with every step. Eventually, the only light in front of them was the faint glow of Siris' tracker.

"What was that?" Siris snapped as a sudden wave of heat hit her from behind. She brought up her free hand, surrounded by a swirl of snow and ice, ready to fight whatever had created the source of heat.

"Whoa, calm down. I just thought you'd need some light." Siris turned to see a small fire glowing from the other girl's palm.

"You should have told me you were going to do that. You don't know when something will pounce at us." Siris paused for a moment. "And be more careful around here. I don't want to have something pinned on me for whatever happens to you. It'd be bad for my family's reputation." Siris sighed.

But as the three of them moved deeper into the cave, Siris couldn't help but admire the true scale now that she could see her surroundings. If the cave looked large at the entrance, it seemed almost gargantuan now. The cave's ceiling stood a few dozen meters above them, with the occasional drip of water echoing throughout the cave. Along its surface stood several giant stalagmites, reaching towards the ceiling like miniature skyscrapers, with a few so high that they almost scraped the ceiling.

Siris turned her gaze back down at the tracker; they were almost there. But then she heard something behind her collapse to the ground.

"We need to take a break. Please, Siris, let's just rest for one moment."

Siris turned to see that the boy had collapsed. He was gasping for air, with the girl next to him not in any better condition. Siris opened her mouth, ready to put them in their place, but paused. Seeing them in their weakened state reminded her of something—no, someone.

"*Ugh.* Fine, you two can rest for a little while. I'll try to find this thing on my own." She relented, storming off deeper into the cavern.

Her teammates let out a sigh of relief. They watched her walk off into the darkness, her sharp footsteps echoing away. The boy propped himself against the wall. It was cold, but it was far better than lying down. Beckoning him over, the girl snapped her fingers, summoning a small mote of fire for warmth. He scooched close, finally able to rest after walking through that hellish wasteland for so long.

"You think she'll be back?" he asked, glancing in the ice mage's direction. They listened closely as Siris' footsteps became fainter and fainter with each step she took into the darkness.

The fire mage thought for a moment, then nodded weakly. "She'd better be. You've seen what she can do; she's literally in her element."

Beep, beep, beep.

Siris walked deeper into the cave, her surroundings becoming darker and darker, the shadows around her growing larger. It was like the murky void was trying to trap her.

"Siris."

"Who was that?" Siris spun around, looking for who had just whispered her name.

Nothing.

Siris dismissed the whisper as her mind played tricks on her in the dark, walking faster towards the target.

"Siris."

"It's just your mind messing with you, Siris. Keep moving forward." She hastened faster as if she hoped she could outrun the darkness.

But the whispers only got louder.

"Will you let yourself be bested by that boy?"

"Leave me alone," Siris yelled, increasing her pace to a sprint.

"He will surpass you, Siris. He is coming. Soon you will be—"

"Just stop!" Siris screamed as she fell to the floor. Shadows, whispers, laughter: it all overwhelmed her.

The tracker beeped.

"Huh?" Giving her head a little shake, she looked at the tracker: the point was right in front of her. But when she looked up, she found herself face to face with a massive wall of ice, nothing more than a dead end. Confused, she checked again. And again. her target was the wall.

"Stupid device." Siris smacked the radar in frustration. "That's what I get for relying on metal junk."

As if in reaction to her statement, the tracker beeped so rapidly that it started to vibrate violently.

"Wait, what's going on?"

The cave trembled. Chunks of ice across the cavern's ceiling crashed down to the floor in a massive shower of ice.

"What the hell is happening? Oh, come on!" Siris snapped up to see a giant stalactite of ice hurtling towards her. By pure instinct, Siris raised both her hands into the air, ripping up a layer of ice from the ground beneath her to form a dome above herself just a mere second before the giant chunk of ice crashed directly onto it.

"Argh!" Siris felt her knees buckle and every muscle in her body strain as the falling debris slammed into her shield of ice. The dome suddenly cracked with a violent ripping sound, a giant gash running right down the center.

But Siris wasn't going to go down that easy. No Vasilyev would let themselves be bested by their element. "Come on, a single chunk of ice isn't going to hold me down."

Siris let out a massive blast of compressed cold air from her hands, bursting through the top of the dome and sending the massive chunk of ice back up into the ceiling, shattering it into hundreds of harmless flakes of ice. But it wasn't over for her just yet, for Siris heard a strange, sharp sound through the cave's rumbling.

The ground itself broke apart beneath her, slowly cracking further and further as bits of it started to disappear into a dark void below it.

"WHOA." Siris flung down her arms, repurposing her dome to create an icy floor beneath her, just barely saving herself from falling and turning into a pile of broken bones.

"Damn it! First the ceiling, now the floor. When will it end?" Siris gritted her teeth and shut her eyes. The strain was becoming greater, the shaking and rumbling getting even stronger. Pain ripped through her body, becoming so unbelievably intense that it seemed as though every muscle would explode just by the sheer amount of force she was pushing against.

Then, just as quickly as the massive tremors came, they disappeared.

"What the... is it over?" Siris opened her eyes and witnessed the destruction around her.

Despite the darkness, Siris could barely make out from the glow of her tracker or how much the cavern had been ripped asunder. The once still and crystalline perfection of the cave was replaced by the broken remains of stalagmites and stalactites littering the floor. And beneath her? A giant gaping maw, its end nowhere in sight, leading down deeper into the darkness.

"Whatever caused all of this"—Siris glanced down at her tracker and immediately confirmed her suspicion—"must've been our target."

But her mind raced even faster when she realized where it was headed: her team.

Its prey.

"...and that's why I'm trying out Bastion," the girl said joyously, her breath forming small little puffs in the air. "I want to explore so many different parts of the world while helping people."

The fire flickered over the girl's hand. The boy rubbed his hands and shivered.

"Well, for me, I just wanna get away from my crazy family." The boy chuckled. "While, you know, also helping people."

The girl laughed alongside him, scooting closer to the fire. "Hey, I never got to ask your name."

"Oh, it's Ben. You?"

"Hana."

"Ah, well nice to meet you," Ben responded, looking back down at the fire. Hana reached slowly into a small satchel by her side and tossed a few bits of cloth scraps into the fire, adding extra sparks to keep it from burning out. The two squatted near the fire for a while in a cozy silence, watching their shadows flicker about.

"Say, where do you think she is?" Ben asked, gazing down into the dark winding path Siris went down into the cavern.

"Well, wherever she is, I bet it isn't nice." Hana glanced into the darkness and shuddered. "But she's probably fine. We have nothing to worry about."

The second she spoke, the ground beneath them started to shake violently.

"I think you spoke a bit too soon."

The two leaped to their feet as the icy floor beneath them start to slowly break.

"What's happening?" Hana panicked.

"Whatever it is, we have to stay calm," Ben shouted back at her. "Shit, just keep an eye on the ground."

With a sound like a whale breaching the surface of the ocean, a creature burst from the ground, crashing through their makeshift fireplace and smashing it into bits.

"Oh lord almighty, what the hell is that?" Ben screamed, staring at the beast in a mix of horror and disgust.

It appeared to be some sort of beetle, only it was the size of a pickup truck. Its carapace was a light blue with white markings across its many legs—fitting camouflage for its arctic environment. Its pitch-black eyes darted around, searching for its prey as the fog drifted from its giant mandibles that were made entirely of ice.

However, the thing that truly sent a shiver down their spines was the remains of some of its unfortunate prey, gruesomely stretched out in full display across its mandibles.

But now wasn't the time to stand idle.

Hana leaped toward the beast and summoned flames from her hand. Ben followed her initiative, pulling out several swirling concoctions from his bag. They weren't going down without a fight.

The beetle clicked in response, skittering rapidly toward the two.

"Here it comes!" Hana charged the flames in her hands, sending several sparks flying as the small mote of fire roared into an inferno. Sweat dripped from her brow as she struggled to hold onto the whirlwind of fire in her hand, using all her concentration to keep control of its chaotic energy while feeding it even more power. Finally, it grew so big that it was beyond her ability to hold onto it.

"Ignis," Hana shouted, letting loose a torrent of fire directly at the bug, engulfing it in a wave of roaring flames.

"Hot damn." Ben watched as every inch of the beetle's body scorched from the intensity of Hana's full magical might. But despite that, it withstood the blast quietly. The more Hana increased the intensity of the flames, the more the beetle appeared hunkered down.

"Why won't you just go down?" Hana screamed, surging all her power into one final inferno.

Silence.

Hana collapsed to the ground, gasping for air as a wave of fatigue pierced every inch of her body. She looked up at the giant bonfire she had turned the beetle into hoping that, just maybe, she had finally defeated it with that final blast of fire.

Screech. The beetle leaped out of its fiery veil, appearing almost completely unharmed. Those few small marks on its shell seemed to only make it even more determined to focus down on Hana.

"Crap." Hana felt the blood drain from her face as the beetle turned its full attention towards her. Its turn to strike had finally arrived. Charging towards her crumbled frame, Hana watched as the insect came closer, looking up at the beetle, it seemed gargantuan to her. She tried to move, tried to dodge in some direction, but her body would not respond to her. Whether from fear or her exhaustion, her legs refused to move. All she could do was watch the beetle's frozen mandibles come ever closer to her, pointed at her like a spear, intent on goring her in one swift attack.

Hana suddenly felt something shove her to the side, just barely edging out the pointed tip of the beetle's mandible.

"Ben!"

Hana turned to watch in horror as the beetle slammed into Ben, pinning him against the wall with a sickening crunch. But instead of ripping into him with its jaws, the beetle leaped back. Shrieking as it swung its frozen mandibles wildly in all directions, an odd substance covering its mouth.

"What did you do?" Hana exclaimed, doing her best to move over to Ben's side.

"I, *ugh,* tossed some of this into its mouth." Ben pulled out one of the concoctions in his bag, wincing in pain. "The one I threw in the creep's mouth was full of acid."

Though relieved that her teammate was all right, something else had drawn her attention.

"Hey, why are you hiding your arm like that?" Hana noticed Ben trying to shift his left arm away from her.

"What are you trying to hide?" Hana looked over to Ben's left arm and upon seeing the state that it was in, immediately knew. "Oh my god! What happened to your arm? It's all twisted."

"*Yes,* I know. But right now, the most important thing is to not let that damn thing get out of our sight." They quickly turned to the beetle.

Its mouth was still covered in Ben's concoction, burning through the beetle's mouth rapidly with a distinct sizzle. The deeper the acid burned into its mouth, the more terrifying the beast's shrieks became. But the two of them could hear the sizzle of the acid growing quieter, the beetle's shrill screams becoming less intense until finally, only a single sound could be heard—a deep, guttural roar.

"What do we do?" Hana panicked as the beetle let out another shrill scream and charged at them. Ben tried to think of some sort of plan to get them out of this situation, but his mind had gone blank.

The only thing he could do was look away.

Boom!

A deafening sound suddenly burst from the ground in front of them, followed by what sounded like a battering ram slamming into a wall.

"The hell was that!?" Ben said.

Out of nowhere, Siris had put herself between them and the beetle, forming a wall of ice just as the beetle was about to rip through them.

Siris let out a pained groan while her hands dug deeper into the wall of ice in front of her. She was doing all she could to hold the beast back, to give herself some more time, but she had something to do, something to say.

"Hana, I need you to summon one of those fire mote things," Siris yelled. The beetle let out another terrifying screech.

"What?" Hana looked at her in confusion, unable to hear her over the shrieks.

"Summon some damn fire!"

Hana stepped back at Siris' command, a mixture of confusion and fear rushing through her. But still, she nodded, pulling out a scrap of cloth and lighting it aflame. "What now?"

"Throw it over to the side, right about...there!" Siris pointed towards the other side of the cave. Hana turned and nodded again, chucking the ball of fire around Siris' crumbling shield.

The clawing and shrieks stopped. Both Ben and Hana looked at Siris, still baffled at what her plan was. But before they could even open their mouths Siris snapped towards them.

"Shhhh," Siris whispered, motioning them to quiet down.

The creature started to slowly turn, shifting its sight toward the patch of fire burning on the other side of the room. And as it did, Siris just smiled, her theory proven correct.

It charged at the flame, clawing and shrieking as it tore through its prey. Both Ben and Hana looked at the beetle, still utterly confused by what had just happened.

"It appears my theory was correct. I thought it was strange that the beetle ignored me and ran away. Then I had an epiphany." Siris watched the beetle aimlessly attack the small fire. "It tracked down its targets not by smell or hearing, but by heat. Such a clever system, perfect for the tundra." Siris walked towards the beetle until she stood just a meter away from it. But still, despite being so close, the beetle didn't turn its attention away from the measly mote of fire in front of it. Siris gave it one last look before she swiftly crossed her arms,

"But it's truly a shame it had to fight against me."

It was quick and deadly, so fast that Hana was barely able to process what had just happened. In the end, all that remained was the skewered remains of the beetle, its body destroyed so quickly that it didn't even have a moment to feel pain. A swift and precise death.

"D-Damn, Siris." Ben looked down at the destroyed remains of the beetle, completely ripped apart by a dozen or so ice spikes, almost feeling sorry for it.

Siris headed in closer to the remains of the insectoid, examining its corpse back and forth as her tracker started to beep rapidly. She looked down at the remains of the beetle's head with disgust and let out a small gag upon seeing a faint blue glow glitter from within. Siris looked back at Hana for a second but decided against it. *Who knows what she might end up doing.* Siris let out one hesitant sigh and reached in.

She cringed as she dug blindly through the gooey remains within its skull until she felt something hard and chiseled brush up against her hand. She grabbed the object, and with a mighty pull, ripped out a strange blue crystal.

"My, would you look at that?" Siris glanced back down at the tracker. One of the three slots above the tracker's radar started to glow softly. It was a perfect match.

The tracker reverted to its normal state once the crystal clicked in, now with only two dots flashing on the screen.

Siris looked back toward Hana and Ben. "You two, let's get going. We can't waste even a single moment if we're going to pass this exam."

Hana quickly pulled Ben back onto his feet and tried to help him walk, but it was too much. Ben collapsed to the ground, unable to go any further.

"What's wrong?"

Ben winced as Siris walked closer. He expected more scolding, more insults, but nothing of that sort came from the aristocrat. Instead, to the surprise of both of them, she knelt next to Ben and carefully examined his bruised arm and leg.

"Ah, you should have told me your wounds were this severe." Siris turned towards Hana. "Do you have any sort of cloth that I can bandage his arm with?"

"Oh! Yeah, let me check." Hana dug through her small satchel and pulled out a few cloth scraps. "Here you go."

Siris grabbed the cloth scraps and partially froze them before turning to Hana. "I need you to cauterize his wounds before I wrap them."

Hana nodded and quickly set to work. Focusing on her remaining strength, she formed a miniature flame and cauterized his open wounds.

"Ugh." Ben winced.

"What's wrong? Does it hurt?" Hana asked, pausing for a moment.

"No, it's fine. Keep going." Ben let out a deep, yet shaky breath. He watched as Hana and Siris slowly patched him up, burning his wounds shut, and then covering them in frozen bandages to relieve them.

"Try and rest for a bit. Do your best to not move. I can't have you collapse on me," Siris ordered Ben, before turning her attention to Hana. "And you, keep an eye on him and make sure he's all right. I'll scout ahead a bit and see where we're headed," Siris said in the sort of tone a mother or teacher would use when talking to a child. "I can't have you two drop out of this match this early, just thinking about what it will do to my reputation is enough to make me wince. So don't even think about failing me now. You hear?"

"Gotcha," Ben and Hana answered blankly.

Siris took that as her cue to head out. "I'll let you two know when we should be good to go."

As Hana watched Siris go, she turned to see that Ben, to her surprise, was smiling. "What's up?"

"Oh, it's nothing." Ben turned to Hana. "It just…"

"It's just what?"

"I kept thinking that she'd leave us behind, you know. Because she probably saw us as nothing more than just baggage. But now?" Ben chuckled. "I think we're gonna be all right."

CHAPTER 6

Kibo stood at the edge of a cliff, looking off into the vast canyon that laid in front of them. Kaze was next to him, tracker in hand.

No matter where one looked, it was just a canvas of beige and brown rock that stretched out endlessly, with enough orange sand to build one hell of a sandcastle. Numerous valleys were sprinkled around the expansive landscape. Within the pockets, hundreds of small stone pillars stood tall. Each one was like an island, hanging above the open abyss.

"Do you see anything in that direction?" Kaze asked Kibo, eyes back down at the radar's screen.

"No, just the same old boring, rocky canyon." Kibo sighed. Despite his relentless scanning of the landscape, he could not find a single creature or anomaly that stood out in the ever-still canyon. They'd been at it for hours now. He couldn't think of what else they could do to prepare.

"Looks like we'll have to go in blind," Kibo said, hopping down from the large boulder he was scouting from.

"You sure?" Kaze perked up. "That sap was the only medical supply we had on hand. If anything happens..."

"Going in blind may be the end of us," Kibo noted. "But what other choice do we have?"

Kaze nodded in agreement. "I just haven't figured out how we're going to get across."

Kaze squinted ahead. The pillars of stone formed a vague pathway from plateau to plateau. They were like stepping stones in a river, only many times more dangerous. Despite his hopes for finding a safer path, he saw no other way through the canyon. He closed his eyes and let out one big breath. "Follow my lead."

"Hup!" Kaze ran towards the edge and, before Rex and Kibo could react, took a daring leap. He landed on the nearest pillar with a resounding thud. Although some dust shook off the pillar, it seemed otherwise stable for the most part. Kaze turned around and gave a thumbs up. "Seems strong enough."

His two companions nodded and followed him.

"Crazy, but it just might work," Arcanus said. *"Just watch your step, kid."*

Kibo nodded and leaped after Kaze. He was right; the rock didn't move an inch. With a hesitant gulp, Rex soon followed.

"Jeez, ya guys sure this is safe?" Rex asked, looking down the side of the pillar.

"We have no other way through." Kaze smirked. "What, are you scared of heights?"

"Of heights? Nah. But if it ain't normal to not be scared standin' on some rickety rock above a giant damn pit, then I don't know what is." Kibo and Kaze chuckled. It wasn't much, but it made things a little less tense.

The group slowly moved from pillar to pillar, taking their time to not slip up. As they moved deeper into the canyon, Kaze would frequently look at the tracker as they got closer to their target.

Before long, they came to a huge plateau in the center of the valley. A glance at the radar confirmed they had arrived. The orange dot was beeping rapidly on their screen. Their target was right in front of them.

However, nothing seemed out of the ordinary. There was only another pillar a step away. They looked at the ground below for clues; nothing there either. Not a single bit of animal or plant life save for a few dried bushes. Kaze sighed before turning his attention over to the tracker.

Rex laid a hand on the wind mage's shoulder. "Seems like we have to keep on going."

"Damn it." Kaze shoved his hand off, scowling. "I know we have to, but I have no clue how to deal with this target. Unless you have a plan on how to find and deal with it, I say that you stay back for now. Because of a *certain someone*, we have nothing to help us now. Charging ahead blindly could get us all eliminated in the blink of an eye."

"Whoa, calm down. Getting angry like that will get us nowhere." Kibo quickly stepped in between the two.

"Hey, man, just saying that we might have to go a little further." Rex waved his hands defensively. "Maybe the freak's hiding or something. That last thing had that special power of...tracking or whatever. Who knows."

Kaze scowled, but he nodded in defeat. Again, no other choice seemed to be available. He crossed his arms. "Fine. You go ahead and waste your energy. Kibo and I will wait here."

"They're like little children." Arcanus sighed.

Rex looked back with a snarky sneer before walking over towards the next plateau on the pillar. Kaze turned around as if to guard the rear, but the annoyed look on his face said otherwise. Kibo rolled his eyes. They *were* like children.

However, Arcanus chirped up in a curious tone. *"Oddly enough, I'm reading heat signatures in the valley. Go check it out, just to be sure."*

Kibo got up and looked at the pillar, then below. The orange rock was bare. Even zooming, he only detected a curious-looking brown lizard crawling on the ground. Not big enough to trip off any sensors.

"Where did you get those heat signatures from? I don't see anything." *That must mean...* "Rex, stop!" Kibo quickly grabbed and pulled Rex back. As he did, the pillar in front of them rumbled and groaned, it's top closing in on itself. The team stared at it, utterly bewildered. They all knew what was in front of them.

This was no pillar.

It was their target, but one far larger compared to their previous quarry. The slender bottom portion of the pillar split apart into four long, rocky legs. The pillar appeared to be its body, with the plateau at the top was a giant mouth that encompassed its entire back. The portions below its mouth slowly shifted to form a smooth yet tough-looking shell. The thing was massive, and this next fight was going to be a whole other ordeal.

The creature looked at Kibo with two giant black, buggy eyes that popped out from beneath its back, staring at the group like a predator that found its next meal. Rumbling with each movement, the beast used its massive limbs to quickly latch onto the other pillars and opened four large cavities across its smooth shell.

"Oh no, I ain't getting eaten today," Rex shouted, taking a stand alongside Kaze while Kibo activated Arcanus, forming a pair of metallic gauntlets.

Yet, instead of charging after them or breaking down their pillar, the thing just stood there.

"Wait, what do you think it's trying to do?" Kibo looked over the edge down at the giant rocky creature. "Huh, is it just gonna stay there?"

"Phew." Rex let out a small sigh of relief. "Guess even that rock knows not to mess with us, huh?"

Buzz.

"Wait." Kibo nudged Rex. "You hear that?"

A faint buzzing, like the buzzing of a beehive, could be heard from a distance. It seemed to be coming straight from the creature.

"*Be ready, Kibo. Looks like things are about to get hectic,*" Arcanus warned, with Kibo bringing up his gauntlets for defense.

The three watched the beast, each of them edging closer to see what exactly the source of the sound was. But the closer they edged, the more cautious they became with each step, watching the still frame as a tense veil hung over all of them. They could hear it, the buzzing growing louder. They all knew something was coming, but they could not simply step away. A tense mix of fear and curiosity drove them to see just what was making that sound.

The beast exploded in a furious, buzzing wave of energy.

Kibo blocked his face as he was assaulted by a torrent of dust, rocks, and dozens of silhouettes flying by. They slashed at him like a tornado of blades, trying to rip through his arms. He dove to the ground and covered his head, only for Kaze to pull him up by the arm.

"Run, Kibo!"

The two bolted in the opposite direction, just managing to jump across onto the pillar behind them.

"Whoa!" Kibo buckled as he landed on the pillar, just barely maintaining his footing on it. His heart pounded as the pillars behind them buckled and crashed onto the ground. It wasn't just them who was being attacked; It was breaking the pillars around them as well.

"Wait, what about Rex?" Kibo snapped back up, looking around for Rex, who seemed to have disappeared from their sight.

"Yeah! Take this, ya flyin' rat." Out of nowhere, Rex crash-landed next to the two of them, along with one of the strange flying creatures into the pillar. "You two see that?" Rex shouted as he smiled up at them, only to be met with a look of bewilderment from both of them.

It seemed that Kaze would have let loose another torrent onto Rex, but was more drawn in by the creature than the troublemaker. The creature, now thankfully slain, vaguely resembled a bat with a rocky shell, and four webbed legs that appeared to be what it used for flying and walking.

"Wow, these things are really something." Kaze looked up at the flying beasts and back at the rocky creature beneath them, and it all suddenly clicked.

"That massive 'thing' must be some sort of hive or queen, and the other creatures must be drones that it controls," Kaze exclaimed, his gaze darting from the hive mother and the swarm, which suddenly turned their attention back towards the group.

"Shit! We don't have the equipment to deal with a swarm." Kaze quickly dashed over to another pillar. "C'mon, you two. Keep moving!"

Both Kibo and Rex followed Kaze. As they did, Kibo glanced back at the pillar behind them. It was swarmed by the drones as it cracked and shattered under their relentless savagery. The giant, rocky pillar fell through the swarm and into the pit below.

"I gotta pick off a few while I can," Kaze quickly pulled out a dozen rounds from his jacket. He placed a bullet on top of his index finger and aimed at the massive mob of creatures. His thumb was slowly enveloped by swirling wind when at last, he flicked it with his finger, sending it streaking towards one of the flying beasts. The bullet went right through its head, a quick and clean kill.

But a single bullet did nothing to stop the horde of drones.

"Damn it, there are too many of them," Kaze shouted as he launched several more bullets into the swarm, but a few rounds weren't enough to stop a swarm of hundreds. "We have to kill the source."

Nodding in agreement, the team began to traverse back to the queen, fighting drones along the way. Kaze picked off as many drones as he could using his bullets. Those who got close were clobbered by Kibo or electrically fried by Rex. However, it was becoming even more difficult as the swarm slowly destroyed all the pillars around them. Their options for a head-on attack dwindled, as did their escape routes.

"The clever bastards are trying to corner us," said Arcanus as Kibo beat down another drone.

The swarm moved closer in a pincer formation, the hive queen slowly closing behind them. No doubt approaching to finish them off.

Kaze shifted his aim towards the queen and fired off a few more rounds only for his bullets to be deflected by its rocky skin if it were nothing. The closest pillars were already cut off by the queen's approach.

"Great job, Kaze. You got us stuck in a corner surrounded by god damn hell bats." Rex said frantically, dropping another drone. "Mother, have mercy."

The hive queen latched onto their pillar and moved closer. As the pillar started to crumble, it opened its maw to reveal rows of razor-sharp, stalactite-like teeth, the kind that looked very painful.

"Wait a minute." Despite their dire scenario, Kibo noticed something vital to their victory. A plan raced through his mind as he realized the queen's fatal mistake.

"Kaze, that thing is crushing the pillars that it is holding on to," Kibo yelled. "If you hit it just right, we can cause that thing to come crashing down."

"What about the pillar we're standing on? It's still holding onto that," Kaze shouted back.

"Don't worry, it's stable enough. Just do it!"

The wind mage looked at Kibo's dead-serious face. They had to try. Nodding grimly, he grabbed three rounds from his bag and aimed. "Cover me!"

Another wave of drones flew towards the group. The two melee fighters jumped beside Kaze, frantically holding them off. Kaze took another deep breath and fired all three bullets in rapid succession. Each bullet struck a pillar right in its weak point, causing each one to collapse in a spectacular explosion of dust.

The queen let out a deafening screech as it clawed frantically at the team's pillar, its last option for stable support.

"Well, now what? How are you gonna get it off our pillar?" Kaze aimed his bullets toward another wave of drones.

He got no response.

"Damn it, Kibo. You there?" No response.

To his shock, Kaze looked down to see Kibo had jumped off the pillar, barreling directly towards the hive mother's limb.

Diving towards the beast, Kibo pulled his arm back and with a perfectly timed swing, slammed into the creature's arm with a resounding boom. Crunching through its thick earth armor and ripping into its fleshy leg.

The hive mother let out one terrifying, ear-bursting screech and buckled, its claws ripped from the pillar. Kibo had done it, but it was far too early to celebrate

"Quick, grab onto that thing, kid," Arcanus shouted.

"Already ahead of you," Kibo shouted back as he reached for the queen. All he had to do was grab onto it and he'd land safely on the ground, victorious over their opponent.

And then the queen gave one last defiant swing.

The blow struck true.

Kibo screamed as he hurtled into free fall. The sheer speed at which he plummeted sent him hurtling in and out of consciousness. He could not think, could not come up with any sort of plan as his mind ripped asunder. He was doomed.

"Wow, you're so cool, Siris!"

The group of children crowded around the young Siris. With the finesse of a sculptor, she molded dozens of snowflakes into intricate designs.

"What did you expect? My father is the greatest mage of all time," she said, beaming with pride.

"Wow, I can't wait to be able to use magic, too," said a small voice.

Siris suddenly stopped, as if catching a scent of a delicious pie, and grinned. She pushed through the crowd to come face to face with a small boy. His face was beyond excited, like he was face-to-face with a celebrity.

"You? Use magic? Aren't you that kid who still can't use magic even though you're eight years old?" Her eyes bore through his soul.

"I-I can use magic. Watch!" Kibo gulped and held his index finger out, concentrating with all his might. Eventually, a little flame sprouted from his finger, dancing faintly in the breeze. He waited for the cries of "Wow!" and thundering applause like they'd given Siris.

But they all laughed at him.

Worst of all, Siris stared at him, a dark smile creeping across her face.

"It probably would have been better if you couldn't use magic." She laughed with the rest of them.

"Stop, please! Watch, I can do more." He tried to increase the intensity of the flame, only for it to lash back at him, burning his finger. He yelped in pain as he desperately tried to salvage the situation. But the only thing it did was make the children only laugh harder.

A gust of icy wind slammed his face into the dirt.

"You will never be as good as me."

He coughed as he gagged on the dirt, tears reddening his eyes. He could only close his eyes and cover his face as the shrill laughter pierced his ears and she—

"Kibo, snap out of it!"

"This is the worst possible moment to be having a flashback," Arcanus yelled.

Kibo woke to his body hurtling towards the ground at terminal velocity.

"Crap, crap, crap. What the hell do I do?" Kibo panicked the ground approached him ever faster.

"Try to land on your feet."

"Land on my feet? What difference will that—"

"Just do it!"

He looked at the glowing triangle in his hand and back at the ground. He had no other option. Moving his body in whatever

Ali Kerem Eke

way he could, Kibo flung and twisted himself until he was standing upright. As he drew closer and closer to the earth, a familiar warmth coursed through his body, pooling down his legs. All Kibo could do was close his eyes and wait to hear a sickening crunch.

But he felt nothing.

Kibo slowly opened his eyes. He was standing upright, every part of his body intact. Other than a slight tingling in his legs, nothing seemed to be in any sort of distress or pain. He seemed...*fine.*

Then he looked down at his feet.

The ground around him had been crushed into broken earth and stone. His feet were covered in a pair of knee-high metal boots. They looked similar to his gauntlet: metallic, intricate, and completely alien.

"Whoa!" Kibo stomped the ground with the new armor. Despite their metallic look, the boots were surprisingly light and comfortable.

"Where the heck did these come from?" Kibo exclaimed, holding his leg up to examine the design better.

"You must have subconsciously unlocked it thanks to that daredevil stunt of yours," Arcanus said proudly. *"Once again, you've surprised me, kid."*

"Let's go check out that beast, I don't want a repeat of what happened last time."

"All right, all right," Kibo agreed, turning his gaze up at the remains of the Hive Mother.

Its massive stone body splayed across the ground, a pool of tar-like blood forming beneath it. Its sharp limbs stood upright, all shriveled up like dead tree trunks, limp and cold. It looked like a partially squashed bug, only it was the size of a frigate ship.

"Well, looks like it's time for us to dig through this thing," Kibo said, letting out a small gag at the thought. However, before he could take a single step towards it, someone called out for him.

"Kibo, damn it. I know you're here," yelled Rex. "Come on. You're not supposed to do the shit I would do."

Rex carefully slid down the rockface, followed by Kaze gliding down with periodic gusts of wind. Rex's eyes darted across the valley frantically until they met Kibo's and the worry instantly dissipated from his face.

"Jesus, man, you scared me." He ran over and gripped Kibo tightly. "Only I'm allowed to do stupid"—Rex's gaze eyes darted to Kibo's feet. "Whoa, where the hell did those come from?"

"Yeah, I imagine you have some sort of explanation for how the hell you survived a fall like this?" Kaze asked from behind, also curious about the sudden appearance of the boots.

Kibo realized he had some explaining to do.

"I have this magic armor. I need it because... "Kibo hesitated for a moment. What should he tell them?

Well, what should I tell them? Kibo telepathically asked Arcanus. *I mean, I don't know if I could even manage to explain this away without raising a few eyebrows.*

Arcanus stayed silent for a few moments like he was trying to think of what sort of answer to give.

"Uh, Arcanus?"

"Aw, to hell with it. I'd just tell 'em at this point. It'll probably do more harm than good to keep it a secret from the two of them for much longer, don't you think?" Arcanus suddenly said, surprising Kibo with his blunt advice.

But deep down, Kibo could feel that what Arcanus said had some merit to it. He closed his eyes and sighed. He had to tell them the truth. "The thing is, I can't really use magic."

They were both taken aback for a moment.

"What the hell?" Rex replied. "I ain't heard of anyone like that. Hell, everyone I knew could at least do a trick or something."

Kaze looked grave. "Need I tell you how dangerous it is to waltz into an exam like this without having magic?"

The two stared at him, demanding an explanation.

"I know," said Kibo. "But it's been my lifetime dream to become a mage. This gear is a gift from a friend. I don't fully understand it, but it's a way for me to achieve that dream. As cliché as it sounds, it's a once-in-a-lifetime chance—my only chance—to get into Bastion. And I intend to use it to its fullest." Kibo looked down at his new boots and smiled. "I think I might be finally making some progress."

The two stood there for a moment, taking in what Kibo had just said. Rex was the first to accept it, nodding proudly at Kibo's fiery spirit. Kaze took a bit longer, scratching his chin in consideration, much to Kibo's worry. Was he going to get angry? Was he going to shout and explain everything wrong with what he was doing?

After an unbearably long silence, Kaze shook his head and sighed. "I wished you'd told me sooner. Seriously, I'm like an inch away from letting out a laundry list of reasons why that's bad. But I'll trust you. For now."

Kaze looked at Kibo and smirked, "So, let's get back to business, shall we?" With the tension finally lifted, the team began their search for the crystal. They all took to searching different parts of its body. Rex clambered on top to search the shell, while Kaze dug through the creature's mouth.

"Took you long enough," Arcanus hummed. *"You gonna tell 'em about me, too?"*

"I don't think they're ready for you at all," Kibo whispered. "Besides, we gotta make sure we stay as hidden as we can. As much as I love Bastion, who knows what they might do to me if they found out what I am—let alone you."

"Huh, I gave you an upgrade no less than five minutes ago and this is how you treat me? Good grief, you're rude." Arcanus chuckled a bit. *"But yeah, you're right. I gotta stay as hidden as I can."*

"Hey, I think I found something." Around the right side of the creature, Kaze motioned Kibo and Rex over. With the tracker in his hand, they saw its dark red screen. "It's somewhere around here."

The creature's rocky side was otherwise bare. They spent several minutes checking for some sort of hidden hole or crevice, but they found not a single lead.

"God damnit. Where could that stupid crystal be?" Frustrated, Kibo stomped his boot right into the creature's shell.

With the combination of his anger and his boots, he cracked straight through the shell with a powerful blow directly into the hive's soft interior, with a gap just large enough for Kibo to squeeze through.

Before the other two could take notice, Kibo hurried inside the hive mother.

He moved through the dark crevices of the creature, noting how they were remarkably spacious, most likely for the swarms of drones. A foul smell emanated throughout the entirety of its body, most likely from all the waste built up within it, much to Kibo's disgust. Fortunately, Kibo managed to find the source of the glow: a peculiar-looking organ that resembled a brain. No doubt the gem was ensconced inside.

"Finally. Let's get this thing and get out of here." Kibo excitedly ran towards the strange organ.

Kibo gagged as he slammed face-first into the squishy tissue, having slipped on a patch of slime. His face was covered in the most disgusting ooze imaginable that both tasted and smelled like rancid onions.

"*Should look where you're going, kid,*" Arcanus said. "*I mean, I could have warned you, But now where's the fun in that?*"

Kibo rolled his eyes, pulling himself out of the organ.

Taking one deep breath, he dug his hand into the creature's brain until he felt something hard inside the tissue. With a mighty pull, he ripped the gem out along with bits of gray matter and ooze. "Okay, I got it this time."

"*Think we got it?*" Arcanus asked.

The slime-covered crystal rested in the center of Kibo's hand. It was warm on his palm, glowing a soft amber.

"We got it all right." Kibo looked down at the gem and smiled. *Only one more to go.*

CHAPTER 7

"Looks like we're almost at the waypoint," Kaze said, sliding down a small rocky hill towards their next target. He checked the tracker again. Two slots were locked in by two glowing crystals. Only one remained empty.

And by the looks of where they were headed, it seemed as though they were entering the very gates of hell.

Before them was a burnt landscape, covered in gray ash and dust. Everything was a mix of gray and black: gray sky, blackened earth, and even the few signs of life were nothing more than the withered, charred remains of trees dotted across the landscape. The ground was parched and cracked as if all the nutrients and water had been sucked out. The few trees, if they could even be called trees, were nothing more than husks of dead branches and scorched bark.

However, none of this was as concerning or frightful as the volcano billowing in the distance, pumping soot and ash into the sky. It would be the last place anyone would want to go.

It was exactly where the tracker pointed.

"You sure we have to go this way?" Kibo asked Kaze, shifting a bit as he looked up cautiously at the brooding volcano.

"It's right where the tracker's pointing so I don't think we have much of a choice." Kaze smirked. "And here I thought that heading through the canyon sucked."

Kaze waited for Rex to slide down and motioned the two of them to follow him. "Come on, the faster we take down this thing, the faster we can get out of this hell hole."

The three walked deeper into the ash-covered hellscape. As they headed closer to their target, the ash in the air got heavier, making it harder and harder to breathe. Eventually, they couldn't walk without one of them collapsing in a coughing fit.

"Looks like the air here is filled with too much ash for us to continue like this." Kaze reached into his bag again and pulled out a few small squares of plain cloth.

"Here, take these," Kaze said, handing both Rex and Kibo a single piece of cloth. "I brought these to use as makeshift bandages, but it looks like we can also use them here to our advantage. Tie them across your face like a bandana. It should make it easier to breathe in this place." The team stopped for a moment, wrapping and tightening the bandanas around their mouths, all while Kaze looked off in the direction of the target. "This area looks even more dangerous than the last. Not only do we need to keep an eye out for the target, but we also need to watch our steps. Meaning I *need* you two to not do anything reckless." He glared at both Kibo and Rex.

"What do you mean *reckless*?"

"Come on, don't tell me I need to remind you." Kaze cut him off with a somewhat tired look.

Kibo paused before going beet red. "Yeah, I guess you're right".

Kaze continued onward. The cracks within the earth only got bigger and the plant life scarcer.

Kaze stopped in his tracks. He took a bit of a look around. It all just seemed the same. No matter how far they went, no matter how many times he looked at their radar, it felt like they were just walking in circles. He turned towards his other two teammates. "We'll stop here for a while, but be ready to head out at a moment's notice. We have to be prepared to fight the next monster."

Kibo cautiously scanned the area before sitting down, afraid the ground would somehow break apart into a pit of lava. Kaze pulled out the tracker and began to fiddle with it, trying to plan out their route. Meanwhile, Rex just laid down on the ash-covered ground and stared up at the gray, murky sky.

Kibo took this moment to observe his teammates, watching Kaze's calm yet puzzlingly intense look as he fiddled with the tracker, in contrast to Rex's laid-back bliss as he rested quietly on the ground. *They are different from me, huh?* Kibo said, leaning back onto a withered, dead tree.

"Well, yeah obviously they are. I mean, it isn't that hard to tell," Arcanus said, as the two of them glanced at Kibo's teammates.

Yeah, I know that. Kibo paused for a moment. "I just don't know if people will truly accept me, not even as a mage, but as a friend," Kibo said telepathically to Arcanus. "It's just been kind of hard. I never really had anyone by my side who I could call a friend. Sure, I have my family, but outside of that, no one ever really hung around me. No thanks to her. It's honestly been a bit overwhelming for me to suddenly be in a team and work with others like this."

Kibo tossed a pebble aimlessly, watching the ashen ground blow away in the breeze. A troubled look rested on his face. *And then I have you. I mean, just think about the position I'm in. I went from being some powerless kid to suddenly having a machine that can transform into a pair of gauntlets and boots. I try my best, but how can I just explain it away when I don't even know how you work? Hell, what even are you?*

"Look kid, you're asking a two-thousand-year-old amnesic robot for help with an existential crisis; don't expect much from me." Arcanus paused as if to reconsider its tone. *"But you shouldn't give up. All you can do is take your tools and run with them because if there is anyone who can figure out how to use and understand me, it's you.*

"And I wouldn't worry about working and bonding with others. You're a bright kid. As long as you help out others, and show 'em some respect, you'll fit in just fine."

Kibo rubbed Arcanus' sigil subconsciously as he mulled over the machine's advice. It had a point. "Heh, guess there's more to you than just being a busted-up machine."

Rex could not sleep. The air was too hard to breathe in, the rocks were all rough and pointy, and he felt as though was going to fall through the ground somehow.

Boredom overcoming his fatigue, he sat up and looked around for something to keep him busy. He finally decided to set his sights on Kaze (not that there was much else within the ash-covered hellscape). Kaze hardly noticed him walking over, too busy fiddling with the tracker while drinking some water from a small metal flask. His gaunt face was in the usual perpetual squint-and-frown, engrossed in whatever he was trying to accomplish.

After a few moments of glancing over at what Kaze was doing, Rex decided to go in for a closer look.

"Hey, whatcha got there?"

Kaze gave an indifferent glance at Rex before turning back to the tracker. "And how will answering your question help me with this?"

"Just tryna figure out what you're doing, that's all. No need to get so defensive." Rex raised his hands in the air.

Kaze placed the tracker down and thought for a moment, staring off into the distance. "I was thinking about how everyone back home is doing, what they must be thinking about me," Kaze replied, gazing down at the ground with downcast eyes.

"I guess one of you was going to ask eventually, so I might as well explain it now." Kaze got up on his feet. "I've been trying to get away from my family."

"What? Why?"

Kaze took a deep breath and continued, "They did things that I don't agree with."

"Huh, what kind of things?"

Kaze shook furiously. "I never saw eye to eye with them, so I left. That's all."

"Oh, sorry about that." Rex slowly backed up a bit.

"What? You expected me to come from a normal, comfortable family like you did?" Kaze snapped at Rex.

"And where the hell did you get that from?" Rex snapped back, much to Kaze's surprise. "Didn't think that I might've gone through some shit myself?"

"No, I just—"

"You just what? All I did was ask you a simple question, and you suddenly got angry thinking about your past like I did." Rex sat down next to Kaze in silence.

They sat there for a while, neither saying a word to the other. The silence pressed down, making it unbearable for both of them. One had to eventually crack under the pressure.

"So, why *are* you here?" Kaze asked Rex, breaking the awkward silence. Rex didn't respond at first and looked off into the distance. "Rex?"

"I made someone a promise." Rex smirked.

Kaze looked over at Rex for a moment, turning his gaze back towards the horizon. "Guess I was wrong."

"Hey, you know where Kibo went?" Rex hopped to his feet, returning to his usual carefree self. As if he had forgotten what the two of them just talked about.

"Oh, I thought he was by that withered tree." Kaze turned around. "He should be right there."

Kibo was gone.

"Where did he go?" Kaze got up to his feet, a sudden twinge of worry piercing his heart. "Kibo!"

No response.

"Where the hell did he go? Ya think he woulda told us where he was gonna head out." Rex peered in the same direction as Kaze.

"You would thi—"

"Get away from there!" Kibo frantically raced away from the two of them.

"Oh boy. I wonder what that's about," Rex said sarcastically as the ground started to shake beneath them, running off in a sprint. Kaze followed suit, bullets in hand. "Do you have any idea what's happening?"

"How about you look down at that radar of yours," Kibo shouted back at Kaze.

"Let me guess, our target is right beneath us?" Kaze looked down at his radar, and sure enough, the dot was smack dab in the very center of the area.

"Do you know what kind of creature we're going up against?"

Almost as if in response to Kaze's question, their target burst from the ground.

The massive creature launched itself several meters in the air, letting out a deafening screech as it exploded from the earth. At first glance, it appeared similar to a large worm. Upon further inspection, they could see several hundred legs running along the side of its body.

It was a monstrously large centipede. With its dark purple carapace and tar-like skin visible through its cracks—a perfect predator for its environment.

"Whoa! Did it just freeze in midair?" Rex looked up at the massive centipede. It stood completely still, locking the carapace into place as it towered over them and their surroundings. It had two sets of glowing red eyes, darting wildly across the ash-covered landscape.

"What's it doing?" Rex shouted, looking at the monstrous centipede with both shock and awe.

"Well, whatever it's doing, I would get down."

The centipede let out another blood-curdling screech as it turned its entire body towards Kaze. Its red eyes glowed with fury, its rancid, glowing maw wide open.

"Arcanus, what's going on now?" Kibo asked Arcanus as he looked up at the Centipede. Trying to figure out all of its movements and actions.

"*Oh no...*"

"What's the matter?"

"*Its entire body suddenly started to increase in temperature,*" Arcanus exclaimed. "*It probably about to—*"

The centipede let out a sudden burst of molten lava from its monstrous mouth, hurling it at Kaze with such force that its body recoiled from the effort.

"Kaze!"

Kaze let out a blast of air at his feet, launching himself off the ground as the ball of lava hurtled towards him. Hot lava splashed onto the earth.

"*Damn.*" Kaze felt the color drain from his face as the lava melted everything, leaving behind a smoldering hole in the ground. Kaze could not help but imagine what would have happened had Kaze been just a second late.

"Don't take your eyes off that thing," Kaze shouted, signaling both Kibo and Rex to the centipede.

When they did, however, it had disappeared into the earth, leaving behind only the giant hole it had burst through. "How did it disappear that fast?" Kibo looked down, bewildered.

"*And without making any noise?*" Arcanus mumbled.

"Shit, that bug must be trying to get the jump on us again," Kaze shouted. "Huddle up!"

Following his command, the group consolidated, each facing in a different direction, ready for the centipede to strike. Rex's eyes darted around rapidly, waiting impatiently for the centipede to strike again. "When ya think it's gonna come back up? Gonna give that thing a pounding!"

The ground rumbled again, getting more and more intense as the massive creature dug around beneath them.

"Well, I think that's your answer," Kaze yelled back at Rex. "Here it comes!"

As expected, the centipede launched itself straight through the surface with a resounding *boom*, letting out another screech as it showered everything around it in a barrage of dirt and stone.

"Watch it! We gotta let it come to us. We can't risk charging that thing head-first," Kaze shouted at Kibo and Rex, holding them back from the lava-drenched centipede. They nodded in agreement, waiting for the creature to rush them like it had before, ready to retaliate.

The beast seemed to not even notice them. Instead, it launched itself over them like a spring. The three of them froze, its body so massive that it almost blotted out the sun. Yet at the peak of its jump, it started to do something quite peculiar.

"Is it spinning?" Kibo looked up, perplexed. But his observation was not wrong. The team slowly backed away from the giant centipede as it started rotating in mid-air. They watched its twisting body out of curiosity, wondering what it was trying to do.

"Huh?" Kaze heard a slight sizzle beneath his right ear and looked over to his side. A small drop of lava fell right onto his shoulder, burning slowly through his leather jacket. At that very moment, it all made sense to him.

"Get down," Kaze yelled at them, diving behind an ash-covered boulder.

"You don't have to tell me twice," Rex shouted back. He and Kibo jumped behind the same boulder, just as the lava splashed onto the ground.

Kibo gulped. Drops of lava sizzled across the landscape, raining down on the team like a volley of arrows—only far deadlier.

It took a while for the rain to stop, but when it did, all was quiet again. The group looked around for a bit, waiting to see if the centipede was preparing to attack them. Yet everything remained calm.

"Is it gone?" Kibo asked, unable to bear the silence. Kaze got back onto his feet and looked around for a moment.

"I wouldn't be so sure."

The ground beneath them suddenly gave way, parting to reveal a magma-filled sinkhole right beneath it.

"Get outta there, kid," Arcanus shouted, giving Kibo that sudden shock to push him into full gear.

"Whoa!" Either by instinct or quick thinking, Kibo jumped with all his might, sending himself far away from the sinkhole thanks to his new set of boots. "That thing won't even give us a single second to think!"

Arcanus snorted. *"What'd you expect? Imagine the calorie intake it needs to maintain a body that big. No doubt it's hungry and looking for prey. Can you really blame it?"*

"Thanks for the *very helpful* biology lesson," Kibo muttered in annoyance. He would have said far more if it weren't for the massive centipede charging at them.

The centipede continued its ceaseless offense. It dove in and out of the ground like a needle through fabric, fast enough to avoid Kibo's and even Rex's lightning-fast blows. Sometimes, it would dive underground for a bit longer, only to burst up again to spew a molten fireball. Other times, it would erupt from the ground and spin rapidly, leaving the two to frantically scatter among the lethal, ranged attacks.

However, one of them did manage to let off a small counterattack.

Four shiny bullets flew towards the centipede, only to bounce off of its thick carapace. No use.

Kaze pocketed his bullets and clenched his fist. His mind raced frantically, trying to think up some kind of plan. Only one thing came to his mind. He refused. It was too risky. There was too much at stake to take a *chance* at landing a single shot at the beast.

But, if I land that hit... Kaze thought to himself.

"Crap! Here it comes again."

The creature fired another ball of molten lava, just barely missing Kibo. Kaze looked at his teammates; they were fine, a little ash-covered, but neither had suffered any sort of injury so far.

They were beyond exhausted, their bodies caked in a mix of sweat and ash. He watched as they gasped for each breath of air, trying desperately to keep going despite being just mere moments away from collapsing. And all of this effort to dodge the centipede's attacks! Kaze closed his eyes.

He had to do it.

"Kibo, Rex, I need you to hold the creature off of me for a while. I got another plan."

He grabbed his right arm and focused all of his attention upon it. Small gusts of wind manifested around his arm, swirling his air rhythmically and purposefully, getting faster with each passing second.

"Know what he's doing?" Rex panted, looking over to Kaze.

Kibo gazed down at Kaze's right arm, now wrapped in a swirling storm of energy.

"No idea, but he looks like he knows what he's doing," Kibo replied. They moved in to defend the wind mage, waiting patiently for the hellish beast to strike again. But nothing came.

"It was attacking us nonstop, and now it just disappeared? Where the hell did it go?" Rex turned over to Kaze.

"Ya see that creep on that map of yours?"

"I think you can tell I'm a bit too busy to be looking at the radar right now," Kaze snapped.

"Oh, come on, please don't tell me they're gonna start at it again," Kibo groaned.

"*Huh, that's strange.*" Arcanus sounded more puzzled than stressed.

"What's so strange about us fighting a massive lava centipede right next to a volcano?"

Arcanus ignored the sarcasm. "*Well, I was trying to scan for the centipede to see if I could pinpoint it, but I noticed that the ground below us is completely hollow.*" Arcanus paused.

"*Hold on a second. That bastard encircled us right above a pressurized chamber of magma. It's trying to roast all of us to a crisp. Move!*"

Kibo didn't have a moment to process what Arcanus had told him as the ground started to crack apart.

"Shit! It must be coming at us for another attack," Kaze said, fortifying his stance. Not knowing that it was doing quite the opposite. In this small window of opportunity, Kibo did the only thing he could.

"Get out of here!" By pure instinct, Kibo dove towards the nearest person as the ground gave way.

Kibo opened his eyes. He was flying up several hundred feet in the sky. The blast of pressurized air had destroyed the ground, leaving behind nothing except a massive pit of lava.

Although he had managed to shield himself with his gauntlets at the very last second, Kibo imagined the rest of his body would be burning with pain, every bit of skin across his body screaming as he was roasted to a crisp. Instead, it felt like nothing had happened at all to him.

Hang on just a second." Kibo's chest, shoulders, and thighs were encased in shining white armor. And he was barreling towards the earth in a freefall.

Come on, land on something solid. Something—

Kibo's entire body buckled even as his new set of armor absorbed almost the full brunt of his landing. He clenched his teeth as every bone and muscle in his body started to burn. He could feel his suit heat up as Arcanus desperately tried to manage not only the new addition to Kibo's armor but also the energy from that impact. Yet he held through.

"Hot damn, kid. You managed to pull out almost the entirety of my combat form with that adrenaline rush of yours. Saved our asses at the last second!"

"Where are they?"

"Huh? What the hell's that supposed to mean?"

"Kaze and Rex. Where are they?" Kibo looked around frantically.

"Over here, jackass!" Kibo whipped around towards the sudden shout. He didn't need to hear it twice to know who it was.

"Rex! Are you okay?" Kibo said, frantically rushing over towards Rex.

"Yeah, I'm all right," Rex sputtered as Kibo slid next to him. However, one look at Rex was all Kibo needed to know that he was anything but okay.

"All right? Look at you. You're completely covered in burns."

While Rex's upper body seemed fine—as fine as it could look for being covered in a mix of ash and sweat—what truly terrified Kibo was the state of his legs.

They were both almost completely ripped to shreds, with large sections of flesh exposed or embedded with shards of rock.

As if that was not bad enough, Rex was losing lots of blood, and fast.

"I...we need to"—Rex gagged through the pain—"get ready for that thing."

"Wait, are you seriously trying to get back up?" Kibo looked down at Rex in a mix of shock and horror as Rex desperately tried to get back onto his feet.

"You aren't doing anything while you look like that!" Kibo turned around to see Kaze shouting at him, his right arm now wrapped in a furious storm of howling winds.

"Kaze! Are you okay?"

"I'm fine, unlike that knucklehead over there." Kaze looked down at his arm. "With this much air pressure wrapped around my arm, all I needed was to let out a small bit of it to quickly get away from that explosion." Kaze turned towards Rex, wincing upon seeing the sheer amount of damage to his legs. "Unfortunately, it seems you didn't manage to get out of there in time. We have to beat that centipede as fast as we can before something even worse happens to Rex."

"Here, take these scraps of cloth I still got on me. They should at least stop the bleeding." Kaze frantically dug through his pocket with his free hand, before ripping it out and tossing several bits of cloth at Kibo.

"Crap. What the hell did they tell me to do in first aid training with an injury like this?" Kibo panicked, desperately trying to bandage and clean Rex's wounds to the best of his ability. Rex winced as Kibo pulled bits of stone out from his legs, trying to say something in defiance, but didn't have the strength to let out even a small mumble. He was far past his limit.

"Wait, won't he just get teleported out of here to safety like that other group?" Kibo asked, desperately hoping there was a way Rex could get some sort of real aid. Though Kaze's outlook was far more grim and likely.

"I don't think so. That other group got teleported out once all of them got knocked out. So unless you plan on giving both me and yourself a concussion, I wouldn't count on it." Kaze looked down towards the giant gaping pit of lava that was now before them. "The only way we're getting out of here and passing this exam is by taking that thing down."

Kibo's mind started to race. The only way Rex was going to get any aid was by them defeating that centipede.

Tossing Rex against a boulder, Kibo sprinted back towards the battlefield. A defenseless Kaze furiously gestured at Kibo; he still needed more time to charge.

As if summoned directly by his thoughts, the centipede popped up from the ground and rushed towards Kibo, almost expecting him to run away. But this time, Kibo stood his ground. This creature was driven by nothing but a sense to hunt and kill. It was just another animal that saw them as nothing more than prey. So why should he have any sort of hesitation when attacking it?

Kibo leapt toward the creature, a rage far beyond what he had ever felt burning throughout him as he charged at the beast. He wasn't going to back down. Not this time.

The centipede let out a blood-curdling scream as it reeled back. Kibo had crunched his armored shoulder deep into the insect's carapace.

The centipede huddled away, and despite its best efforts to cover its wound with its mandibles, Kibo could clearly see the full extent of the damage he had done. The carapace on its face was shattered, revealing the soft pink flesh beneath the cracks now present on its head.

The centipede gazed down at Kibo with a look of rage, almost as if it was unable to comprehend how such a small thing could manage to gravely damage its shell. It only made it more determined to finish off its prey.

Whether he intended to or not, Kibo had gotten its attention.

The centipede charged towards Kibo, screeching and clicking the giant pincers by the sides of its mouth. But none of it put even the slightest dent in Kibo's armor. His mind was set,. He knew what he had to do, and that he had one shot to do it.

"What are you doing? We have to move. That thing is gonna crush us into a million bits." Arcanus panicked but Kibo had a plan.

"I'm gonna grab that thing by the mouth."

"By the—do you see that thing? I'd give you a twelve percent chance of even grabbing one of those pincers," Arcanus shouted at Kibo, utterly bewildered by his insane plan. Nevertheless, Kibo refused to back down. Hearing those odds only seemed to make him more determined to hold his ground, as if to prove that he could beat those odds.

"Come on." Kibo watched the centipede draw in closer to him by the second. A hundred different calculations flowed through his mind of when to strike as he waited.

"Closer." He could feel the sweat drip down the side of his brow.

"Closer." His heart pounded as though to burst from his chest.

"Closer..." His hands trembled as the centipede drew so close that Kibo could see the very center of its small, beady red eyes.

"Now!" Kibo threw out his arms as the centipede lunged with all of its primal fury, bringing in its mandibles to crush him in one swift stroke.

"There we go," Kibo screamed as his legs buckled. His bones creaked as he grappled the raging centipede. It attempted to close its pincers, to shake Kibo away violently, but to no avail. Kibo held fast, his feet digging deeper into the earth as it desperately tried to reach for him. And as it did, its long, segmented body slowly scrunched up more and more, revealing the soft fleshy skin underneath its tough carapace.

That was all Kaze needed.

"Hold him just like that, Kibo," Kaze yelled from behind.

"What does it look like I'm doing?" Kibo held onto the centipede for dear life.

Kibo felt a sudden blur fly over him, only to see Kaze slam directly in between the massive carapace plates, smashing the whirlwind of energy around his arm directly into the small opening of soft, vulnerable skin.

Like a balloon, the plates expanded as the pressure inside its body increased tenfold. The centipede reeled back into the air as it realized what had happened. But it was far too late for it to do anything about it.

Kibo stumbled back as a giant chain of shockwaves suddenly blasted out from the centipede. With a mix of morbid curiosity and awe, he watched as the centipede flailed around in the air, screeching in agony as its entire body was destroyed in a chain reaction. Segments of its body blew up one by one, leaving nothing but its blown-out shell.

"That was something." Kibo looked down at the remnants of the centipede. Its smoldering exoskeleton lay on the ground, its remaining lava-like entrails spilling out on the ground.

"Wait, where's that other kid?" Arcanus said.

Kibo turned his attention up to the sky and—just as he guessed—Kaze was still up in the air. Far up in the air. Yet, he didn't hurtle towards the ground like a streaking bullet, but rather floated down gracefully, using the last bits of energy he had to slow his descent.

"Kaze, you all right? That was one hell of an attack!" Kibo ran over to where Kaze had landed.

"Yeah, I'm all right," Kaze rasped in between small gasps of air. Despite being within point-blank range of the massive explosion, Kaze was mostly fine. The most damage he had sustained was to his jacket's right arm, which was destroyed, exposing his bare, but uninjured arm.

"Hope that's the last time I gotta do that," Kaze gasped. "Go check on Rex, will you?"

Kibo nodded and dashed over to where he had left Rex, and it didn't look pretty. Rex's legs were covered in a mix of blood and sweat. And worse, every part of his body had gone pale.

"Shit, he doesn't look too good, kid." Arcanus almost sounded as though he was sick at the very sight of him.

"You don't think I can't tell that just by looking at him? We gotta get him out of here as quickly as possible!" Kibo reached for Rex. "Jesus! He's still conscious?" Kibo jumped back. Rex jolted upright. He had not expected for Rex to even be able to move, let alone be conscious.

"I'm up. I can still help...with..." Rex's words were jumbled, though the fact that he could even speak only further surprised Kibo and Arcanus.

"I'll be damned. If there's one thing I can say, that kid's got quite the spirit. But I don't really think he can get anywhere with just that."

"Because of the fact that both of his legs are stabbed by like a dozen spikes and he's probably bled out half of the blood in his body?" Kibo snapped at him.

"Yeah, I guess you could say that," Arcanus replied sheepishly.

"Well, we should probably get going then." Kibo reached for Rex and put him over his shoulder. Rex's response was a slight mumble, as though he meant to say something in protest, but could only weakly concede.

"Okay let's see if Kaze's got the gem," Kibo said enthusiastically as he started walking towards the blown-out carapace of the giant centipede. However, as soon as he placed Rex on his back, Kibo felt as though he had hauled up an entire boulder. His legs strained just from the weight of Rex's body, despite him being the lightest member of the group.

That thing really wore me out, Kibo thought to himself, his breath coming more uneven with every step he took.

"I don't think it takes much imagination to see that holding onto a massive bug for that long would tire you out," Arcanus replied jokingly.

"Yeah, I know." Kibo rolled his eyes.

"But seriously, that was something else. The fact that you managed to hold onto that thing for that long should have been physically impossible. Well, unless one had a massive spike of adrenaline. But even then, your body would need to be pumping so many hormones that... You know what? Forget it."

Kibo looked down at Arcanus, confused. "What do you mean?"

"I just said forget it. It's as simple as that, kid."

Kibo opened his mouth to prod further but stopped. He shouldn't push it. Still, he couldn't help but wonder what Arcanus was going on about.

All he did was just try and hold back that giant centipede, but something did feel off. That thing was not only several times larger than him, but it was on a full-blown rampage. How was that possible?

Kibo shook his head. He had more pressing matters to focus on, such as finding his other companion.

"Kaze, where are you?" Kibo shouted out into the ash-covered landscape. He didn't see a single person.

"Right over here." Kaze rested by a small boulder, scrubbing away at something in his hand.

"All right, almost...there!" Kibo grunted as he put Rex up against the boulder and let out one long sigh. Despite not saying a word, it wasn't hard for Kaze to see that Kibo was absolutely exhausted.

"Whatcha got over there?" Kibo said, looking down at Kaze. To his surprise, he saw Kaze was already fiddling about with a gem in his hands.

"Wait a minute. You already found it?" Kibo said as he looked over Kaze's shoulder, almost unable to believe that Kaze could have found their target that fast.

The little gem was covered in a mix of blood and ash. Despite being covered in so much grime, Kibo could clearly see it shining a bright red. Kaze looked down at the red gem in his hand and smirked. "Yup."

Finally, their last challenge was complete.

As Kaze inserted the crystal onto the last slot, he watched the screen in his hand turn a deep blue instead of the default black, like it had been washed over by a great tsunami. At the very center of that vast ocean remained one small white dot, beeping faintly. "Huh, would you look at that?"

"What's going on?" Kibo asked.

"My best guess is that's where the central facility to finish this exam is." Kaze hopped back onto his feet. "The interesting thing is the place it's showing us is in the exact direction we came from. All we have to do is retrace our steps."

"That sounds easier than I thought it would be," Kibo said, looking down at the tracker.

"Well, we can't sit here and think about it. Come on. We don't have a single moment to waste."

Kibo nodded and placed Rex back up onto his shoulder. Well, at least we won't be fighting any massive monsters at this point."

And of course, the ground below suddenly started to shake again.

"Oh, you have to be kidding me. Don't tell me it's another one of those bugs," Kibo groaned.

"Uh, no it's not," Arcanus spoke up. *"The magma vent below us is getting more and more unstable by the second from all the tunneling that thing did. Meaning you gotta start running, kid"*

"Kaze, move," Kibo shouted and sprinted away from what was surely to become another fiery pit of lava.

With every step he took, Kibo could hear the ground behind him break apart, erupting into a deafening roar as waves of magma and earth slammed into each other.

"Watch your feet, Kibo. One wrong step and we're—"

"Oh, shit!" Kibo and Kaze screamed as the ground below them suddenly broke away from the surface, launching them high into the sky by a blast of immense air pressure. *"Stay upright, Kibo!"*

"I know" Kibo shouted back at Arcanus as he spun around in the air. He barely managed to position himself upright as they started to freefall toward the ground. All he could do now was hold onto Rex with all his might and pray that he would land on solid ground.

"Oh boy, get ready kid. This is gonna be one rough landing." Kibo slammed into the earth, his feet digging deep into the ashen soil below him as a painful sensation burned through his body. But he held through yet again as his armor absorbed most of the impact of the landing.

"Kaze, where are you?" Kibo looked around frantically, before seeing that Kaze had landed safely a few meters in front of him. Letting out a quick sigh, Kibo ran over to Kaze, who had his eyes glued to the tracker.

"We gotta keep going if we want to get Rex to safety. Come on!" Kaze motioned as he sprinted towards the exit, tracker in hand.

The ground shook furiously as he slung Rex on his back in a fireman's carry, hurriedly running behind Kaze. Kibo's heart pounded to the rhythm of the earth's rumbling as he turned to look over his shoulder and saw the devastation. Everything behind them had collapsed in on itself, leaving nothing but a roaring lake of lava.

He could not look at the devastation for long. For time was not on their side.

CHAPTER 8

The flickering light of a line of small projectors illuminated the dark, dusty room. Each was playing different recordings onto the gray wall, each focused on one of the ten teams. Staff members paused and played the recordings frame by frame, methodically scratching notes on clipboards and muttering to each other about their analysis.

However, one peculiar member of the horde of staff was fixated on projector ten. He watched curiously as the armored figure took the full brunt of a lava blast, escaping completely unharmed. He took further interest as he skipped forward to another clip, where the examinee rushed through the forest, carrying an injured comrade without slowing down.

"So that's the final group?" a staff member near the man asked.

"Why, yes it is. Group 21 is quite an interesting bunch, aren't they?" the man mused, intrigued by the examinee. "Never seen so many potential candidates."

"That was the point of the written exam, no?" a voice toned in from the back of the room. His deep vocals rang through the room, even with how packed it was. All with the slightest hint of a German accent. "They're all interesting—the aristocrats, the clean slate, the nature mage from the arctic."

The more the voice rang throughout the room, the more members of staff recognized it, including the young man. Pulling himself away from the screen, he turned towards the back of the room. *He* was here.

"S-Sir," he said, adjusting his tie before he gave a crisp salute. The other staff followed, standing at attention. The dim lights illuminated the gruff officer's face—a deep frown and even deeper battle scars.

"At ease," he said, waving his hand dismissively. He crossed his arms and asked the young man. "Sidorov, if you would, please elaborate on group 21."

Sidorov fiddled with his pin and nodded. "Well, one member of the group that particularly drew me in was Kibo Kozlov, a boot-camp flop who lacked even the most basic control of any magical power. While he isn't the first non-mage to apply, there is something very peculiar about his equipment."

"I'm guessing that armor isn't some rusty steel plate. How young is he?"

"He's pretty young, eighteen—oh, you'll want to see this." Sidorov leaned over and rewound the videotape. They watched a clip of the team's battle with the forest beast. "The armor seems to regenerate during battle, and it appears the examinee can retract the suit at any time."

Sidorov pressed a few buttons and rewound again, this time in slow motion. The officer watched as the forest beast lobbed its brutish fist at Kibo's gauntlet, smashing the intricate plating clean off, but within seconds, the mangled gauntlet regenerated back to its original shape to such a perfect degree that it looked like it never broke in the first place.

"It's similar to the properties of Sanoium metal, but that only makes me ask even more questions." Sidorov scratched his head. "How could someone like him have acquired such a large amount of Sanoium? Or better yet, be able to craft such an intricate suit of armor from it?" Sidorov looked on, equal parts impressed and concerned. "While I can't be certain, it seems that the suit is somehow evolving." Sidorov looked up at the recording and back down at his notes, almost as though he couldn't believe what he was saying.

"I mean, a pair of gauntlets, next greaves, and now almost an entire suit. I've never seen anything like it."

"Indeed."

The projector flickered from scene to scene. Kibo punching the forest beast. Kibo leaping from the cliffside at the hive mother. The group's fight with the last creature moment by moment. Sidorov edged closer to the screen to witness the entirety of the desperate battle the team fought through until the reel had reached its end, with Kibo and his team heading into the central building as the scene slowly disintegrated into white static.

"Well now." Sidorov turned to his superior, scanning his now-illuminated face for any additional orders. The veteran's face was still stoic, but he furrowed his brow as he smirked: a glimmer of fascination.

"Sir, do you want to start any sort of investigation? It's just far too suspicious for a commoner like him to have such cutting-edge tech." Sidorov waited for a reply, but only silence from the officer. "We should at least take Kibo out of the exam to study the armor. If anything, we'll walk away with some more work for the guys at Research & Development."

His superior shook his head.

"You can give all the new guns, armor, and spells to R&D after this exam is over," he said. "Go and keep an eye on Kibo, but let him stay. I have a gut feeling that there's more to him than just a fancy set of armor and a few strong punches." With that, the officer turned towards the door.

"Sir, with all due respect"—Sidorov hesitated for a moment as he met the officer's piercing eyes—"I don't think command will be happy with this."

The officer faltered for a long moment. It looked like there was almost a hint of uncertainty in his eyes, but it vanished as quickly as it appeared.

"Tell them that when *Lieutenant* Batros ignores protocol, it's for a damn good reason. Kibo is off limits until I say so, and that goes for the rest of his team. Got it?" Before Sidorov could retort, he gave Sidorov a snappy salute and walked off.

As he left the observation room, Batros tightened his hand into fist. His mind wrapped in a veil of thoughts swirling around in his head.

That group better be worth it.

It could've been minutes, days, or weeks since they woke up. They really didn't care. All that mattered was the medical report. Kibo and Kaze waited outside the medical ward to hear what Rex's condition was.

How do you think Rex is? Kibo asked Arcanus telepathically.

"Well, all I can say is I hope the kid's all right. Considering how he was still going despite my readings, I believe he has around a fifty-six percent chance of making it out unharmed."

"Fifty-six percent!?" Kibo exclaimed. Only to quickly clasp both his hands over his mouth. The guard by the door glared at him.

"Uh, sorry," Kibo apologized. The guards had told them to stay put and be quiet, much to Kaze's chagrin. But there was little they could do to retort them and their rifles, leaving the wind mage quite vexed.

To take his mind off his current situation, Kibo took in the insides of an actual Bastion facility. Its white concrete walls were covered in many of the recruitment posters and messages that he would often read or see as a little kid. He even smirked a little when he saw one with a picture of the Red Cossacks, or another with The Lightning Wonder.

"What got ya smilin' like that, kid?" Arcanus asked

It's nothing really. I just happened to see a few posters that remind me of the shows and pictures I saw as a kid, Kibo replied fondly.

"Really? Which ones?" Arcanus prodded further, genuinely curious.

Well, that one over there is the Red Cossacks. I used to listen to them on the news to hear all the cool stuff they did as a kid. They're a group of Russian agents who work for Bastion and the Russian government. They help so many different people and countries all the time. Kibo paused for a bit, almost as if he was taking a moment to savor the memories flooding back to him.

And the other one's The Lightning Wonder. And even though she's a Commonwealth agent, she still works to uphold Bastion's principles even when working right here in Russia. I would hear all about her and the crazy stuff she did to help people and take down any rogue mages and baddies that are around."Hm, they sound like good people," Arcanus said.

Yeah. That's exactly why I want to join Bastion. Because when you're there, it doesn't matter what country you're from or who you are. You are fighting to protect the world from harm and help people. A lot of countries often have many of their top agents work for Bastion from time to time as a sign of goodwill and to show that they care about upholding the world order and peace," Kibo exclaimed, getting giddy with excitement at talking about Bastion.

"Now, hypothetically speaking, what would happen if, say, one were to put agents into Bastion to further their agenda?" Arcanus asked,

Well, if they tired, not only would they run the risk of damaging their own reputation on the global stage, but it would result in getting banned from Bastion permanently. That would further mark them as an unreliable nation to work or trade with and keep them from being able to easily communicate with other countries on the world stage.

"I see..." Arcanus trailed off a bit, sounding somewhat skeptical. *"Well, that's interesting and all, but I think you should check your friend over there. He seems agitated."*

Kaze paced back and forth in front of the medical ward. He was alone with his thoughts, which lead him to further worry.

Damn. It didn't have to be this way. Kaze pondered to himself, his thoughts clearly on full display across his troubled face.

"What's wrong?" Kibo whispered to him.

"It's nothing really. Just wondering if I could have done anything different back there during our fight with that last thing." "I think you did pretty well." Kibo chuckled quietly.

"What do you mean?" Kaze asked, somewhat intrigued by Kibo.

"I mean, if it wasn't for that quick thinking of yours, all of us might have been roasted to a crisp *and* failed the exam," Kibo said. "And not only did we all make it back, we passed the test and got Rex to the medical ward just in time."

Kibo paused for a moment, "So, if you ask me, it couldn't have gone any better. Well, other than you know... but I'm sure he's fine. Rex's a tough guy! I'm sure he'll pull through. For heaven's sake, that guy stayed conscious after having both his legs get messed up like that!"

Kaze chuckled at the memory. "You're right. You know, I thi—"

Kaze was cut off as the door to the medical ward swung open. Kibo and Kaze both froze; neither of them could believe what they were seeing.

Rex stepped out of the medical ward, fit as a fiddle. His ragged and damaged clothing was gone, replaced with a loose hospital gown. His entire body, which had been covered in bruises, cuts and blood, looked fine. Other than a small scar above his right hand, it seemed as though nothing had happened at all.

The two sprinted toward Rex before slowing down to a walking pace as they passed the guard. The two of them sheepishly earned another scowl. They examined Rex's injuries, or rather the complete lack thereof.

"Are you all right?" Kaze inspected his legs, marveling at the lack of burns. "One hell of a medical team they got here."

"We were both worried." Kibo chuckled. "I mean, are you sure you feel all right?"

"Guys, guys, I'm fine. There ain't a single thing loose in me." Rex laughed it off, waving nonchalantly. "I actually woke up an hour or two ago. I feel fine, but the doc said I needed to lay down for a bit." Rex shrugged. "So, how were you two doin'?"

Kibo and Kaze looked at him blankly, almost as if they didn't know what to say. "Well, we just waited for you I guess."

"Guess I shouldn't keep the two of you waitin', huh?" Rex smiled. "Gotta say, good to see we're back together now. Where can I change into something a bit more of my style? Let's see..." Rex walked down the hallway with a bit of a bounce.

Kibo and Kaze cringed, having witnessed the unfortunate scene that was Rex's open-backed gown.

"*I didn't need to see that.*" Arcanus gagged a bit. "*Huh, though I think I'm hearing some feedback.*" And he was not wrong, as the PA system above Kibo and Kaze crackled on.

"Congratulations to all who passed the first portion of the physical exam. All examinees must report to the Debriefing Room."

"This is the room, huh?" Kaze said. "It's, uh, really big."

It was a massive auditorium with a podium and large blank screen located at the back. The room held a sizable number of students; Arcanus gave a count of about sixteen examinees.

Considering the initial number of try-outs, this exclusivity was nothing to scoff at. Each examinee stuck to their own group, and the loud buzzing from earlier was replaced with fatigued murmurings and tired silence, interrupted by the occasional hearty chuckle. Not only were these potentially among the best the exam had to offer, but each seemed to have forged strong bonds with their teams. Kibo's group quickly took their own seats, wondering what exactly they were in for.

Rex tugged at his white shirt, which he had picked out at random. Though he had little time to pick out what he wanted, he was satisfied with his choice.

Meanwhile, Kaze looked like a laid-back thug. An aura of intimidating confidence radiated off him: leaned-back posture, the straight line of his frown, and a pair of disinterested eyes, despite being surrounded by the most talented mages in the world. Yet the impatient *tap, tap, tap* of his foot hinted otherwise.

Kibo glanced around the room, looking at the lucky few who passed. Trying to see who had passed and who didn't. But part of him was watching out for Siris, hoping that some miracle occurred and she did not pass. Such wishful thinking. There she stood, just across the room.

Despite her teammates' bickering and gossip, Siris stood silent. All she did was sit straight and keep her focus on the stage ahead, with a look on her face that made it seem as if she were above whatever petty gossip they were sharing.

Then her gaze clashed with his.

On instinct, he snapped his head forward and acted disinterested, like he had never seen her in the first place. But a seed of dread had planted itself inside him. Several different scenarios of what she would do raced through his head. Perhaps she would call out some boastful challenge or mercilessly belittle him. Maybe she would try to attack outright, furious at how such a 'lowborn' like him got so far.

But it never came.

Cautiously, Kibo turned around again, only to find her staring back, fixated on him. He couldn't believe what he was seeing. She wasn't mad, or fuming. Not even a small twitch in her eyebrow.

She still had that mildly-condescending, aristocratic frown. But those eyes were definitely something else. Kibo felt as if she was gazing directly into his soul, her eyes a dark spear gutting through him.

Thankfully, Siris' stare was broken by the sound of the auditorium doors swinging open.

Do you know what's happening, Arcanus?

"How should I know? I'm not some clairvoyant being. I'm just as clueless as you are," Arcanus exclaimed, trying to figure out who had just stepped in.

It was the official who had led them through the first part of the exam. He was slowly making his way to the front of the stage. As he stepped up to the podium, he took a moment to survey the group of examinees, giving a slight nod before clearing his throat.

"Congratulations on passing the first part of the physical exam. I hope you all had a good rest. You still have one more trial to pass before you can join Bastion in full force," he announced joyously. The man pulled out a small remote from his jacket and pressed a button. The large blank screen behind him flickered and an image slowly came to focus.

It was a blank tournament bracket. The audience murmured anxiously.

"While the last exam was a way of seeing how well you all function together as teams, this next portion of the exam will test your individual skills. Being a part of Bastion will also mean that there will be times when you cannot rely on your fellow agents for help. Rather, you will often find yourselves behind enemy lines, isolated from any sort of back up or aid." The man pointed up at the screen. "So, in order to test your individual skills and abilities, the second part of the test will be tournament-style, with one-on-one matches between examinees," he stated. "The winner of their match will progress to the next round."

He pressed the button again, with the screen now displaying two silhouettes in combat stances facing each other. "This test is meant to score fighters within a point system based on several criteria: skill, strategy, and tenacity." He paused, letting the murmurs die down. "And should you lose early on in the brackets, well. Let's just say that your chances of getting into Bastion can be quite slim."

The crowd was enraptured. Point system? Rankings? This seemed to be both the simplest and yet most mysterious part of the exam. Kibo, Rex and Kaze were leaning forward in anticipation. Kibo noticed the whispers were more excited, hopeful.

"The rules for the matches are as follows." The official's smile disappeared, his expression now far more serious. He switched to the next screen, showing a crossed-out skull. "Rule number one: any sort of fatal injury or intent to kill is strictly prohibited. You may beat and break as many bones as you like, just as long as your opponent is alive and conscious."

The crowd became silent. Kibo drew in closer, wanting to hear every detail of information that he could. The next screen displayed several weapons and items crossed out. "If any weaponry is found on you while entering the ring, you will be automatically disqualified." The screen shifted again, this time displaying a man standing over his knocked-out opponent. "The third and final rule: in order to win a match, you must defeat your opponent by either knocking them out of the ring, neutralizing them so that they are unable to continue fighting, or having your opponent forfeit the match."

The original warm smile returned to the man's face. "Now then, any questions?"

Not a word in response.

Answered by the silence, the man pulled out the remote and pressed the button yet again. "Now then, here are the selections for the matches in the first round." The screen flickered and displayed the same tournament bracket, now filled with the names of those who would face off in the first round. As the candidates rushed towards the front of the stage, the man slowly walked away from the podium, saying, "No need to rush, the listing isn't going anywhere."

As Kibo looked frantically at the board, a thought raced in the back of his head. Despite how slim the chance was, he just couldn't let go of it. He might face Siris in his first match.

"Come on, not Siris." He looked frantically down the list until he saw it.

MATCH 8
KIBO KOZLOV
VEGAR EYOLF

Kibo exhaled as he wiped his brow. He was thankfully facing some random kid.

At least I have a chance of getting out of this match alive, Kibo thought. However, Arcanus brought up a grave point.

"I know you're happy and all that we don't have to face that scary bitch, but trust me, it's going to get a lot more difficult from here on out," Arcanus mumbled. *"Check out your teammate Kaze over there."*

Kibo turned to see Kaze staring at the board as well. But rather than seeing his calm and collected demeanor, he seemed distressed. His impatient foot-tapping combined with the worried expression on his face seemed quite far from what Kibo had expected.

"What's wrong with him?" Kibo asked, perplexed.

Arcanus let out a sigh of annoyance. *"Were you listening during the presentation? The second rule stated no weapons are allowed into the match, otherwise you get kicked out. My best guess? Kaze planned on using some stuff he had or could have gotten from Bastion. I mean, he's not exactly a hand-to-hand fighter like us."* Arcanus' point flashed a thought into Kibo's head.

"Wait, what about you?" The sigil on his hand was gone. Kibo looked around frantically at both of his hands to see where Arcanus was. His arms, legs—he could not feel him anywhere on his body. And that was when he suddenly heard a familiar voice in his head.

"Let me guess, you were thinking that they would find me and disqualify you for thinking I was some kind of weapon?" Arcanus smugly asked. *"I think you forgot that I'm not just some disembodied voice and suit of armor, I'm a part of your damn body."*

Arcanus suddenly rematerialized into his palm. That machine truly was strange.

"Now then," the presenter exclaimed "Who's ready for the first match?"

CHAPTER 9

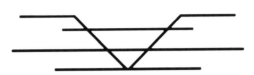

Match one is about to begin," the speaker boomed. Kibo looked around to soak in the true scale of the arena he had walked into. It consisted of a ring, which was a large circular concrete floor about half the size of a football field, and two massive doorways standing at either end. Along the top of the arena was a giant ring of seats where the other examinees could watch. A massive glass dome encased the top, allowing sunlight to illuminate every corner of the ring.

Despite the massive size of the arena and spectator ring, it was almost eerily empty, occupied entirely by a small group of examinees in groups of two or three waiting for the match to begin.

The only sound in the stadium was the occasional hushed whisper, which soon fell silent as the doors opened. Before long, the first two examinees stepped out.

"Match one fighters: Rex Ricci and Tanveer Khatri," the speaker announced.

As the two walked in, one could see just how different the two of them were from each other. Rex took a moment to stretch and scan the giant ring they were going to fight in. He seemed almost completely disinterested, in comparison to his opponent.

Tanveer stared Rex down, analyzing his every action and move as if expecting to get some minuscule advantage from watching his movements. His entire body seemed to be tensed up, his golden-brown face scrunched up in a mix of pure focus and stress. It seemed almost like nothing would stop him from winning this match.

"Yo, no hard feelings if I beat ya." Tanveer snapped out his trance to see his opponent standing with his hand stretched towards him.

"*If* you beat me, that is," Tanveer said, his dead-serious expression changing to a smug one, almost as if he was amused by Rex's challenge. He gripped Rex's hand with all his might and gave it a mighty shake, all while staring him down with a clever little smirk.

"Examinees, please take your positions." Tanveer pulled his hand back and slowly moved back to his corner of the ring, his eyes still full of determination. This was it. The moment he would finally prove he had the determination and tactical skill to join Bastion.

Jeez, he didn't have to break my hand like that, Rex thought as he walked back to his side of the ring, gripping his bruised hand with a pained expression, "Let's get this over with." Rex let out a slight yawn as he did a few last-second stretches before the match began.

The crowd watched from the edge of their seats, waiting for the fight to begin. The unbearable silence slowly built more tension, with each passing second feeling longer.

Above the flock of examinees, from a small spectating room, Lieutenant Batros looked down at the arena. He was surrounded by other Bastion staff and personnel, who all frantically took notes and opened files on the fighters. None of that mattered to Batros, for he had already picked his team. All he was doing was confirming if his decisions were the right ones.

"Now then, let's see what you're made of."

Then it boomed from above.

"Begin!"

Rex and Tanveer stood still, calmly and intently staring at one another. They started to slowly circle the arena, waiting to see who would initiate the first move. Every spectator amongst the stands and beyond held their breath, waiting to see who would finally break the immense silence that permeated through the building.

In a split second, Rex crossed his arms and rushed at Tanveer, charging him with as much speed as possible. Kibo jumped up from his seat in excitement, watching Rex draw in closer to his opponent.

"All right. If Rex gets into close range, he's got this." Kibo exclaimed.

"I wouldn't be so sure."

Kibo turned around to see another examinee with a look of utmost focus.

"Who are you?" The examinee shifted back a bit, somewhat startled by Kibo's question.

"I, uh, was with Tanveer during the first part of the physical test." He looked back down towards Tanveer. "I gotta say, he's a pretty damn good mage."

Kibo looked back down at the stage, this time with a hint of doubt. "I don't think he would let your 'friend' get in that close so easily. Just watch."

Tanveer smirked and flicked his hand. Several small shards of ice formed around him. Moving around in odd, slow orbits, they were different shapes and sizes. But each and every one was pointed directly at Rex.

"Crap! He's probably gonna fire off a volley of those crystals." Kibo panicked. Yet, instead of firing the ice crystals at Rex, he positioned the crystals in an intricate pattern. A beam of light fired from one of the crystals, searing through the ground where Rex stood, rupturing the earth into a giant cloud of dust.

Kibo leaned toward the edge of his seat, trying to comprehend what had just happened. He was familiar (rather traumatically) with ice magic, but he had never seen it be used quite like this.

"What was that?" Kibo said, confused. "He didn't move an inch, and yet he somehow fired off an actual laser beam at Rex."

"What did I say?" The examinee smirked. "You shouldn't underestimate any opponent you go up against."

Tanveer's shots were almost machine-like and methodical. He was taking every moment to line up his shots and firing endlessly into the dust cloud. It seemed as though every single action or motion he did had some purpose, as though none were wasted. It all made Kibo think. Just how was Rex going to get out of this mess?

Rex charged out of the cloud of dust, sending a powerful drop kick directly into Tanveer's chest. The force from his blow hurled Tanveer off the ring and into the wall behind him. Kibo looked in complete shock at the attack. Even with Arcanus' aid, he couldn't tell how Rex was able to move that fast.

Rex must have covered about fifteen to twenty meters in a split-second! but how? It shouldn't be possible for a person to move that fast, Kibo thought, bewildered.

Rex let out a deep breath and collapsed to his knees, his body drained of every last ounce of stamina with that final rush. His skin was covered in several small, cauterized wounds. He had been hit by at least five—no, eight—of Tanveer's lasers just to land that hit on his opponent. But surely that blow must have finished Tanveer off?

"Hot damn, he's still movin'?"

Somehow, despite taking the full brunt of Rex's attack, Tanveer still managed to pull himself to his feet. But it already was too late for him. He no longer stood in the arena and the fate of the match had already been decided.

The loudspeaker thundered from above. "Winner of the first match, Rex Ricci, will proceed to the next round."

Tanveer closed his eyes. To put all that effort behind his attacks, just to be eliminated that quickly. He sighed; he still had much more to learn. Yet, as he turned towards the exit, he heard a voice call out to him.

"Hey."

Tanveer watched as Rex walked up to him. "You beat me, isn't that enough for you? What are you gonna do now, humiliate me even further?" Tanveer scowled.

Rex let out a deep sigh and looked at the ceiling. "While you and I were fighting, I realized that you and I aren't that different."

Tanveer was surprised by the statement, he expected Rex to pull some kind of witty remark or comeback, not calmly converse with him. Tanveer shifted a bit closer.

"Well, what makes you think so? Do you know what it's like to spend countless hours training in order to obtain even a fighting chance?"

"Well, yeah, that's pretty much what I did." Rex let out a small chuckle. "On its own, my ability pretty much sucks. It is hard to control, very risky to use, and it hurts like hell when it snaps back at ya. The only way I got here was through serious training, and even then, I still have a long way to go." Rex looked at his leg, which was covered in several cuts and burns from not only Tanveer's laser, but also his own lightning. "So, what I'm trying to get at is I hope we can face off against each other again, once we both get a bit more experience. What do ya say, huh?" Rex stuck out his hand.

Tanveer looked at Rex hesitantly, but walked up to him and grabbed his hand, shaking it firmly. "You better be ready next time, 'cause I'm not gonna lose," Tanveer said with a smirk. "We'll see about that!"

"You caught that, Sidorov?"

The subordinate looked up from his clipboard and shook his head in confusion. "Caught what, sir?"

Barros watched calmly outside the observation window. "About once every four seconds, Tanveer would stop shooting for a millisecond to blink. That Rex kid was waiting for that exact moment his opponent would have a gap in his attacks and threw himself at Tanveer with that speed of his. In just those few milliseconds, he shifted the fight in his favor, knowing his opponent wouldn't be able to react fast enough. Had he attacked at any other moment, the kid would have been Swiss cheese."

Sidorov looked at Batros in amazement. "That's insane. How would you notice such a small detail, sir?"

The veteran turned towards his subordinate and simply smiled.

"I have a keen eye, that's all," Batros replied. He turned back to look out the window, eyes narrowing at one particular candidate. "But I'm still quite curious about one other examinee."

The examinee seemed to be quite unaware of his surroundings. His full attention was directed at the palm of his hand, which had a soft blue glow radiating from its center. But Batros knew exactly what that glow came from and stared down at it with a look of both excitement and caution.

"Don't disappoint me."

CHAPTER 10

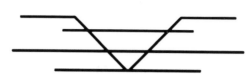

The arena was covered in cracks. Rubble and shards of stone were scattered everywhere. In the center was a large crater, where the unfortunate loser lay, covered in several bruises and blood. The victor blew at his fist like a cowboy after a quickdraw, burnt and smoking from the sheer speed of his attacks. He had completely and utterly defeated his opponent.

The speaker finally broke the pause. "The winner of the second match is Ukrit Tanet, who will proceed to the second round."

Ukrit looked down at his opponent and scoffed. "Pitiful." Ukrit slowly walked to the arena's exit as medical personnel rushed in with a stretcher. Kibo looked in complete shock, attempting to find some sort of sensible conclusion from this insane match.

"How? He crushed his opponent in less than a minute. And for it to be so one-sided? How strong is that guy?"

"I can't wait to face him in the next match, he's going to be real fun to beat," Rex said excitedly. Kibo turned around to look at Rex as if he had lost his mind.

"What?" Rex asked, wondering what he might have said or done in order to warrant such a reaction.

"Didn't you see what that guy did? He *crushed* his opponent. He could have killed him if he wanted too," Kibo said in complete panic.

"And that is exactly why I'm excited to fight that guy," Rex responded smugly, barely able to hold back his excitement. Kibo sighed and just gave up, realizing that it was pointless to argue against him. Besides, he had the next match to focus on.

A rumble permeated through the crowd's idle chatter, the arena slowly molding itself into shape. Cracks, holes, and dents—from the smallest to the largest—were slowly covered up as concrete rose from beneath the ground to level the floor, like a stress ball retaking its initial shape after being squeezed.

Kibo looked at the arena in complete wonder. He had been accustomed to watching people use magic, from construction workers using fire magic to weld to farmers using nature magic for bountiful harvests. But a repair process completely automated by magic? That was a marvel of design and magic, and a testament to Bastion's cutting-edge resources.

"Amazing, isn't it? What people can do with magic?" Kibo sighed in admiration.

Arcanus scoffed. *"Yeah. Real helpful when running a fight club."*

Don't you disrespect Bastion like that, Kibo snapped back. *They help maintain world order, so they have to make sure whoever they recruit is up to the challenge.*

"So what? You think turning a bunch of kids into soldiers is a good thing? Sounds to me like they want their soldiers young because they're clueless and impressionable."

But that's what this whole exam is for; to make sure the recruits are leadership material and strong-willed. Remember what I said about the Red Cossacks? Bastion teams like them are supposed to be independent. It's one of the reasons why they get things done.

"Hmph, I suppose so." When they were hiking to the third gem, Kibo told war stories to the group to pass the time. The Red Cossacks was one of them. Acting on investigative instinct, the Red Cossacks broke into a home and stopped a plot to assassinate the German prime minister. Had they waited for backup or bureaucratic approval, the prime minister surely would have been long dead. Kibo had been excited to share the story and it was (to Kaze's dismay) the first of many. In retrospect, Arcanus realized just how much Kibo cared, how truly devoted he was to Bastion.

"Okay. Tell me then, where you heard those stories again?"

The state radio, where else?

"Okay, I don't think I should have to explain what propaganda is, right?" Arcanus said, somewhat bewildered.

I don't follow. Kibo shifted a little on the bench. *They actually did that stuff. I don't see why the government wouldn't report on it?*

Arcanus sighed. It seemed to be a lost cause. *"I can't really stop you from doing what you want, kid. But just think for a moment if this Bastion thing is something you want, not somebody else."* Kibo paused for a moment. *"Guess the world hasn't changed much in two thousand years,"* Arcanus sighed just as the speaker boomed from above.

"Thank you for waiting patiently for the arena to be refurbished. Please welcome the fighters of the third match: Hana Oginska and Akira Kaze."

The crowd was larger. Off-duty soldiers and staff trickled into the arena, swelling the stadium seating with curious, bored, and excited faces. The crowd was louder as it roared. The fighters had walked onto opposite sides of the arena.

Hana stood at the ready, smiling. She tapped her foot anxiously.

Kaze stepped forward, and stared back, gauging her to see if she would be a tough opponent. *Confident posture. Tapping feet could be fear or excitement. Smiling like a psycho? Not a good sign.*

He then called out to her. "I heard that one member of your team is friends with one of mine. And if she's anything like him, she must be one hell of a fighter."

"You bet she is! At first, I was scared of her, but she helped us through the first part of the exam." She pointed at Siris in the crowd and gave a friendly wink, to which Siris just quietly groaned. "Honestly, I'm just happy to be here."

Kaze was taken back, expecting a far more confrontational response. "You know we're about to fight, right? I was expecting more of an attitude, I guess," Kaze said, although a little sheepishly.

"What? Why would I do that? You don't seem like a bad guy, so why should I treat you like a bad guy, *da?*" Hana responded cheerfully.

Kaze stumbled backward a bit, not really sure how to respond.

"Fighters, please take your stance," the announcer declared.

Kaze shook his head and regained his focus. He stared down his opponent, observing her for any sort of weaknesses or hints she may give off. Hana nodded back with a determined smile before crouching into her unorthodox stance.

Kibo looked in curiosity at Hana, wondering what kind of fighter she was.

"I hope she won't be as tough of a fighter as Tanveer was. Kaze was the one who kept us all together, so I bet he'll get through this fight." Kibo looked at Kaze hopefully. However, Arcanus seemed a bit more skeptical.

I wouldn't be so hopeful, kid. You can never be sure about something until it happens, and that applies to this fight as well," Arcanus stated. But Kibo was not swayed.

"Well, we'll see."

The speaker boomed, "Begin."

Hana slammed her hands on the ground. Flames burst from her hands and encircled Kaze. He was trapped.

What could she be trying to do? Maybe she wants to trap me? Or is she gonna pull off some sort of special spell or combination of many? What could it be? Kaze's mind raced. His opponent, on the other hand, seemed far more relaxed.

"How about we swing into gear?" She rotated her hands in front of herself and aimed her open palms at Kaze. A massive flamethrower burst from hands, engulfing the entire ring into a storm of flames.

Kaze blasted a front of air at the flames, redirecting it safely around him. *Getting matched with a fire user was one hell of a lucky draw.* Kaze quickly wiped his brow. *All I need is one good blast of cold air and I'm good.* He squinted back at his opponent.

His counter only made her smile. "Well, looks like you know the basics." She leaned forward. "Let's move onto something more interesting now."

What could she possibly be planning? he wondered, whisking the air around him for another attack. Hana grabbed the two edges of the ring of flames pulled backwards. Streaking through the air, the ring of fire split in two and flung toward her, rapidly thinning down into long, controlled strips of flames. Hana raised her right arm and swung the flaming line, causing it to crackle and sizzle. She smiled.

Her special technique: a pair of flaming whips.

"Flame weavers, you say?" Batros scratched his scruffy chin.

"Yes, sir," Sidorov explained as he read from an open file. "An ancient clan from eastern Europe who spent their childhood controlling and honing their fire powers. They are given first ropes to burn and control their flames, then strings, and finally practice with nothing. It is one of the most difficult to use, yet powerful techniques in the known world. And it seems she has managed to master it."

Batros looked on at the field blankly.

"She is still at an elemental disadvantage. Unless that technique can make up for it, she won't make it through the match."

Hana charged towards Kaze, letting out a flurry of flaming whip lashes. Each strike left behind a large searing mark upon the ground. Kaze was barely able to deflect or dodge her strikes. His cool composure slowly cracked as he was pushed farther back. He was especially unnerved by the unnatural precision of Hana's attack. His blasts of air were not enough to hold her back.

She moves so damn quick! All of these attacks barely give me a chance to even keep some spare energy in reserve. But all of those constant attacks can't be easy to pull off, she's gotta be tiring herself out, and fast. If I can just keep her at bay, it'll all come together." And his assumption was correct.

Hana felt her own body start to buckle, her breathing becoming more irregular with each passing second. She knew that she had to get him sooner rather than later.

Crack!

Kaze blasted air from his hands and deflected both of Hana's whips searing into the floor ground, all while sending Hana right back to the spot she started in.

"I gotta admit, your whips have quite some power and speed behind them. But your attacks are too linear, too easy to figure out a pattern," Kaze said as he stretched one of his shoulders.

Yet, instead of being distraught, Hana smirked. She reeled back her whips, and called out to him. "Not bad. But can you take me down? I've still got plenty of gas left."

Kaze did not respond, only prepared for another attack. She frowned, expecting a response. "You know, there is more to me than a few techniques and moves." Hana grabbed both of Kaze's ankles with her whips, and with all her strength, slammed Kaze onto the other side of the ring with such force that she cracked the concrete floor, creating a thick cloud of dust.

Hana pulled back her flaming whips, confident that she had defeated her opponent. Painfully, Kaze hoisted himself up. His body was laden with injuries, chunks of concrete stabbing into his bleeding wounds, but he stood to his feet, eyes brimming with resolve.

Hana looked at him, almost sick. "Look, Kaze, I think you should forfeit. You barely seem to be able to stand, let alone even move. It won't be fair to hurt you more. Both of us know who's gonna win this match."

"Yeah, me," Kaze grunted, his face stone cold. Hana stepped back a bit. His emotionless look sent a chill down her spine.What was he gonna do? He was at his wit's end. A simple gust of wind would topple him over. Hana took a step forward, her whip in hand, ready to finish the match.

Except she didn't have a whip in her hand: they had both vanished.

"Seems like it was a smart idea for me to set up a small little trap before the start of the match, just in case things went south," Kaze said, wincing as he ripped out a chunk of concrete lodged in his arm. "I had to make sure you were exactly where we started the fight, and just in time to spring it." Kaze pointed at the whirlwind surrounding Hana. "I surrounded you in a miniature vacuum, without any oxygen to sustain your whips or your body. Oh, and don't even think about running out. Because the second you do, you'll find yourself ripped into a hundred pieces by razor-sharp winds."

Hana looked at Kaze in shock, unable to think up a witty retort. She thought she was pressuring him, that she had cornered him like a wounded dog. Yet, this whole time, it was her who had been slowly pushed back and cornered. She tried to think of a way out, a way to turn the tide in her favor, but only gasped for air, unable to think or move. She was out of options.

"I forfeit," Hana sputtered out with the last bit of air in her lungs, collapsing onto the ground. Kaze quickly dissipated the trap that had surrounded Hana. The speaker crackled on.

"Winner of the third match, Akira Kaze, will move to the second round."

A confident smile was plastered on Kaze's face. *Looks like it all worked out in the end. Always nice to have a plan b, huh?*

Hana gasped for air on the floor.

"Need a hand?" Kaze extended his hand toward Hana. Reluctantly, she grasped and hoisted herself up. Now face-to-face, Kaze smiled. "That was some good fighting," he said. "Honestly, I'd say that was pretty close."

"Why did you have to beat me with such a dirty trick?" she cut him off, pouting. "I gave you a fair fight and how do you repay me? By springing some dirty, no-good trap. You're dishonorable, two-timing cheat," Hana blurted out as she stormed off, leaving Kaze in stunned silence. The crowd snickered at the exchange.

"Well, that's one end to a match."

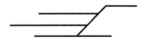

Sidorov watched Batros. The lieutenant, relaxed in his leather office chair, was on his smoke break. He read the report quietly in between huffs of his cigar. Seeing he was not needed—and how awkward the silence was—Sidorov saluted and turned for the door.

"Where are you running off to?" His superior's words suddenly pierced into his back.

Sidorov froze and immediately snapped forward and returned to his superior's side. Batros continued to read quietly. Sidorov stood, fidgeting impatiently. The silence and smoke were beginning to choke him.

"Sir? I don't mean to be out of line, but I feel that smoking that much can't be any good," Sidorov murmured. It made him cringe, but it was better than silence. "Inhaling that much smoke can't be great in the long term."

Batros looked up at Sidorov and quietly chuckled. "And soldiers don't have a long-term lifespan. I don't think a cigar's what's gonna kill me." Batros took another puff, turning back to his reports.

Sidorov felt a little embarrassed and stood quietly, fidgeting again in the silence that followed. He decided to try a second time.

"Quite the fight, wasn't it? For a second, I thought that Ogianska would beat Kaze," Sidorov said.

"She did," Batros stated, to Sidorov's confusion. "In terms of raw power, Ogianska outclassed him, despite a bad elemental matchup. She got out unscathed too. Kaze, on the other hand, is giving our boys in the medical ward a hard time." He chuckled again. "But that's what I like about him. He's willing to get his guts kicked in, and he uses his brain on the field to beat her. If he were to train his powers and gain more mental fortitude, Kaze would make a great leader both on and off the battlefield." Finished with his cigar, he gently laid it onto the ashtray, and returned to reading. "He passed my test."

Sidorov nodded. "I agree, sir. For a pretty unassuming background, his skills are nothing to gloss over."

Even as the smoke dissipated, the bitter scent of cigars still burned Sidorov's nose. But he stood still, content he heard Batros' input.

The veteran stirred. "Oh, before I dismiss you." He produced an unopened cigarette pack from his breast pocket and extended it to Sidorov. "Something more your size."

Sidorov chuckled and took the pack. As he stepped out into the hallway, he took one last look at Batros. He saw the curve of a smirk beneath Batros' stoic face before quickly vanishing behind a flurry of papers. But a second was all that Sidorov needed to see and think, *Heh, guess he isn't all that tough.*

CHAPTER 11

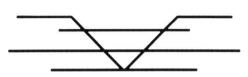

"He will be fine. He's not ready for visitors, so please come back later."

Rex and Kibo (and Arcanus) nodded, somewhat relieved. The medic nodded back and returned inside the room, closing the door.

"I'll wait for Kaze. I'm sure you're tired of waiting here," Kibo said, sitting down on the bench. "You can go watch the fights."

Rex sighed and nodded. "All right, let me know if you need anything." Rex got up. "I'll give you the highlights later, 'kay?"

"All right."

"Who exactly is that energetic young man?" Batros asked, leaning toward the window inquisitively. Sidorov sifted through a file, and soon found the answer.

"The examinee's name is Max Garret, a young man from Australia. He was born and raised in the scorching Australian outback on a ranch. He's somewhat of a local celebrity for having an undefeated winning streak fighting both men and"—Sidorov paused for a moment, staring at the file with a puzzled look—"Kangaroos? He also owns a pet emu. I hardly see the relevance of any of this." Sidorov closed the file, dumbfounded.

Batros let out a small snicker. "It's quite simple, really. It helps give us a gauge on what kind of person he is. Based on that information, we can understand if the person we are recruiting really is who they say they are. It allows Bastion to see if they fit the criteria for a good soldier and leader." Batros thought for a moment, and then snapped his fingers. "I suppose the pet emu suggests Mr. Garrett here is not as much of a bonehead as he seems. Taking care of an animal, much less a wild and extremely dangerous one, is no brute's task. Even heard the Aussies lost a 'war' to them."

Sidorov listened to Batros, in awe at his superior knowledge. *He really is one of the best, huh?*

"All right," the veteran said. "What about the other one?"

Sidorov reached for the other folder laying on the desk, quickly sifting through it. "He is Kyung Sang-Ho, born in Seoul, Korea to a wealthy family who owns a multi-billion-dollar construction company with lots of projects and connections all over the world. He is quite the prodigy—passed several exams with full scores and even finished college at Oxford at the age of seventeen, studying military history and architecture." Sidorov looked up from the file. "In other words, he's one smart kid."

Batros looked at the arena with a small smirk on his face.

"But not a fast one it seems."

Down on the arena floor, Kyung's unconscious body lay slumped down on the arena wall. His opponent stood in a set of spike-ridden boney armor, his outstretched fist still hanging in the air from his blow. The fight was over in one swift, powerful strike.

"The winner of the fourth match, Max Garret, will move onto the second round."

"Yeah," Max shouted at the top of his lungs, drowning out the speaker. He flexed his muscles and drank in the roar of the crowd, celebrating his glorious victory.

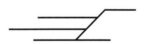

"That was one hell of a match," Rex said as Max started doing some strange victory ritual.

"Yeah! Can't wait to see what's gonna happen in the next match," Hana said as Ben stood behind her observing the field. "That Max guy pummeled the other kid."

Hana and Rex snickered like hyenas. Ben considered letting loose on them but reconsidered. "I gotta say, that *was* one heck of a fight, but you guys gotta look at the bigger picture," Ben said. Rex and Hana looked at him curiously. "The reason Max won this fight wasn't because he was physically stronger or smarter, mind you. It was because of his mental fortitude during the fight. Even when he was pressured by his opponent, he remained calm." Ben glanced toward Kyung's crumbled body being carried away on a stretcher.

"While on the other hand, Kyung started to panic the second the tables turned against him."

Rex just stared at him blankly. "Uh-huh. Well, that guy was pretty similar to one of my buddies on my team, Kibo."

Ben just sighed. "Kibo? What is he like?"

"Are you sure you can walk?"

"I'm fine, jeez. Are you my mother or something?"

The halls were empty except for Kibo and Kaze. Aside from bandages on his hands and face, Kaze appeared to be doing fine. Bastion healing magic did wonders for a quick recovery. Then his stomach growled.

Kibo snickered. "All right, fine. But I think you need a snack or something." Kibo smirked.

"Damn, you heard that too?" Kaze sheepishly scratched his chin. "Well, I guess I could use a sandwich. How about you, Kibo?" No response. "Kibo?"

Kibo stopped dead in his tracks. Why, why was *she* here?

Siris walked around the corner right in front of them.

Kibo's brows furrowed and his fist clenched up. Sweat dripped down his forehead as she walked closer, until she stood an arm's length from him.

Kibo waited like he did back in the orientation room, waiting for her to assault him with a torrent of insults. But, just like then, she didn't. She stared Kibo down. He gulped, fighting the urge to look away. His arms and legs quivered ever so slightly, but he stared back into Siris' icy eyes. He would not back down, not anymore.

"Well, uh..." Kaze watched the scene unfold before him. He could feel the intensity between the two. It was like there was an invisible fight occurring between the two. Not a word was spoken. None were needed.

"Tsk." Siris finally relented. With a scowl, she turned and walked briskly past them. All the while, Kibo just stared off into the distance, hearing each and every one of Siris' footsteps echo away into the distance until they were finally gone.

"Oh god." Kibo let out one shaky sigh. Despite his best attempts to hide it, every part of his body was shaking uncontrollably. That look seared right into his mind. It was full of malice and rage. Like she would stop at nothing to eviscerate him into tiny bits. Never had he been this terrified of her, and she didn't even speak. A veil of impending doom hung over him, ticking down as his match drew ever closer.

Kaze hesitated. "Hey, Kibo?" Kaze gripped Kibo's shoulder.

"AH! Oh, it's you. What up?" Kibo responded, a slight warble in his voice. Kaze looked at him for a moment. His mind went blank.

What do I say, what do I say? Come on Kaze. Kaze let out a slight cough as he awkwardly scratched the back of his head.

"How about we get you a sandwich?" Kaze said, putting together the first thought that came to his mind. Kaze felt his ears burn as he did, slightly regretting his choice of words. Yet in a way, that made Kibo feel just ever so slightly less on edge. To have his comrade—no, his friend— by his side. It felt good.

"Yeah, why not?"

CHAPTER 12

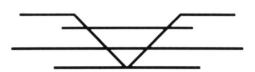

Ben sat in the medical wing of the facility, his body covered in bandages and bruises, but seemed to be relatively fine. Hana sat next to him, attempting to comfort him.

"It's all right, Ben. There's still a chance you'll get into Bastion," Hana said as she patted Ben on the back. It did little to boost Ben's mood, and he remained slumped over.

"I really could have won. If I had pushed myself a bit harder, I would have been able to beat him," Ben said, disappointed with himself. "He was one heck of a fighter. I can see him making it well past the second round."

Before Ben could dwell on his mistakes any longer, a nurse walked by, surprised that they were still here. "You should hurry along if you don't want to miss the next match. You already missed the last one." They nodded and thanked the nurse before going back into the stadium.

Hana and Ben struggled through the crowd towards Kaze, Rex, and Kibo, who were waiting for the match to begin. "Hey guys," Hana shouted out to the trio. Both Rex and Kibo turned to wave, while Kaze quickly turned around as though he hadn't noticed the two.

"Hey, nice to see you two again," Rex said casually, pausing as if he was trying to remember their names.

"Hana and...?"

"It's Ben," he stated, annoyed. He and Hana sat down next to the group and observed the ring. Just as they settled into their seats, the speaker boomed from above.

"Begin!"

Batros looked at the folders so intensely that Sidorov thought that they would catch on fire. "That is my next candidate."

"What, sir?"

Batros opened the folder and pointed at the picture at the top of the page. "Siris Vasilyeva."

Sidorov was surprised. It seemed to be a no-brainer for Batros to be interested in such a skilled and known candidate. However, what seemed so odd was the troubled expression on Batros' face. This was the first time Sidorov had seen the lieutenant genuinely conflicted.

"She really is one of the greatest mages of her generation, and it isn't a risky bet to say she'll win this tournament."

"Well then, sir, why do you seem so troubled?" Sidorov asked.

"She's too much of a loose cannon. Combine that with her latent talent and overwhelming power, she ends up doing more harm than good." Batros started with a deep sigh. "It was reported that she damaged private property in several cases and injured or attacked several people without provocation. If it wasn't for the fact that she was part of one of the most powerful aristocratic houses in Russia, she would have probably been rotting in some prison or asylum." Batros fixed his eyes on the arena, which was still undergoing maintenance. "If she manages to overcome her hot-headed nature, she'll become one of the greatest mages in the world. One far beyond even me."

"Sir, you don't mean?"

"Yes, a Mage of Mass Destruction, an MMD."

"Hey, good luck out there. I hope you win." Siris turned to see Hana running up to her.

"You think I need luck to beat my opponent? They'll be the one needing it."

Siris took in a deep breath and opened her eyes. She stood in a dark hallway, light pouring in from the arena. Her foot tapped impatiently, her mind muddled with distractions.

"What kind of mage will I be up against? It'll be bad if I go up against an opposing element. But I can't hold my guard down even if I get a favorable matchup," Siris mumbled to herself. "But even if they were a bad matchup for me, I'd still easily crush them. I shouldn't even have to think about losing this match."

But what if she did?

Siris shook her head.

"No, the Vasilyevs never lost to anyone. I have nothing to worry about." Siris quickly marched onto the stage, almost as if she was trying to outrun her thoughts. As she stepped into the bright lights of the arena, the speaker crackled from above, signaling her arrival.

"Fighters of the seventh round, Siris Vasilyeva and Raluca Diaconescu."

Siris sized up her opponent. Raluca was hunched over, staring at the ground aimlessly. Siris was unnerved; something felt incredibly unnatural about her, as if a blanket of darkness surrounded her. But something about her also felt strikingly familiar.

Raluca lurched upward and stared back with lifeless eyes. She had large bags underneath them, her face thin and pale from malnutrition. Raluca dragged herself closer to Siris until she stood centimeters away, muttering some odd words. An unbearable stench lingered over her. Siris leaned back, filled with a mix of pity and disgust, and she wondered just when that girl would back away from her.

Then, as if satisfied with her analysis, Raluca jumped back and looked at Siris with an eerie smile plastered on her face.

"You're like me, aren't you? I can see it, the pain and anger within you." Raluca's raspy voice rang in Siris' ears. Goosebumps slowly formed on the ice mage's arms, yet Siris maintained her composure.

"And how exactly am I similar to a wretch like you? You don't look like you've seen the sun for years."

Raluca seemed unfazed by the jab. Her soft chuckle transformed into hysterical laughter. "You have the same power within you. But you're hiding it away, suppressing it. Why? Why would you hide your power? Let it out," Raluca rasped. Siris tensed up, the fear slowly building within her. How could someone that weak and pitiful be so terrifying?

"Fighters of the seventh match, take your stance."

Fortunately, Raluca's advance was halted by the speaker. Raluca slowly moved back to her side of the arena, and dropped to the ground, taking a snakelike stance, crawling on her hands and feet. Siris stood upright. Her entire body was on alert, ready for whatever Raluca would throw against her. As they got into position, the speaker crackled on.

"Begin!"

Raluca stared at Siris with a sinister smile. "The Swarm consumes all, until all that is left is the truth. They will bring it out."

Siris felt as though her entire body was grabbed and constrained by several chains. A cloud of darkness surrounded her, tightening its grasp around each and every part of her body. Siris tried to open her mouth to speak, yet nothing came out. Instead, something spoke for her.

"You're scared, aren't you? You fear that he will see you lose? That he will abandon you like the runt you are?" The disembodied voice pierced her mind. Siris stared into the darkness in panic.

Who are you? Leave me alone. "Why do you suppress yourself? Do you really think you can beat her with just this small portion of your power? Let go. Let your true power flow through you. Make him regret ever doubting you."

Stop it! Siris thought to herself. She looked at the darkness, which stayed silent, as if it obeyed her command.

Then they all flooded in. Dozens of voices yelling at her in unison, drowning out her own thoughts.

"Do it."

"Crush her."

"Show him how—"

"Enough," Siris screamed at the top of her lungs. A massive burst of cold air-launched toward the swarm. She stared at Raluca in rage as she slammed her hands onto the ground.

"Glacius!" A whirlwind of ice and snow exploded from Siris, sending a storm blizzard across the arena. Within seconds, the entirety of it had been transformed into a frigid hellscape, everything covered in a thick blanket of snow and reaching to the very edge of spectator windows far above. Her opponent? Where she once stood, there was a massive glacier with Raluca entombed in the ice like a statue. It showed her final moments as she tried to raise her arms and legs to block the blast.

Siris collapsed to her knees, out of breath and exhausted. "Shit, I went too far with that move. I can't let myself get carried away like that again." Siris' mind raced. She covered her mouth and coughed, her hand covered in blood.

Thankfully for her, she had already won the match.

"Winner of the seventh match, Siris Vasilyeva."

Everyone was staring at the frozen arena. A stunned silence hung over the whole stadium. Siris' left the frozen arena. Kaze looked at the glacier in complete amazement. The ability to produce this much ice and snow within seconds was something that he may have heard of in theory, yet Siris did it like it was nothing. Kaze turned towards Kibo, only to see him drenched in sweat.

"Guess I can see why you're so damn scared of her. I don't think I could hold a candle to her even if I spent all my life training."

"Y-yeah, well a-at least you're going to be able to train." Kibo stared at the ground in a state of panic.

"If I lose in the first round, I won't have to face Siris, but I can't join Bastion. If I win, I'll probably never walk upright again." Kibo pulled at his hair, stuck in a dilemma.

"Crap, crap, crap." A jolt of electricity tazed him.

"Kid, get a hold of yourself. Are you seriously gonna give up your life's dream because you might get hurt? Trust me kid, you'll regret abandoning your life goal over a single fight."

Yet, instead of being inspired, Kibo started to laugh.

"Hey, what's so funny, jackass?"

The thought that I'm getting advice from a machine who's lived under a rock for two thousand years and probably had almost no knowledge of the outside world was just so funny that I couldn't help but laugh! Kibo wiped a tear from his eye. He leapt off his seat and looked off to the arena. *But yeah, you're right. We still gotta get ready for our fight.*

"That's the spirit, kid! Now show them what we're made of." With that, Kibo rushed towards the exit, full of energy, and the determination to win. And as he did, a figure watched him from above, smiling.

"Now then, let's see what you're capable of, Kibo Kozlov."

CHAPTER 13

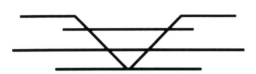

So, this is the screening room, huh?

"Looks like it."

Kibo let out a sigh and looked at Arcanus, his eyes full of worry and anxiety. *Will they even let me go through? What if they find Arcanus? How will they react? Will they disqualify me?*

"Kid, trust me, they won't find me. I'm just gonna lay low until we get the clear," Arcanus said as he disappeared into Kibo's body.

Kibo took a deep breath and walked through the enameled glass doorway into a tiled, whitewashed room. Completely empty save for one thing, a security officer who sat on a small bench in a corner of the room. The officer read a file in one hand while taking a few sips from a mug of coffee he had in the other.

"Kibo Kozlov. Is that right?" the security officer asked, looking back and forth from the file to Kibo.

"Yes, sir."

The officer put the file down and motioned Kibo toward a circle on the ground. "Stand there."

Kibo moved to the circle and stood still, holding his breath intently. Several thoughts coursed through his head, both good and bad, as he waited for the security officer to search him.

Ten seconds...

Thirty seconds...

A minute...

The officer still sat at the bench, going over Kibo's file and drinking coffee. Kibo looked at him, somewhat perplexed. "Sir, aren't you going to examine me?"

"What do you mean? I've already examined you." The officer took another sip of coffee from his mug.

Kibo looked at him puzzled. "Wait, when?"

The officer chuckled. "This is Bastion, remember? I did a full body and residue scan with that bad boy." He pointed at the ceiling where a camera hung. Its shutters opened and closed, glowing runes and incantations inscribed on the rim of the lenses, examining every inch of Kibo body to see if it had missed any possible contraband.

"Did I—"

"No need to ask. You've passed the screening." The officer pointed to the left. "This way to the arena."

The wall in front of Kibo parted from the middle, revealing a large dark hallway. Kibo thanked the officer and walked towards the dark passageway. As he entered, the walls closed behind him. The only way out was the arena. There was no backing out now.

His footsteps echoed through the dark hallway. The crowd roared louder with every step he took, until the shouting was so loud it drowned out his own thoughts. Kibo took one final breath before stepping out into the arena.

Blinded by the intense lights of the stadium and the excited clamor of the crowd, all eyes focused on Kibo, but the warm buzz in his hand urged him on.

"Fighters of the final match of round one: Kibo Kozlov and Vegar Eyolf."

Kibo studied his opponent. Vegar had quite the physique. His body, while lean, was well-built. His face was quite relaxed, yet his eyes seemed full of energy and focus. His clothes consisted of a simple red shirt and a pair of loose trousers. A strange pendant hung proudly from his neck.

Kibo walked over to him and extended his hand. "Hey, the name's Kibo. Nice to meet you."

"Hail and well met, Kibo, son of Kozlov." Vegar gave back a smile and gripped his hand, giving Kibo an excruciatingly firm handshake. "I hope for us to have an honorable and glorious fight. May the gods bless our fight."

Kibo, though his hand was becoming sore from Vegar's iron grip, was infected by Vegar's confidence.

"Well, I'm eager to prove my worth against the gods," Kibo said boldly and slammed his fist against his chest. "Let's test your faith."

"Us mortals often underestimate the influence of the gods. I hope that your body is as strong as your words."

The two let go as Kibo gave a quick nod, followed by a bow from Vegar.

"Way to show it to him, kid. That doesn't mean much until we see what kind of power is hiding inside him. Religious types like him tend to be esoteric, but they still aren't something to be trifled with." Kibo had a determined smile on his face and settled into his combat stance, his hands to his chest.

"I was kind of nervous at first, but I feel really pumped," Kibo said excitedly. "And now that we're fighting people, I'll be able to actually use my training." Kibo looked across the ring at Vegar, who had also taken a stance just as the speaker crackled once more.

"Fighters, take your stance."

Kibo and Vegar stared down at each other, an intense aura surrounding the two fighters. The crowd watched in silence, waiting impatiently for the speaker to initiate the match.

Finally, the silence broke with a deafening boom.

"Begin!"

Kibo stomped his feet and Arcanus' gleaming armor formed around him. The audience was in uncharacteristic silence, wowed by the alien suit. Rex excitedly nudged a wide-eyed Ben and Hana.

"Told ya he was something." He cheered.

Kibo's opponent was no less impressive. He formed a pair of blades from his hands made of pure electrical energy crackling loudly across the arena. Kibo stood back, taking a more defensive stance, a plan forming in his head. Vegar looked at Kibo with a serious glare plastered on his face and charged Kibo. Vegar launched a furious rush of sword strikes and stabs. Kibo managed to deflect almost all of them, only a few blows grazing his armor.

Just a little more, Kibo thought as he dodged a strike. Vegar got more daring with each strike, frustrated at how such a heavily-armored target could evade him. That was when the opening that Kibo was watching for revealed itself.

Vegar lunged at Kibo's face with his blade but instead of slashing his opponent's face, he split away.

"What the?" Vegar gasped for air as something tightened around his neck. It was Kibo, with both of his arms locked around Vegar's neck. Kibo had caught him in his trap.

"Systema?"

"It's a collection of different Russian martial arts adopted by the Russian military after the Great War. It focuses on grappling techniques to disarm and immobilize any enemies one may encounter, and it seems Mr. Kozlov has a pretty good handle on it after spending two years in the militia." Batros coughed.

"Well, that's quite interesting to see, sir," Sidorov said. "Even at a young age, he seems to be using it quite well."

"Yes, it seems so. Considering that Kibo's opponent is also a close-combat fighter, it appears that he is in an advantageous position." Batros leaned in a bit closer, taking a look at Vegar fighting back fiercely against Kibo's grip.

"But this fight is not yet over."

The Nordic fighter's face grew a bright red, gasping for whatever air he could take in. Despite this, Vegar continued to struggle with all his might, pulling forcefully at Kibo's tightening arms. "I am Vegar Eyolf, warrior of the gods." Vegar suddenly grabbed and wrenched Kibo's armored hands off of him, as if renewed with supernatural strength. He shouted his rage. "I won't be defeated so easily!"

Vegar flung Kibo over his body and several meters across the area. Kibo shook his head, his vision and mind disorientated by the sudden and powerful throw. A large blur streaked above him, surrounded in a storm of electrical energy.

"*Crap.*" Kibo panicked as Vegar slammed both of his fists into the ground. Kibo barely dodged the attack as Vegar's fists ripped through the earth, creating a sunken crater on the arena floor.

What kind of attack was that? If I hadn't jumped out of the way, even you wouldn't have protected me! Kibo's mind raced as Vegar stepped out of the large crater morphed into a completely different person. As though his body were a Tesla coil, sparks of electrical energy radiated from his skin. Vegar's shirt had been torn to shreds, and his muscular physique was now visible to all. His electrical blades were replaced with fists of brilliant electrical energy.

Vegar slammed into Kibo. Kibo grit his teeth as his arms felt like though they were on fire; the armor on his forearms had been scraped clean off from that single blow.

How did he damage me this much in one strike? He hits as hard as the creature we faced in the woods. I gotta think up some sort of plan. Kibo had little time to strategize. Vegar charged towards him once again, slamming Kibo with another fury of blows. Kibo was completely on the defensive.

"Wow, that guy's pretty strong," Hana said excitedly, watching Vegar land blow after blow on Kibo. "You think he actually has power from some god?"

"He gets power from his faith," Ben noted. "If you're that fervent and strong-willed, it shouldn't be that hard to push your body past its limits with a bit of your resolve. I'd say things are only gonna get worse for Kibo."

"Yeah, he's losing focus," Rex said. To their surprise, Rex was watching the match with a stern poker face, completely engrossed. "That charge of his did quite a lot of damage, but that was because he shifted all of his weight against his shoulder. But if ya don't control electricity, it can do a number on ya system," Rex stated, much to the group's surprise. "He's so caught up in a rage that it's frying his brain—he's gone berserk. I should know, cause I've done it too."

They all looked down at Vegar. Rex's assumption seemed to be correct. While Vegar's blows were heavy and powerful, he'd gone wild, each attack becoming less accurate. Kibo realized this as well, noting how each dodge or parry required increasingly less effort. Seeing an opportunity, he launched his fist into Vegar's gut.

Vegar hunched over in pain and stumbled back, giving Kibo a few precious seconds to regain his footing and some distance. His mind raced wildly to think up a plan in this small window of opportunity.

"WHOA, watch it Kibo. You almost stepped out of the ring," Arcanus yelled at Kibo, waking him from his panicked state. Kibo looked back at the edge of the arena. *"You almost gave the match to Vegar. Focus and rush him while he's weak."*

"Nope. I think I got a better idea."

"What? But then he'll—" It all clicked everything together. *"All right, kid, but I'll tell you this: you're taking one hell of a bet here."*

Kibo nodded at Arcanus as he yelled at the top of his lungs, "Come on, is that all you got? I thought a servant of your gods would be stronger than that!"

"What did you just say?" Vegar jolted upright. His once tired-and-ragged breath stilled, his eyes full of rage. Kibo stared Vegar down with a smirk. He had him hooked. All that was left was to reel him in.

"If the servant of the gods is this weak, what might that say about your gods then? Maybe they are just a pile of rocks and statues some old Vikings in a frozen hell decided to call god," Kibo taunted.

"Such heresy! You are no worthy opponent. You are a defiler, one who spreads lies and deceit," Vegar said, his rage boiling over. "There is only one way to cleanse heretics from this world. Death!" Vegar slammed his foot into the ground and launched himself towards Kibo.

"Arcanus, I need you to bump up my power for a second," Kibo stared down Vegar.

"All right, you got it!"

Kibo felt a sudden boost of energy flow through him and took a stance. Vegar charged toward him at full speed. He held his breath.

This next move would decide the match.

The room shook with a resounding *boom* as the two fighters were wrapped up in a swirl of dust. As the dust parted, Vegar, the mighty Nordic warrior, lay on the ground in a small crater outside of the ring, completely and utterly beaten. Kibo had triumphed.

"Winner of the eighth and final match of round one, Kibo Kozlov, will move to the next round."

"Good job, kid!" Arcanus congratulated Kibo, a slight hint of pride in his voice. *"I gotta say, Kibo, even when you have the*

most batshit-crazy plan, you always get them to work in the end."

Kibo let out a small chuckle. "Yeah, but I don't think I planned for every outcome."

"Huh, what do you mean, kid?"

"Well, I didn't plan for, uh, wetting myself."

Batros looked down at Kibo intently, his eyes glancing back and forth from the file in his hand to the arena. Sidorov stared at Batros, he seemed conflicted.

"Hmmm," Batros stated, leaning back in his chair and staring at the ceiling. "He was able to take the heavy hits that Vegar threw at him and held his ground, which is perfect for a grappler like him. He needed to be able to tank such hits in order to get close to his opponent. Those years of training in the militia seemed to have helped hone his mind and body quite a bit, allowing him to perform those techniques with decent execution." Batros paused. "However, he doesn't seem to have anything that really makes him stand out. That armor of his lets him really absorb blows and take down his opponent up close, but he lacks any sort of powerful magic or ability that give s him an extra edge."

"So, what do you plan to do with him, sir?"

"I don't know yet." Batros leaned back in his chair as Kibo exited the Arena. "But we still have many more matches to go. Let's see what else you're capable of, Kibo Kozlov."

CHAPTER 14

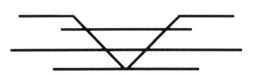

"Winner of the first match of round two: Arex Ricci." Batros' ears perked up as the speaker announced the match. Holding Ukrit's and Rex's files in hand, he turned his attention to the arena, curious to see how the match ended.

Ukrit's unconscious body was firmly planted in the ground. Rex stood above him, covered in burns and bruises, victorious. Just as Batros expected.

"Pitiful," Batros said. "With that level of arrogance, I was surprised to see him get past the written exam, let alone the physical portion."

"I wholeheartedly agree, sir," Sidorov said, taking a glance into the arena. "Though I wonder who Mr. Ricci will have to fight in the next round now."

"We shall see." Batros got up from his seat. Reaching for two other files, he took a quick peek at both labels and smirked.

MATCH 15
AKIRA KAZE
MAX GARRET

"Because this next match could go either way."

Kaze stood still, looking Max Garret straight in the eye, his hands crossed.

"Well then, look who I've run into."

"Hor are ya, mate?" Max blew away Kaze in one shout.

"Can you not yell at the top of your lungs when I'm literally right in front of you?" Kaze grumbled, massaging his ears.

"Oh, sorry about that. My ears don't have the best of hearing, mate," Max said sheepishly. Kaze groaned slightly, somewhat relieved.

Huh, he's more understanding than I thought. Kaze returned to his brooding state. Max stepped toward him and gave him a thumbs-up,

"Well then, I hope for us to have a bloody good fight. I think we both know who's going to win this match."

"How could we, *mate*? We haven't even faced each other, and we both probably haven't seen all the moves we have at our disposal, so it's impossible for us to guess who might win," Kaze stated in a bit of an annoyed tone.

Max pondered Kaze's words, scratching his chin. "You know what? You're quite right. Guess we really can't tell who will win a match until we're really in it." Max seemed quite impressed by Kaze. As Max continued thinking about Kaze words, Kaze slowly backed up, hoping to get as far away from him as he could. But right as he turned around, Max called out to him, "Hey, mate. You don't have to force yourself to act that way, you know. If ya go down this road, you'll find yourself alone with no mate to help ya."

Kaze furrowed his brow, considering the advice, before jolting back upright. He walked away, albeit now much slower, each of his steps echoing of wariness.

"You don't have to force yourself to act that way, you know." Kaze was going over what Max had told him, tapping his foot impatiently. Each tap echoed throughout the dark hallway leading to the stadium floor. *What did he mean by that? This is how I normally act. Anyone can tell that,* Kaze thought to himself, letting out a small grunt in frustration. Yet, the more he thought about it, the more conflicted he became. *Why the hell*

does it bother me so much? Kaze thought as he slowly walked towards the ring, clearly troubled by Max's words.

"Fighters of the second match in round two: Akira Kaze and Max Garret." Kaze woke up from his confused stupor from the sudden boom of the speakers above and moved his gaze from the ground toward his opponent.

Max had already put both fists up, moving from side to side out of excitement as he impatiently waited for their match to begin. Kaze entered his combat stance, yet he wasn't able to concentrate, his mind distracted by Max's words.

Do I really want to fight to protect people and uphold justice and peace? Kaze thought as he stared blankly into the distance.

"Fighters, take your stances."

Kaze shook his head and regained his focus and resolve. *I've got a match to fight. I can think about this later!"*

"Begin!"

Max quickly covered himself with his exoskeletal armor and charged Kaze. Max brought back his fist and layered bones on top of each other until his arm became a large, white battering ram. Max threw his enlarged fist at Kaze while screaming at the top of his lungs.

A flurry of wind exploded from Kaze's arm as he struck Max with every bit of force he had right into his chest. The pressure unleashed from his attack rippled through the arena, leaving behind a cone of destruction that originated from his fist, turning half of the arena into rubble. At the other end of the ring lay Max Garret, his armor cracked and damaged, his body on the ground, still and unmoving.

Good thing I stored up some wind pressure around my arm while the match was starting. Hopefully it's enough to finish him off. Kaze gazed down the arena at Max Garret's battered body. Many in the crowd were starting to murmur and talk amongst themselves, seeing that the match was already over.

The speaker crackled from above. "Winner of the second match—"

"Wait!" Everyone in the stadium looked at where the shout had come from. Max stood upon his knees, coughing up blood all over the floor. He had a massive, cracked hole in his chest, right where Kaze had slammed his fist. Max stood on his two feet: his body thrashed, pieces of his exoskeleton falling to the ground. But he was standing regardless.

"Yeah! Now this is the kind of fight I was searching for. That punch was nothing like what those small-timers threw at me," Max yelled at the top of his lungs, still in his old, hyped-up self. Though one could easily tell that he was in pain, his body trembling, his breathing ragged. It seemed like none of it affected him one bit. He motioned for Kaze to attack him, but Kaze just stood frozen in place, his face plastered with shock.

How did he manage to get back up? I crushed a giant centipede with that attack, yet Max is still able to stand? Kaze was baffled and unable to think or plan what to do next. His legs shook with fear.

"So, you ain't gonna attack, huh? Guess I'll take that as my cue." Kaze snapped upright to see Max charging toward him at full speed. It sent his mind into overdrive, thinking of some kind of solution.

What should I do? I could charge up another attack or lay down a trap, but it might backfire and hurt me. I could stall, but that'll only tire me out. What do —"

"HAAAAAA!" Max yelled on the top of his lungs as he launched his entire body at Kaze, throwing a singular punch with all his remaining strength behind it.

"I forfeit!" Max's fist stopped centimeters from Kaze's face. Max slowly moved back as Kaze crumbled to his knees, his face pale and drenched in sweat.

The crowd looked on in awe. Kaze, who had blown away Max in one punch, who had left his opponent barely able to stand upright, gave away the match. As the onlookers watched in silence, the speaker crackled on, echoing through the stadium.

"Winner of the second match of round two, Max Garret, will move on to the finals."

With the speaker's announcement, Max smiled for one final time as he collapsed to the ground, victorious. Kaze stared off into the distance blankly as medical personnel rushed into the ring to aid Max. He had been completely and utterly beaten.

"Those were some pretty serious injuries you had there. If you weren't protected by that armor, I'm afraid even the strongest of healing magic and equipment wouldn't have saved you," the doctor told Max, who was sitting down on a bed, nearly recovered from his fight.

"Bloody hell, thanks for getting me back on my feet, doc. If ya need any help, just call this chap back over here," Max said joyously. The doctor smiled and shook Max's hand.

"I appreciate the offer, Mr. Garrett, but we seem to be quite fine with the workload we have now. If we happen to need any manual labor, we will give you a call." The doctor chuckled.

"Now then, have a good day." Max headed out of the med bay while waving back at the doctor for his help. At the exit, Max was surprised to see a certain individual waiting for him. It was Kaze. Instead of glaring at him or yelling how he'd beat Max next time, Kaze just sat there, his face perturbed.

"How did you get back up after an attack like that?" Kaze asked, getting straight to the point. Max sighed, put his hands on the back of his head and looked up at the ceiling.

"If I'm gonna be honest, mate, I don't really know." Max paused for a bit and scratched his face. "Why'd you ask?"

"Whenever I'm in any sort of situation, I try my best to come up with a plan. When you got up after that attack, I couldn't think up anything. It just seemed so improbable." Kaze drove his hands through his hair in distress.

"And now, I don't know what to think anymore. What do I do when my plans fail? Will I have nothing to fall back on? I'm just *lost* when I can't predict or plan ahead." Kaze slumped down, a veil of despair hanging over him.

"All I can ask is, when nothing goes the way I intend or plan, what do I do?" Kaze asked Max, not even expecting an answer. But fortunately for Kaze, Max perked up.

"Actually, I think I do have an answer to that, mate." Max sat down on the bench and started talking. "Someone told me a long time ago, "Son, if you ever think you're about to lose, that you've been beaten into a corner and nothing will work, it's at those moments that you'll be at your strongest. After that day, whenever I got into a fight, whenever I got a hell of beating, I would stay on my feet and hold my own," Max reminisced fondly. "So even if things don't go your way, mate, just keep fighting through. Cause ya never know how it'll turn out." Max extended his fist, though he expected that Kaze wouldn't return the gesture. To his surprise, Kaze returned the gesture, the troubled look on his face now replaced with one of purpose.

"Thank you, Max. I think I understand what I've been missing." Kaze said as he turned back towards the stadium.

"It ain't a big deal...uh, what's your name again?" Max asked him. Kaze paused for a moment. He turned and smiled.

"Oh, it's Akira."

"Busy day, huh?"

"You bet. Holding back those swarms of recruits really was a hassle. You know, I don't get why the higher-ups have all applicants come on the same day. It must swamp the offices with a ton of paperwork."

Two guards were chattering amongst themselves, both of them on watch at the entrance of the Bastion testing facility.

"I've heard that they've had some unusual recruits this year. One guy is some crazy Australian fighter, another apparently can make a bunch of whips from fire."

"No kidding. Well, I saw a French examinee today and it kind of made me homesick. I wonder when our country's military rotation is up."

"Apparently the big one a lot are talking about is Siris Vasilyeva."

"A Vasilyev? Hot damn, didn't think I'd hear that name here." The other guard whistled.

The guard looked around to see if anyone was around and motioned his fellow guard over to him. "Apparently, from what I've heard, she froze the entire arena during her fight in a single second. They had to dig out her opponent from a slab of ice."

"Huh, what else do you expect from somebody from that crazy house? Every one of them might as well not be even human. They're all walking natural disasters," the guard quipped.

"If there was anyone I would put my money on to would win this exam, it'd be her. Chances of her losing sounds like one in a million," the other guard joked, but his buddy seemed to think otherwise.

"Then what about that Italian kid, Rex Ricci? Apparently, he beat the living daylights out of both of his opponents. They say he moves so fast they couldn't even see him half the match," the guard said.

"Well, he'd have to get close to even land a hit on her. In practice, that would be near impossible when she can just freeze the whole damn ring over," the other guard stated. His friend took a step back and looked up at the evening sky.

"Well, that is a pretty compelling argument, but I think we just have to wait a bit more before we come to any sort of conclusion," he said to the other guard, but he heard no reaction and turned his attention back down. He looked at the ground, absolutely horrified. The guard lay dead. His neck had been snapped, a small pool of blood forming around his body.

"What the hell—" Something sharp sliced his neck. As he fell to the ground, coughing and gasping for air, a cloaked man held a blade covered in blood. The man looked around to see if there were any other guards, then signaled to someone out of sight. Several dozen men appeared from the surrounding woods, marching past the dying guard to the entrance. They were heavily armed. He watched in horror as they stepped past him, his consciousness slowly fading until everything went dark.

The assassin looked around and nodded. They were ready to proceed. He turned to the rest of the militia, a mixed bag of vagabonds and mercenaries. Their only similarities were the rifles they held, but they'd get the job done.

"It's showtime, laddies! No movements until you get the signal. Keep close and your bloody jabbers shut. Today is the day we strike back against oppression, against *them*. For the revolution!"

"Death to the Tsar!" they cried.

He gave more signals, and each partisan quickly formed off into squads and snuck to their positions. As they all moved in, he pulled out a communication device hidden beneath his coat.

"This is 'Halifax.' Operation Sideshow is a go. Keep forces on standby."

"Artur Sokolov, a nature-magic user from frozen Siberia, won the last match? How interesting," Batros scoffed, reading through the documents his assistant gave him.

Sidorov handed him a coffee. "He has all the qualities you're looking for, sir. Why haven't you picked him to join your team, sir?"

Batros turned to his side and pointed at the projector. "He lacks cooperativeness." Batros got up and went next to the small projector, turning it on. As the projector flickered on, Batros motioned Sidorov over to a seat next to him. They both sat down and watched the recording of the first part of the examination, seeing the multitudes of examinees fighting the even more numerous exotic creatures in the arena. Suddenly, Batros tapped the pause button and pointed at the freeze-frame.

"There were supposed to be eighteen people at the start of the second part of the exam, but we had only sixteen, and it was because of this."

Sidorov looked at the scene and saw what he meant. In the middle of a lush jungle, two people stood at the jungle floor and were attacked by a massive swarm of small raptors. However, their attention was focused not on the ferocious horde, but on their other teammate. Their faces filled with anger, as if they were shouting and cursing at him. Upon closer inspection, that teammate was Artur Sokolov. He was using vines to swing away from the horde—and his team. The radar was in his hand, each slot filled with a gem.

"He made it to the second part of the exam, but at the cost of his team. He didn't even think about saving them or helping them. He only cared for his own well-being. He left his team for dead. If we hadn't teleported them out of there, they would have been ripped to shreds."

Sidorov nodded. "I guess those two fighters aren't similar at all. Kaze, at least, worked alongside his team."

"Of course, the exams are to see how skilled mages are in certain environments, and Sokolov does possess a great strategic and rational mindset. With his self-sufficiency and speed, he could sneak into anywhere Bastion wanted with little effort. He would do well in the Magehunter Corps. He has the skillset to take down his targets quietly and efficiently." Batros leaned forward and resumed the recording, letting it play until the end. They both watched the next segment, consisting of

Kaze, Rex, and Kibo. They watched the three of them struggle, fight, and work together to reach the end of the exam. Batros sipped his coffee and stood up.

"They could have left Ricci behind at the very end there, but instead they instinctively saved him, because he was their teammate. This is why I want all three of them to join me. Not because of their individual powers or talents, but because of their ability to cooperate and to stick together as a team. Ricci, Kaze, and..."

"Kozlov."

Batros turned to see who had called out Kibo's name, and instantly a smile cropped up on his face, causing Sidorov to spit out his coffee. "Nima! It's been a while. How have you been?"

Nima leaned against the doorway, staring at Batros with a little smirk.

"I've been well, but let's cut to the chase. You know why I'm here."

Batros stopped, his once joyous demeanor instantly replaced by a stern and murky expression.

"Um, sir? Do you need—" Sidorov interjected.

"That won't be necessary, Sidorov." Batros trudged towards Nima and came face-to-face with her. They stared at each other intensely, not saying a single word. Sidorov felt himself slowly being crushed under the intensity around the two of them. At last, Batros relented.

"Fine, but let's get something while we talk. Sidorov, I'll be back in a few minutes. I expect to see more reports for me to read."

Nima walked out of the room. Batros followed, glancing back at Sidorov. Sidorov couldn't exactly tell, but it almost looked like there was a sense of regret in Batros' eyes. Before he could say anything, Nima grabbed his shoulder.

"Let's move. Command is giving us an hour."

Sidorov watched his two superiors leave with a worried frown; something felt off.

He just didn't know what.

CHAPTER 15

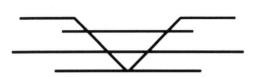

"The final match of round two is about to begin, the final match of round two is about to begin."

The speaker's chant rang through Kibo's ears. He stood at the entrance of the arena, taking an uneasy look down the stretch of the massive arena floor, but he didn't need to see who was on the other side. He already knew who he had to face.

"So, this next match against Siris..." Kibo muttered, running his hands through his hair. He felt his heart beating irregularly and his palms sweaty. Arcanus had gist of what was going on in his head. "I swear that last match went quicker than the rest of them."

"Listen, Kibo, I know you have quite the history with this person, but you've gotten much better over the course of the exam," Arcanus exclaimed. *"I'm just letting you know, you've got higher odds at winning this thing than you think."*

"I know that, but I have this feeling that I just-I just can't push away. Like there's something wrapped around my chest, squeezing me inside out." Kibo put his hand on his chest.

Zap.

"Ow! What the heck was that for?" Kibo said, both bewildered and annoyed by Arcanus' sudden shock.

Arcanus piped up, *"Kid, no matter what happens, I know you won't regret going into that arena. You have the strength and willpower to face things even scarier than her—I've seen it myself. Don't tell me some damn fleshy is gonna beat you."*

Kibo looked at the ground and exhaled. Arcanus was right. Step by step, he marched slowly towards the entrance of the arena and into the light.

Under the blinding sun, surrounded by massive walls and the deafening sounds of the crowd blaring from above, none of it mattered except the figure in front of him—Siris Vasilyeva.

Siris' eyes were cold, empty of all remorse or mercy. She looked down at Kibo with a smug sneer, expecting him to cower in fear. Instead, he stood upright, staring directly into her eyes with a fierce determination. Siris was taken aback by it. The person she believed would always fear her was not reacting to her presence. It seemed she needed to poke a bit further to make him crack.

"Well, I guess you could say I'm quite impressed by your newfound ability, just like how one may be impressed by a monkey who can draw," she taunted, yet Kibo gave no response. It only further served to make her angry. "Just because you've acquired this power doesn't mean you're anywhere near my level, you hear me? I'll show an underling like you where you belong." Siris saw a flash of fear across Kibo's face, yet he remained stalwart. Her face turned a bright red. He was a non-magic user, someone she would always be better than. Yet, in such little time, he grew powerful enough to crush someone who was a lightning-charged bull! And if he, someone who could do nothing more than create the smallest flicker of flame, grew to be stronger than her, what did that make her?

"You're nothing without your name."

Siris quickly shook her head, driving away the dark memory. Instead, she turned her anger towards Kibo. "I'll show you! You—"

"Are you done yet?" Siris looked at Kibo in shock. Did he just talk back to her? She watched, bewildered, as Kibo walked slowly towards her. It was as though he were getting larger and larger, until he towered over her.

"Listen, I'm not really the kind of person to hype myself up or be all talk. So, if you want to show me, then show me in a fight," Kibo uttered, not stuttering once. As he walked back to his side, Siris looked at Kibo, dumbstruck at what she saw.

"Fighters, take your stance." Kibo took a low stance, guarding himself with both of his arms. Siris shook her head and directed all of her focus at Kibo. Even though the match hadn't begun, the crowd understood that they were about to see one hell of a match.

"Begin!"

Kibo charged towards Siris, keeping himself low to the ground. Siris responded with a flick of a single finger at Kibo, launching a wave of massive ice chunks. Kibo, instead of dodging the attack, took it head-on. The spectators watched in shock as ice slammed into him, launching large amounts of dust into the air.

"He took that attack head-on! Is he crazy?" Ben said, bewildered by Kibo's seemingly brash decision. Yet, he saw that Rex was watching the fight with a giddy smile, as though his friend didn't suddenly get crushed by a wave of ice. "Why are you smiling? Didn't you see what just happened to Kibo?"

"Just keep watching," Rex said as he continued to watch the arena. Ben turned back to look at the ring and saw why. Kibo rushed out of the massive cloud of dust, jumping from crystal to crystal, undeterred.

But why would he take the risk of getting hit by those crystals rather than just dodging that attack and resuming his attack? He must know something that the rest of us don't, Ben thought. Though he didn't know it, Ben's hunch was correct.

I've been watching Siris use magic ever since I was seven years old. If anyone would know her weaknesses, it'd be me, Kibo thought to himself frantically as he ran on top of the ice crystals.

She always relies on her power at range to keep her opponents at bay, because you can't jack in close range. I can't wait a second trying to dodge or move away if I am going to try and close the gap between the two of us.!"

However, Siris caught on with what Kibo was trying to do, and summoned several icicles around herself, ready to launch them at Kibo. With a crunch, Kibo grabbed a large chunk off an ice crystal and threw it at the Siris, forcing her to block them with the icicles. Ice and snow rose into the air, obscuring Siris' vision. This was all part of Kibo's plan.

Kibo landed a powerful roundhouse kick against Siris. She barely managed to block it with her arm. She flew to the side of the ring, nearly getting knocked out of the ring but for the crystals she summoned behind herself.

She massaged her arm, biting down the pain. *Damn, even with all that ice,* she thought. *"But he doesn't have ranged attacks. Why else would he throw a piece of ice to attack me from the range? All I have to do is keep the brat away from me and I'll beat him.* She raised one hand towards the sky. A large wall of ice ravaged the arena towards Kibo, who once again jumped over the attack. But Siris was prepared this time.

A swarm of icicles flew at Kibo at an alarming rate. Kibo quickly dropped low to the ground, blocking his face with his arms, and rushed towards Siris once again. But no matter what he tried, he couldn't move. Kibo looked down at his feet and was struck with horror. Both of his legs were frozen from the ground up, all the way to his knee, holding him to the ground like an anchor.

Siris let out a chilling laugh as she rose from the ground. A thin layer of frost froze the ground in front of her. "I knew you would try to rush me head-on, so I turned your own strategy against you. I threw those icicles at your face, knowing you would be forced to block them or take fatal damage. That in turn obscured your vision and let me freeze the ground and you to it. You may have that fancy armor, but you're still the same in the end: a failure."

Kibo started to sweat profusely, knowing that staying still was the last thing he should do while fighting Siris. Kibo tried to bring his arms up to protect himself, but they would not budge. Kibo started to panic. it was going to happen all over again. Him on the ground, beaten and defeated. Siris gloated over him, kicking him in the gut. Kibo couldn't let that happen. Not anymore.

Arcanus, I need you to give me a power boost.

"What do you mean? You're already at your limit!"

Kibo's heart dropped. Even with all that, he still couldn't break free from Siris' icy prison. Siris stared at Kibo with glee, watching him struggle and squirm like a rat in a trap. The crowd roared from the spectator booths.

"Looks like this is the end of the line for you once again, Kozlov." Siris summoned a large spear of ice in her hand and aimed at Kibo. "Time to end this little bout."

Siris threw the spear with no hesitation.

"Kid, move, struggle. Do something or that spear is gonna skewer you like a wild boar!"

Nothing mattered to Kibo. Not the panicked advice of Arcanus, not the cheers or screams of the spectators, not even the spear that was hurtling towards him at remarkable speed. All that mattered was his unbearable, festering hatred against Siris.

He thought maybe, just this once, things would go differently. That he had finally gotten stronger and could stick it to Siris. But, just like every other time, she crushed him into the ground yet again. It seemed so unfair, unjust! How, after all this, could he still be beat so easily?

No, he would not be beaten. He wasn't going to let her roll over him, not anymore. He would do anything to beat her. Kibo felt his body slowly burn as he put all of his strength into his right arm in one final attempt to break out. The crowd stood at the very edge of their seats, watching the spear hurtled ever closer to Kibo's face. A shower of ice shards exploded across the arena in a hundred different directions. Siris threw her arms over her face, shielding herself from the blast. When she lowered her arms, she saw Kibo holding her frozen spear, half crushed in his right hand. But none of that was more impressive or surprising than the futuristic-looking helmet that had formed upon his face, its brilliantly blue visor shining in the arena's lights.

Kibo stared out through his visor in shock, the sudden evolution of his suit washing away his anger. Strange words in a long-forgotten language whizzed past him in a vertical motion, surrounded in a veil of zeros and ones. Images of strange bits of technology flashed sporadically on his screen as well: a pair of strange metallic batons, beams of light firing from a well, and a picture of a clock with its hands moving in erratic directions burst across his screen. Then, all images disappeared, leaving the visor blank, save for a few bold words.

>>*Combat form completed. Energy efficiency: optimized. Upper limit has now been increased.*

Kibo was at first perplexed, but seemed to quickly grasp what the heads-up display, or HUD, was displaying. "All right! That means I can use more of the suit's capable power, right?" Kibo said excitedly. But he wasn't the only one who was jubilant; Arcanus shone brightly in giddiness too.

"*Yup, you got that right, kid. You've completed your combat form. Now let's show that bitch what we can do.*" Those words woke Kibo from his excited trance, remembering that he was in the middle of a match. With a vicious crack, Kibo crushed the spear, shattering it into pieces.

"Let's finish this, Siris."

"How? No, I won't let you win this match. I swear on my family name that I won't let a runt like you ever beat *me*," Siris screamed, enraged by Kibo's sudden burst in power. Siris slammed her foot into the ground and threw her hands into the air, splitting the arena with a wall of ice stretching from one side of the arena to the other, leaving no route for Kibo to attack her.

Power coursed through his veins as he drew his fist back, and slammed it into the frozen wall.

Like a battering ram breaching a castle, Kibo punched through the hole, crushing the ice to bits with his armored boots and fists. Right across the gaping hole was Siris, in total shock.

Siris felt a weight crushing her; her body was sluggish and tired. Casting such a mana-intensive and powerful spell had drained her. She frantically started to think up a way to defend herself. A way to beat back Kibo. As these thoughts ran through her head, an icy hand grasped her shoulder. A haunting, dark voice whispered in her ear.

"Looks like the master is now hunted by the hound. I warned him that he would finally rival your power. If you are to defeat him and show him his place once again, you need to go deep within." She felt goosebumps down her back. *"Let out your true power, the one that lets you destroy all who are beneath you. Let it control you, make you become what you truly are."*

"No!" Siris shook the dark spirit away. Siris woke up from her trance at the exact right moment, just as Kibo was throwing a powerful hook with his fist. Siris just barely blocked the heavy blow. The ice on her hand cracked. Kibo didn't relent, launching a powerful flurry of blows at Siris and chipping away at the sheets of frozen ice that were her final layer of defense. However, another plan dawned on Siris. Kibo was moving slower than before.

Ignoring the increasing pain, Siris froze the ground beneath them once again, covering Kibo's body in thicker and thicker layers of ice, slowing him down immensely. Taking advantage of the distraction, she retreated to a safe distance.

Kibo instantly ripped his legs from the frozen trap, staring directly into Siris' eyes.

"That move won't work on me twice." Kibo leaped into the air. Siris looked up to see Kibo aiming an axe kick directly where she stood, just barely side-stepping the attack.

Kibo landed with a boom, shattering the concrete floor beneath him. Despite dodging, Siris had been hit by debris, covering her in cuts. Her hands were dangerously pale and frozen; she was at her limit. Between those and the bruises from his hits, Siris seemed to be standing on her last legs.

Yet, Siris remained undeterred. She grit her teeth and ignored the pain, her expression in a ferocious snarl. Was it her pride and willpower that kept her fighting? Or was it the fact that she refused to allow herself to be beaten by the one she saw as inferior to herself? Whatever it may be, it kept Siris standing on her feet.

She gripped her pale hand, turning the budding frost on her fingers into sharp, frozen claws. Before Kibo could realize it, she charged forward and slashed at Kibo's face. But she missed Kibo's visor by mere centimeters, and her reckless attack left her wide open. The crowd watched with bated breath—Kibo had a clear shot to end the fight with a single, unimpeded attack. But the armored fighter stumbled backwards, scrabbling frantically at his face.

A devious grin crawled across Siris' face. "Fool. I wasn't planning on hitting you with a weak attack like that. It wouldn't even scratched that helmet of yours. All I wished was to blind you, and it looks like it worked."

Kibo blindly lunged in the direction of Siris' voice, but Siris dodged the attack with ease and quietly slid behind Kibo, drawing back her fist.

"Goodbye, Kibo." Ignoring the increasing pain, she launched a powerful blast of frozen wind, launching Kibo out of the ring and into the arena wall. Kibo flopped to the ground, defeated.

"Winner of the final match of round two, Siris Vasilyeva, will move on to the semi-finals."

Siris collapsed on the floor, exhausted from her fight with Kibo. But she had to get up, she had to see it. She sat up to look at Kibo. She had to see that sweet, sweet expression of defeat. He had put up more of a fight than she'd hoped, but here he was again, on the ground, crying and—

Kibo was standing. He wasn't groveling on the floor in anguish but standing tall. He scraped the ice off his visor and retracted his suit with a slight grin, before quietly stepping out of the arena.

Why is he grinning? I showed him his place by crushing any hope he had at winning and yet he's still smiling. What's going on? For the first time, she didn't know what Kibo was thinking, and nothing scared her more than that. All she could do was watch him leave the arena, too shocked and exhausted to say anything.

Kibo walked along the dark tunnel without a word. Arcanus seemed worried about him, having still lost to Siris despite his newfound power. But, despite this, Kibo didn't wear the face of someone who was distressed or troubled. *"Hey, you okay?"*

"I don't know. It's just- I mean, can't you tell by just reading my mind?" Kibo said with a bit of a snarky tone.

"Just because I can, doesn't mean I will," Arcanus said, not a hint of anger or sarcasm in his voice. He just answered Kibo's question calmly. *"That would be a bit too invasive, don't ya think?"*

"Oh, I guess you're right." Kibo looked off into the distance sheepishly, somewhat embarrassed. "I guess I'm all right. Honestly, I can't really tell."

"But you lost! You weren't able to one-up that bastard."

Kibo stopped and took in a breath. He seemed deep in thought.

"I'm not even that close to Siris or the other fighters that I've met in this tournament." He sighed. "Despite the fact that I lost that match, it didn't really feel like I did." Kibo put his hand over his chest and smiled at Arcanus.

"All I can say is, I didn't regret it."

CHAPTER 16

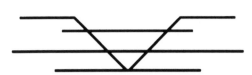

"Winner of the first match of the semi-finals, Rex Ricci, will move on to the final match." Sidorov looked down at the stadium as the speaker announced the winner of the match. Rex, bloodied and bruised, just barely managed to stand on his feet and stared down at the pummeled frame of Max, surrounded by the ruins of his armor. The warrior was beaten at last.

"What a fight!" Sidorov smirked as he glanced at Rex. It was a tough fight between the two, with Rex constantly trying to pierce Max's armor, while Max was trying desperately to land a hit of the speeding bullet that was Rex. For a while, he really couldn't tell which way the match could've gone.

"Heh. If Batros were here, he'd make some sort of quip about Rex's victory and then give a dozen reasons why he knew he was going to win." Sidorov let out a nervous chuckle as the smile faded from his face. That look on Batros' face, that rush, the tone he spoke in—it all left a sense of worry in his heart.

"Just where is he?"

"I do miss being boots on the ground. Even rucking through the Swamplands. Can you believe that?" Nima chuckled.

The meeting had started out as a pre-deployment briefing for the upcoming operation, but Nima managed to wrap it up in record time. Batros realized why she was rushing, why she chose a diner as a meeting place. The table was crammed with a variety of dishes of local snacks and foodstuffs. She picked one randomly, throwing a fistful of pork rinds into her mouth.

"It pays more, but I don't feel like I'm making a *difference*. All because they *still* don't think I'm cleared. I've done it before, and I'll do it again." She took a swig of off-brand cola.

Batros nodded politely, taking a sip of plain coffee. He didn't mind catching up. "I miss it, too. I don't like this...whatever my job is now."

"Coordinator. For the drafting season. Doesn't seem fun either." She gave a sympathetic shake of the head, before taking a bite from a sausage. "But who knows? Maybe we'll get a team after this exam is over. It'll be like old times. Your team and mine: back in the field."

Batros raised an eyebrow. "You're saying that you're as old as me."

"Hey, I've seen some stuff too, old-timer. Worse than you, for sure." She laughed quietly. Batros didn't laugh, however. Nima squinted her eyes and they gleamed for a few seconds. She extended a hand beside the table as if about to catch something, much to Batros' confusion.

"You're quieter today. Gonna share?" she asked.

"No."

"Tell me. I would offer a beer, but it's against regulation."

"You're still a rule freak, huh?" Batros looked out the window of the diner, impatiently tapping his foot, wishing to move on from the subject.

But Nima didn't relent. "You're not gonna share with your old pal?"

"Oh, quiet you!" Batros slammed his fist on the table, causing a plate of sandwiches on the edge to fall. The plate neatly fell onto the younger officer's extended hand. She grabbed a piece, tossed it into her mouth, and handed it towards him.

"You've gotten better at temporal branches," he said, impressed. He took one and ate it slowly.

She tapped her rifle, beaming proudly. "I know, right? I barely feel it anymore."

Batros nodded. "I too have been keeping my spatial magic sharp."

"C'mon, don't change the subject! Tell me."

The older veteran was silent, but he noticed Nima's eyes. That reassuring and calm look was all too familiar. It brought back old memories on the battlefield of a warrior's trust.

The Great Swampland, some years ago...
Click.
The enemy soldier fell, but the submachine gun was out of ammo. Batros could reload, but he was restrained on the ground. A rock mage's doing, no doubt. A grenade sailed through the air towards his foxhole. He was screwed. The soldier closed his eyes and waited, ready for oblivion.

Only it never came. Instead, the grenade exploded midair, plucked out of the sky like a duck shot down by a hunter. A pair of strong hands grabbed his shoulders and lifted him to his feet. The cavalry has arrived: Nima's squadron along with a platoon of Allied soldiers.

Nima smiled back, her eyes glowing. She'd shot down the grenade. She gave a playful salute and reloaded her rifle, ready to turn the tide.

He sighed in defeat. He had to tell her. "I'm worried. About Sidorov."

"Because of the you-know-what?"

"Yes. I don't wanna see any more of my men getting hurt. You'd think after twenty years of service it gets easier. It doesn't. At all. Each time I have to send someone home on a stretcher or in a body bag it still hurts. And this recruitment program makes me think about what those poor kids are getting themselves into."

There was a pause as Nima contemplated his words. It was quiet, except for the comfortable clamor of a restaurant.

"Batros, you know what you signed up for. I know what I signed up for. So do your soldiers, the new recruits, and every man and woman in Bastion." She placed a comforting hand on Batros' shoulder. "It's a sacrifice that we all willingly take. For Bastion."

"But sometimes I feel the sacrifice isn't worth it."

"I understand. But I'd keep quiet about that. You wouldn't want it to happen again." Her tone was serious, Batros sighed in defeat. She was right. "Trust in Bastion, like I do. They're the closest thing to the 'good guys' nowadays."

They finished their food in silence, the only sounds the clink of the plates. The baked potato tasted delicious, at least. It would have been tense, but a military armored personnel carrier rolled up beside the diner, its Bastion emblem on the hull gleaming in the afternoon sun. Nima got up and left a few coins for the food and slung her battle rifle over her shoulder.

"Let's go. The operation is starting."

CHAPTER 17

"I forfeit this match."

The crowd looked at the ring in silence, Artur had given up on the match before it even began. Siris appeared somewhat surprised at first, but then smiled devilishly.

"Someone finally realized that facing me would end badly for them."

"That's exactly right," Artur said. "You had zero trouble dealing with the two fighters before, even when it seemed like they had the advantage against you. It would be foolish for a nature user like me to go head-to-head with you. If I had encountered a situation like this on the field, I would immediately disengage and call reinforcements to help deal with you."

Siris looked at him, conflicted. It didn't feel right to win this way. She didn't know what to feel. Should she be angry at the nature mage for sapping away all the joy she would have gotten from teasing him? Or take the compliment with pride?

Regardless, she didn't know how to respond. Siris awkwardly cleared her throat. "Well, it seems that you are quite a knowledgeable fellow, choosing not to fight me."

Artur raised one eyebrow, clearly not intimidated by Siris, much to her irritation.

Damn it! Why does it feel like I'm the one on the losing side despite winning each and every match? Siris thought to herself as the speaker announced her *victory.*

"Due to Artur Sokolov forfeiting the match, Siris will move onto the finals and fight Rex Ricci!"

Siris awoke from her anger-induced stupor upon hearing the name of her next opponent, Arex Ricci. *Now then, to see just how good he actually is.*

From somewhere in the stands, Rex leaned back in his chair, staring down at Siris. "That rich chick, huh? I've been waiting to fight that spoiled brat. I'll beat her, no sweat!"

"I wouldn't be so hasty in your judgment, Rex," Ben said.

Rex scoffed. "Why's that?"

"Siris crushed the monsters we fought during the first part of this exam on her own. All we did was slow her down." Ben smirked. He put his hand on Rex's shoulder. "She's not like other guys you fought. She's not an up-close fighter like Max or Urkit, or a weak caster like Tanveer. And you've already seen how she decimated the other fighters, no wonder the guy forfeited his match immediately without even trying. The odds are heavily stacked against you, my friend. She's a gifted prodigy with ice magic."

Rex just looked on and smiled. "Even if you told me I had a one in a million chance of beating Siris, I'd still go up and fight her. Because I don't really give a damn about winning against her. I just want to prove something to someone."

Rex got up and headed to the exit. Ben pondered for a moment, before suddenly jolting up from his seat.

"Don't tell me you're fighting her for Kibo's sake?" Ben exclaimed.

Rex turned back and shrugged his shoulders. "Who knows?"

"You can't be serious! You'll be endangering the lives of several hundred civilians and Bastion personnel."

Halifax pressed the revolver into the official's skull. "Shut up and open the gateways, or the last thing you'll see is your brains splattered across this desk."

The official was shaking in fear, his white-collared shirt drenched in sweat. However, Halifax didn't show a shred of mercy behind his mask. He slammed his fist on the man's desk.

"I said get to it, or I'll just grab another hostage to do it for me."

The man yelped, whimpering a bit. He hesitantly began to configure a control at his desk. He was shaking so much so that he kept fumbling, occasionally pressing the wrong buttons. But the feeling of cold iron on his head compelled him to do as he was told.

Several different doors opened in a room below into what appeared to be the unending void. The official turned back at him, and despite the sheer terror upon his face, continued talking. "Why do this? There are only a few high-value targets within this facility. Attacking here would barely do anything to Bastion."

"Ah well, that is far too classified for you to know, my friend." Halifax frowned. He motioned over to his teammate, who was guarding the room's entrance. "Aye, Ripper. How about you reward our prisoner's cooperation?"

Ripper scoffed, taking a cigarette out of her mouth. "What's the matter, Halifax? Still too new to take out an innocent bystander?"

Halifax stared at Ripper intensely. She raised an eyebrow. The hostage kept his mouth shut, nearly pissing his pants in fear.

Halifax chuckled and turned to the hostage. "Oh, don't mind her. She's a little snarky that the operation is led by a promising newbie like me, instead of an old, loyal vet like her."

Ripper sighed and went back to smoking.

The official watched in horror as hundreds of armed insurgents poured into the gateways, disappearing into the void. Halifax gave a mocking pat on his back. "Well then, thank you for being so helpful to us, my good sir. But it appears the time has come for me to leave. I hope you spent some quality time with your loved ones before coming to work today, because now I'm afraid you'll be taking quite a long nap."

Halifax moved in to quickly knock him out. Before he could reach him however, Ripper fired off two shots into the man's stomach from her submachine gun.

"Wait!" The official lurched back as he grasped his stomach, eyes widening. He looked at his shaking hands. Blood.

"You promised that you wouldn't do anything if I did as I was told!"

Ignoring his pleas, Halifax gave Ripper an annoyed look. "Should've saved your ammo."

"What? Too afraid to kill? There shouldn't be any witnesses." Ripper snorted and eyed her partner carefully. "Go on, finish the job. Headquarters is waiting."

"Please! I don't want to die." The official coughed up blood and looked at the insurgents with desperation, praying that they might spare him. But that was not the case.

"What a bloody shame."

Halifax hesitated for a moment before shoving the revolver's barrel into the back of the staff member's head.

Bang!

"Introducing the fighters of the final round of this exam: Siris Vasilav and Rex Ricci."

The crowd exploded into cheers and jeers as Siris and Rex stepped into the ring. They'd clawed their way up to the final round, and both seemed as though they would put their lives on the line to win the match.

Ugh, why did I have to go up against such an idiot? It's going to feel really good to wipe that smug grin off his face when I crush him in one blow, Siris thought to herself when Rex jerked himself in her direction. Siris expected him to taunt and joke around in his usual carefree manner, but instead he looked full of conviction and intensity. Rex walked slowly towards her. She could tell that he was barely holding himself back.

"I heard you've been around Kibo since you were both kids. I could tell just by the way he looked at ya that you must've done some pretty shitty things in your past."

Siris' face twitched. "So? Why should one care about the ants they crush beneath their boots? They are nothing compared to the power and strength of man."

Rex glared at her, rage clearly visible on his face. Siris smiled gleefully at the reaction and decided to push a little further.

"What's the matter, can't handle the truth? Well face it: your friend is nothing but a coward who hides behind his armor. He has no power, no conviction."

But instead of exploding with anger, he smiled, which only served to perplex Siris.

"Heh, I didn't think Kibo had wounded that damn pride of yours so badly that you'd lie straight at my face." Rex moved closer. Siris' tough façade slowly started to fade as she stepped back, as though she was being pushed by an invisible force.

"You may have beaten him, but he left that fight a different man. I know that you would have to be dumber than that fella Max to realize it," Rex stated. And as one final bit of salt on the wound, he threw another jab at Siris. "Oh, and don't expect ya dad to come running in here to save ya when I kick your ass."

Rex gave a little salute to Siris and moved back to his side of the ring. Siris looked at him, bewildered. *Kick my... that simpleton! I'll show him what happens when you talk like that to a Vasilyev."* Siris slammed her foot and quickly put both of her arms up, ready for the match to begin.

Rex turned around and smirked. "Look who's ready to fight all of a sudden? Guess I must've pissed ya right off."

"Shut up!" Siris yelled at Rex, her face bright red in anger.

But Rex found her expression funny and laughed, further angering the ice mage. Rex wiped a tear from his eye and got into his combat stance.

"Guess I shouldn't keep this kid waiting any longer or else she'll have a tantrum. Let's get this match started!"

The speaker crackled on from above. "Fighters, take your stance."

Siris seemed as though she would burst at any moment, her writhing anger exuding from every ounce of her body. Yet, Rex kept the innocent smile on his face, pissing her off even further. Both Kibo and Kaze looked at Rex as though he had a screw loose. What the hell was he thinking?

"Begin!"

Before Siris could muster her attack, Rex launched himself at full speed towards her, slamming an incredibly powerful knee directly into her face. Siris staggered backwards, barely managing to block the blow. They both took the full brunt of Rex's attack, leaving them bruised and bleeding. Without letting her regain her bearings for a second, Rex threw a barrage of strikes at Siris, each one landing with the ferocity and speed of a cobra. Siris felt as though every single part of her body was both in pain and not at the same time, her nerves numbed by Rex's attack.

An earth-shattering crack filled the ears of the spectators as a massive spike of ice speared through the arena floor right where Rex stood, who would have been hit if he hadn't stepped back at the last second. Despite barely dodging the giant spike of ice, Rex continued to smirk at Siris, taunting her. "What's wrong? I thought you were one of the best fighters alive. Ya still couldn't hit me with an attack that big."

Siris slammed her hands on the ground and launched a wave of ice towards Rex, more reckless after her fight with Kibo. The wall of ice spread out in random directions, crashing through the arena with enough speed and force that it pierced through the glass ceiling, shattering it into several shards of glass. Several spectators watched in awe as the shards of glass created an extravaganza of color and light, distracting the crowd from what happened to Rex Ricci.

Kibo looked into the arena in both awe and horror, searching for Rex. However, a sudden blur caught his eye moving at blazing speed towards Siris near the top of the arena, instantly realizing who it was—Rex. He dove toward Siris at breakneck speed.

An explosion of electrical energy and debris flew across the already shattered ring. As the dust cleared, Rex stood tall and proud with Siris was on her knees several feet away, bloodied and bruised.

Rex looked confidently at the battered frame of Siris.

One small chop and I'll win this thing, Rex thought as he stepped towards Siris.

"Thought it would be that easy?" Rex suddenly felt a sharp pain pierce his right leg, sending him stumbling to his knee. A giant shard of ice poked out from both sides of his leg.

"What wrong? Unable to move?" Rex turned to see Siris, who had a terrifying smile etched across her mouth.

"At first I thought it was quite strange how you were still standing after I stabbed your leg when you slammed into me, but even the great Rex can only withstand so much damage." Siris tossed back all her hair and raised her fist at Rex. A sudden surge of adrenaline rushed through Siris. "Come on, then, show me if you can hold your own against a Vasilyev!"

Rex pulled out the shard from his leg and quickly wrapped up his wound with a piece of cloth ripped off his shirt. Rex smirked at Siris, but it was not a taunting look. Rather it seemed that he acknowledged her.

"That's more like it. I accept your challenge, Siris." Rex rushed her, a sudden burst of electrical sparks emanating from Rex's body.

Their fists clashed with a shockwave of sound that rattled the tempered glass surrounding the spectator stands. Rex looked at Siris with a smile and drew back his fist. Siris had encased her once defenseless body in a layer of thick ice and frost, turning herself into an armored knight.

"Well then, seems like you should have no problem with me going all out then?"

"Who said you had to go easy in the first place?" Siris retorted.

Siris had never felt this way before. It was as though a beast had awakened inside of her. She wasn't afraid of defeat, yet she was not confident that she would win. This uncertainty was something she had not felt before. That feeling of excitement and drive, the very essence of competition, had awoken within her.

Siris slammed her fist into Rex.

The crowd watched in shock as Rex skidded across the ground, landing several meters away from Siris. She looked at Rex with a gleeful smile. The ice that encased her fist shattered, but that didn't matter, she had landed her blow against Rex. And her reward for doing so? Rex lay on the ground, panting for air and clutching at his side.

"I watched your match against that unintelligent brute, Max, and wondered how you could maintain that devastating speed while attacking him with your electrical blows. Then I realized halfway through that you weren't running past him, you were gliding. You used your momentum to launch yourself into the air to maintain your speed and launch your deadly attacks," Siris said as she walked up to Rex, who was trying his best to get back up.

"But there was one little problem with your strategy: you couldn't dodge his blows while in midair, meaning if someone were to predict when you were airborne, they could land a guaranteed blow." Siris loomed over Rex. She expected him to look back at her with some cocky smile or throw a quick little jab at her, but he was still, silent.

Siris raised her mace of a hand into the air, ready to smite the elusive beast that had dodged her attacks.

"This ends here, Rex," Siris yelled at the top of her lungs as she threw a devastating punch directly at Rex.

Siris screamed as she reeled back in anguish. The armor around her arm cover shattered, only to reveal her now horrendously disfigured arm, broken at several different joints. Meanwhile Rex's right hand was covered in blood, his fingers broken and blackened as though they'd been burnt.

"How did you do that so fast?" Siris broke in a cold sweat as Rex raised his broken hand and closed it into a fist, despite his clear pain. However, Rex then broke out into a smile and stepped towards Siris.

"Sometimes you need to sacrifice a little to get an edge over ya opponent. I've suffered worse. Now where's the cocky look ya had?" Rex taunted with a grin.

Siris stepped forward, her once confused and shocked expression now one of burning fury.

"Don't you lecture me about being cocky, you bastard!" In an incredibly grotesque and sickening fashion, Siris locked her arm back into place, surrounding her arm once again in ice to support it. But instead of writhing in pain, Siris just smiled, her eyes lit up with excitement.

They circled each other, neither ready to give in. Then suddenly, both of them stopped moving, seemingly ready to clash once again. The crowd looked on with their breaths held. The battle between these two titans seemed to be coming to a close. This next set of blows would surely determine the victor.

"I give up," Rex said, raising his hand to signify his forfeiture. The crowd—Kibo, Siris, everyone—was shocked that Rex stepped down.

"Winner of the final match, Siris Vasilyeva, has finished the final exam in first place."

Siris should celebrate, yet she gritted her teeth, her fist clenched in anger. "Damn it, why did you quit? Why didn't you keep fighting?" Siris yelled at him as she grabbed him by his shirt. "Didn't you want to beat me, you idiotic simpleton?"

"Who said I didn't?" Rex turned away and limped towards the exit, but not before tossing a smirk in Siris' direction.

Siris smacked Rex across the face and pushed him toward the ground, despite her many injuries. But, as Siris raised her hand to hit Rex again, she couldn't move. She was locked in some sort of stasis. Two Bastion personnel ran into the room and grabbed Siris, dragging her frozen body away from Rex.

Rex coughed. *Well, guess I should also head back to get these wounds patched up.* He crawled backward before getting back to his feet. But even as he walked out of the ring, Siris' gaze burned into his soul.

Kibo and Kaze looked down at the arena, a look of complete disbelief on both of their faces. Despite what the speaker may have said, they knew who the real victor was. At the end of the final match, it crackled on one last time.

"The selection exams have come to an end. All spectators please exit the stadium in an orderly fashion."

"We gotta go check on Rex. He got pretty beaten up back there," Kaze said as he and Kibo ran toward the medical room.

"Yeah, for sure—"

Both Kibo and Kaze fell to the ground in pain as a sudden terrible screech emanated from the speakers. Kibo covered his ears and gritted his teeth, the terrible sound ripping through his eardrums.

As quickly as the speakers exploded, they were followed by silence. Kibo and Kaze looked up, confused and worried.

"There is no need to worry folks. Everything is fine," a voice said over the speakers. It was smooth and relaxed, not the same robotic droning that had been used for the rest of the exam.

Kibo let out a nervous sigh and continued to walk again. "It must have been a technical problem with the equipment. I guess there's no need to worry."

"I wouldn't be so sure," Kaze said as he pulled Kibo towards a random closet and locked the door.

"Hey! What's the big idea?"

Kaze motioned Kibo to stay quiet and pointed to a small hole in the closet door. Kibo looked through to see two soldiers who wore dark-colored camo and military gear, assault rifles in hand. They were pointed at Bastion staff.

"Hey, where are you taking us?"

"None of your damn business, that's what," one of the soldiers roughly responded as he slammed the butt of his rifle into the official's stomach. The official groaned in pain and fell to the ground, with the other two hostages quickly turned around and shoved forward.

Kibo stepped back as Kaze put his ear next to the door to listen. "What the hell is going on?" Kibo asked, perplexed. Kaze just continued to listen to the sounds outside the door, slowly grabbing a few bullets from his ammo pouch.

"I can't say for sure, but there's one thing I know: those soldiers aren't here for a friendly patrol." A soft breeze swept through the tiny closet. "And that we need to be ready."

"For what?" Kibo asked in a slight panic.

Kaze only smiled and looked out the small hole, a bullet in hand.

"A real fight."

CHAPTER 18

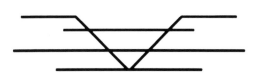

"Sir, I got us some coffee. I guessed that you like it black, so I..."

Sidorov was surprised to find Batros packing up. The lieutenant was neatly stacking some files into a suitcase. His face was blank as ever, but his eyes were serious. "I have to go."

"Who will be in charge?"

He closed the briefcase. "You will be. Your orders are still the same: keep the tournament running."

"Any reason why you're going?" Sidorov was shocked at the sudden change. What was going on?

"It's classified," he replied, abruptly. Batros put on his beret and sighed.

"Oh." Sidorov grinned. "I get it. You're on a spec-ops mission. Did they finally call you back?"

"I wish, kid." Batros picked up his suitcase and walked up to his junior. He lay a hand on his shoulder. "Sidorov, I want you to know that you're a good man. You have a lot of potential."

"T-Thank you, sir," the junior officer stammered. "But why the sudden sentimentality?"

Batros stared at Sidorov. His face was still blank, but Sidorov could tell something was off. A hint of sweat dripped down the veteran's forehead and his scarred hands shook ever so slightly.

"It's nothing."

Batros quickly stepped out of the room, leaving Sidorov on his own.

"I'll be fine!"

Rex winced as he ripped the bandage from his arm. The doctor offered to help, but Rex waved her away. After doing a few stretches, he thanked the doctor and left the medical bay with a spring in his step. But he bumped into a certain someone when he stepped outside. Siris leaned against the wall, arms folded.

"You seem quite pleased for someone who lost the final match." Siris' expression was stoic, but she held a hint of venom in her voice.

Rex clenched his fist. Siris scoffed in response.

"Really? Do you think I would attack you here?"

"Well, ya weren't above fighting out in the open," Rex retorted. "Like back then."

Siris maintained her composure. She stepped closer and leaned forward until her face was mere centimeters away, her cold, blue eyes were locked onto his. Rex instinctively leaned back, still tense.

"Why did you let me win?"

"Are you gonna move?"

"Answer me, simpleton."

"Listen, *your highness*, I'm not gonna get into a shouting match with ya. I think it would be better for both of us to walk away. *Capisce?*"

Siris seemed disappointed.

"Hmph, go your way then," she said. "And it's supposed to be *your well-born*."

Siris watched as he walked away. "But I will say: whoever taught you to fight was a half-wit."

Rex stopped and slowly turned around. "What the hell did you just say?"

"You heard me. Your teacher must have been a fool to make a lousy fighter like you."

Rex grabbed Siris by the shirt and slammed her into the wall.

"You gonna disrespect my old man like that, you evil Cagna!" Rex shook with the rage of a demon.

Siris smiled devilishly. "Hit a soft spot, did I? Bet that old bastard ran off just like Kibo's terrible excuse of a father, leaving you all alone—" Siris fell to the ground, a bright red mark planted across her face. She looked up at him in shock.

"Oi, what's going on here?"

Before she could process what had happened, a group of armed men hastened down the hallway. They looked different from the Bastion guards, dressed in a mismatched set of combat gear. Similarly, their weaponry was just as mismatched, ranging from stout assault rifles to knives and wired explosives. All of their faces were concealed behind balaclavas. Siris felt a little flustered. How much of the conversation did they hear? Their masks didn't show it, but what if they had caught an aristocrat acting so unladylike?

Rex quickly turned to the guards as though nothing had happened, slipping his shaking hands behind his back.

"We're fine. All is good here. Yup."

"You're guardsmen, correct?" Siris said, too busy worrying about her image. "There's nothing here. Carry on."

Two of the soldiers looked at each other, bemused. Their leader stepped forward, a taller man with a beret and a submachine gun. He looked down at the two of them as though they were nothing but children. "We're Russian special forces, and we have been ordered to gather everyone up, including the potential recruits," the man stated.

Siris and Rex looked at each other. Something was off.

"For what reason?" Siris asked, narrowing her eyes,

"For your safety, of course. We've received reports that there's going to be an attack on this area." He glanced around. "Come on. We'd better hurry."

Siris walked up to their leader and pointed at his gray fatigues, mismatched with a green chest rig and camo cargos.

"My family has presided over plenty of military parades and I've never seen that sort of uniform."

"We're special forces, your grace. It—"

"...it's supposed to be your well-born," she cut him off.

"Ah. Forgive me, your well-born. It wouldn't be a covert uniform if we flaunted it around."

Rex gulped. Several of the soldiers had those long, slender battle rifles with a detachable magazine and carry handle. He'd seen it before. It was a common rifle in the western bloc countries. It wasn't Russian.

"Why does one of you have a British accent? And isn't that rifle from the Commonwealth?" Siris grew even more suspicious.

A tense pause. The soldiers glared at them, their hands gripping their weapons tighter.

The leader stepped up to Siris, his calm façade replaced with a grim stare. He aimed his submachine gun at her chest. "Listen, lady. If I were you, I would just put my little head down and walk with us, or we might have a little accident here."

"Threatening me now, are you? What happened to your grace? Even the lowliest of Russians would know how to address one of the high-class." Siris stepped toward the man, unfazed by his attempts at intimidation. "The best way to show low-lives like you the difference between us is through sheer power. So, if I were *you*, I would walk back out if I planned on leaving here safely."

Siris and the leader glared at each other, intense auras clashing with one another. One side was an increasingly agitated mob of armed soldiers, trigger fingers twitching. On the other, Siris clenched her fist, an icy fog flowing from it. Rex, too, was already in a combat stance.

"To hell with it," a soldier in the back shouted with a panicked voice. Within a split second, he let loose a burst from his rifle, and others began to do the same.

Rex's reflexes kicked in and he ducked. Siris slammed her hand on the ground, unleashing a massive blast of icy wind. The scene afterward was surreal: everything in front of the two was encased in ice, frozen in time. One soldier was reaching for an explosive on his chest, while another braced himself against the blast. The leader, eyes half-closed as though he was flinching, had already pulled the trigger. The bullet was held aloft in a trail of ice, a hair away from Siris' head. Rex looked at the scene in awe. A single moment, frozen in time.

Siris smirked. She lightly tapped the suspended bullet, shattering it into little pieces.

"Well now, what do you think about the power of the Vasilyevs?" she said.

"Okay, I guess." Rex chuckled. "Should've left some for me."

"'Okay? I save you and this is what I get? How utterly ungrateful. I should smack you right now for being such a—"

"Relax! I'm sorry." He raised his hands. "Listen, I don't know what's going on with these soldiers, but I'm pretty sure they ain't the only ones here. Instead of fighting each other, we need to work together so we can get out of here and not get, you know, killed." He extended his hand. "C'mon. No hard feelings."

Siris frowned, but all she did was clench her fists angrily. He had a point. Begrudgingly, she extended her hand and shook his.

"Fine."

Rex sighed with relief. "Well, first things first. How about we figure out what is going on? Let's look for something like..." Without finishing his sentence, Rex rushed down the hallway, leaving Siris to reluctantly follow behind.

"Wait! We should plan this out first."

"Don't have to, just look for radios. Walkie talkies." He grinned. "Improvise!"

Siris groaned. She was going to regret this.

The whole facility was plunged into chaos.

Pockets of resistance formed by candidates, Bastion soldiers, and staff were scattered throughout the compound as they fought a confusing and close-quarters battle with the mysterious attackers. The chain of command was broken and they were left to fend for themselves. The insurgents were swift and well-trained, locking down the facility with cold-blooded efficiency.

"All right, ya bastards. Show me what ya got!" Max charged head-first into a squad of soldiers. They fired their guns with calculated accuracy, but the bullets harmlessly deflected off of his thick, bone-plated armor.

"Lay down more suppressive fire! Don't let him break through," a soldier down the hall yelled. He ducked as Max threw one of his comrades over his head, as though he was made of paper.

Another called back, firing his shotgun frantically. "We're trying, but we can't."

Max grabbed the shotgunner's head and smashed him into the ceiling and floor several times, leaving him a broken and bruised mess.

"Damn it," another insurgent cried. He unpinned one of his grenades. "Didn't want it to come to this but get down, lads!" He lobbed the grenade at Max, which exploded with a resounding *boom.*

"Is he gone?" The insurgent looked up, hoping they had subdued the juggernaut. Yet, as the dust settled, the frame of a giant great-shield slowly emerged.

"Would've got me if ya weren't so slow," Max yelled as he pulled away the boney great-shield. "C'mon, is that all you got?"

The rest of the troops looked at the Australian juggernaut in fear.

"Withdraw," one shouted. "We need reinforcements!"

They all broke rank and swiftly withdrew from the fight. The one leading the retreat turned around the corner at the end of the hall, only to see two flaming whips lash out.

"Oh, running already?" Hana yelled as she grabbed the insurgent and threw him into a wall. "The fun's just started!"

Hana grabbed the other two soldiers and tossed them into a door behind her. They crashed through in a flurry of splinters. The remaining insurgents fell into formation, back-to-back, aiming their guns at both Hana and the ominously advancing Max.

"This isn't what I signed up for at all. Where the hell is our backup?" an insurgent shouted.

"Right here." Kaze appeared behind Hana, tossing the limp body of another soldier onto the ground.

"Shit!" The soldiers sprayed bullets from their guns. Kaze hit them with a gust of wind, letting the guns fire harmlessly into the ceilings, floors, and walls. The troops dropped their guns and fell on their knees.

"We surrender! Please don't hurt us."

Kaze looked bemused. *So arrogant at first, and now they won't put up even a slight bit of resistance.*

"Tie them up. Don't want to give them any funny ideas," he said, signaling Hana and Max to help him.

Max laughed as he restrained two soldiers, both of them cowering in fear from his sheer stature. He folded up his visor like a knight's helmet, revealing his wide grin. "Akira! Hana!

Didn't think I'd see ya here. You know what the bloody hell is going on?"

"We don't know," Kaze said, tying up an insurgent. "Radios are jammed, and the PA system hasn't said anything. Kibo and I had to fight our way through a few others like these men here, and we ended up coming into contact with Hana."

Hana came right up behind Kaze, grabbing onto his arm, smiling. "Such a gentleman, isn't he? He insisted that I come along, even though I was doing quite fine myself."

"I said it'd be better if we stuck together," Kaze stated sheepishly, his face beet-red.

"But you said to Kibo that you *vowed* to protect—"

"Hana, can you tighten that guy's binds, please?"

Max and Hana erupted into laughter, much to Kaze 's bashful annoyance. Just as they finished tying up the last of the men, Max looked around with a confused look.

"What is it?" Kaze asked.

"Well, I was curious where that metal mate of yours was. Didn't ya say he was with ya two?"

"Ah, Kibo. Well, we decided that the plan was to try and find everyone. We decided to split up and find the others. We'll meet up at the rendezvous point." He stood up and looked down the hallway with an anxious expression. "He dashed off towards the medical wing to find Rex and Siris. He seemed worried."

The ground shook, accompanied by a distant explosion. Muffled gunfire could be heard as well. Hana activated her whips and Max put back on his armor, ready for action.

"I hope they're okay."

Kibo ran across the hallway as fast as he possibly could. He had already activated Arcanus' combat form since he had split up from Kaze, yet, he still felt a hint of fear and anxiety within him, as if it wasn't enough to protect.

"Dang it, where the hell could they be? Arcanus, pump up my output."

"Kid, I already told you: anything higher than your standard limit would drain you way too fast," Arcanus replied. *"You'd be tuckered out in about twelve-point-five seconds."*

Kibo sighed as he looked around rapidly while running down the hallway. "Have you at least detected any trace of them through heat or sonar?" Kibo asked impatiently.

"Well, I've detected something *ahead of us, but I don't believe it to be them."*

The interface on his screen disappeared, replaced by a mix of blue, green, and orange, along with a thin line of flashing white text at the top of his visor stating that infrared vision was enabled. Around a corner, there was a large cluster of orange signatures, each armed with various guns—no doubt the insurgents. The cluster was surrounding a single signature. Kibo put his back to the wall as he came to the edge of the corner, moving as quietly and slowly as he could to figure out who the insurgents were aiming at.

"I said let him go," one of them shouted. Yet, under his stern voice was a hint of panic. "I'm giving you three seconds or we'll shoot!"

Who's making them so worried? Kibo peeked around the corner.

The soldiers were surrounding a young man not much older than Kibo. He was motionless. He held a sweating insurgent in a chokehold. His other hand was wreathed in a floating ring of fire. However, the feature of this strange fellow that had truly intrigued Kibo was his face. It seemed so familiar to him, yet try as he might, he could not recall where he saw it. The young man's eyes were full of ravenous hunger. His mouth formed a discomforting smile as he lifted the limp insurgent into the air. The other soldiers stepped back, all of them unnerved by him.

"I'm serious, drop him now." The group of insurgents readied their rifles. "One!"

The young man furrowed his brow.

"Two!"

"Cowards."

"Three!"

Suddenly, the arm holding the unconscious insurgent also went up in flames. He threw the burning corpse toward the soldiers. Half the soldiers seemed as though they had already soiled their pants, immediately breaking rank to sprint away.

The rest wildly sprayed bursts of bullets at the young man, who only smiled as he summoned a scorching blast of fire from his palm, turning the bullets into melted piles of lead. The soldiers screamed for their lives, begging for the pain and misery to end.

But it seemed that the boy was in pure ecstasy, hearing the soldiers beg and die in the most painful way possible. He couldn't get enough of it.

"Well, what are you waiting for, kid? Let's get the hell away from that damn psychopath!" Kibo silently agreed and turned to escape from the scene.

However, a voice suddenly called out to him. "Well now, where are we running off to?"

Kibo froze in place, his heart beating so rapidly that he thought it might burst. Kibo turned around slowly, fearing the worst. Yet he saw something...surprising.

The once aggressive and unsettling look on the young man's face was gone, replaced by a jubilant smile. The man stood in a more polite and docile manner, hands held together before him, like a butler waiting to answer any of his master's needs. After standing awkwardly for some time, Kibo managed to finally string together a sentence.

"Um, have you seen anyone?"

"Looking for a few friends, are you?" the mysterious figure replied, looking at Kibo with the same warm smile. But only one look at his eyes let Kibo see he held no emotion or joy, as though he was completely devoid of life. "By chance, I happened to come across two other people not long ago. A young man and woman who seemed to be looking for someone as well. I believe the name they mentioned was Kibo."

"That's me!" Kibo cried out excitedly as he looked down the several different hallways. "Which way did they go? Do you remember?"

"I believe they went down the path right behind you, toward the communications and examination room." The young man pointed over Kibo's shoulder.

Kibo waved goodbye at the mysterious stranger and ran down the hallway, only for a question to suddenly pop into his head. "Wait, I forgot to ask you—" But when Kibo turned around, the young mage had disappeared. Kibo felt a sudden shiver down his spine, remembering the haunting face the stranger wore as he slaughtered the soldiers. The sudden shift in the young man's tone after the fight was even more unsettling.

"Wake up kid! We gotta get going if we don't wanna lose your friends!" Kibo shook his head. He had greater things to worry about and set off after Rex.

"Got what you came for, Halifax?" Ripper tapped her foot impatiently, waiting outside the room her superior had gone into. She was flanked by half a dozen guards or so, all keeping watch. "That man told me he would have been in and out in just a second."

"All right then, I've got it." Ripper turned to see Halifax step out the door, a smug look on his face. Ripper wasn't exactly pleased.

"What took you so long? If it was going to take this damn long, I would've gone in with you."

"Oh, nothing much. While I was grabbing a layout of this place, I ran into some, how shall I put it, *resistance*. But I dealt with that quickly." Halifax grinned. "Now then, let's move down to the comms room. It's time to put the plan into action."

Ripper motioned the guards to follow, weapons in hand toward their target. The troops quickly trailed after her, taking one final peek back into the room.

"Just couldn't let me through, could you?" Halifax looked grimly down at the floor. It was Sidorov. His bruised body lay on the tiled white floor—cold, limp, and alone.

Well, I got everything I need. Better move on before they grow worried. Halifax shut the office door behind him, running after the rest of the soldiers. But he just couldn't help but think, *he'll be pissed, all right.*

CHAPTER 19

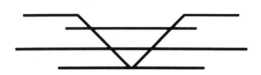

"And that's fifteen."

Rex tossed an unconscious insurgent onto the floor, watching him slowly slump to the ground in a pile of other unconscious insurgents. "Guess we're even now, huh?"

"Well, that's *only* because you kept getting in my way." Siris casually dusted her hands before tipping a frozen soldier onto the floor. She studied the body curiously. *Who the hell are these guys? They seem to be well-trained, but they're getting floored by a bunch of recruits.*

Siris crouched down near one of the soldiers that Rex had knocked unconscious and examined his gear. *These weapons—some of them look Commonwealth, but some of them are from other places, too. Lots of older models. From the black market, perhaps?* Siris examined the rifle next to the soldier. She looked over two other nearby bodies and their equipment. One of the guns stuck out to her. It looked like the standard Kalash of the Russian army, only decked out in fancy attachments. Upon closer inspection, she noticed a Russian proof mark—it was authentic Russian equipment. Siris initially ignored it, assuming the unconscious insurgent just happened to be rich or had connections. But upon closer inspection, many others had legit tactical equipment as well. Her eyes widened. *A lot of this is Russian made. Some of them are the latest equipment for special forces. But that doesn't make any sense. It would be incredibly difficult to find this stuff in the underground market, let alone supply an entire insurgent group with it!*

"Whatcha looking at?" Siris turned to see Rex standing over her shoulder, staring her right in the face.

"Could you not come so close to me? Jeez! Haven't you heard of personal space?" Siris said as she shoved Rex back.

"Well sorry, your well-born. Seemed like something caught ya eye in those guys."

Siris sighed and decided it would be better to explain what she had uncovered. "I initially believed that these soldiers or insurgents, or whatever they are, to be Commonwealth agents. Their weapons are black market-sourced and a lot of them have accents from Commonwealth nations."

"Well, what about it? Get to the point," Rex said, much to Siris' annoyance.

"But there's an alarming amount of state-of-the-art Russian gear, definitely not items that your average group of insurgents could get their hands on." She got back on her feet.

"Maybe they've got criminal connections like the mafia or the cartel," Rex said, shrugging. "You know how rich those guys are. They can get their hands on anything."

"That's what I thought too, but stuff like this is hard to get—and expensive. If they do get their hands-on high-grade equipment, the bosses usually keep the fancy toys for themselves. There's no way this many insurgents could have been outfitted with this much top-of-the-line equipment." She frowned. "There's something very odd about this whole ordeal."

"Rex! Siris!"

Kibo rushed toward them so quickly that he could barely stop himself. Kibo had to slam his feet into the ground to stop himself from crashing into them, ending up planting face-first into the ground.

"My man! What's up?" Rex said with a laugh as he helped Kibo onto his feet. Kibo let out a sheepish chuckle as he grabbed onto Rex's hand.

"Couldn't be any better," Kibo said as he smiled. However, Siris seemed to be less than amused by Kibo's sudden entrance and turned away coldly, not wishing to speak with him.

"Wasn't too much of a pain to deal with her, was it Rex?" Kibo whispered as he looked over at Siris, who was brooding in a corner.

"Nah, but it's pretty funny to watch her get mad."

"You know I'm right here, you dolts!" Siris said as she smacked both of their heads.

"Jeez, sorry to get your panties in a twist, *your well-born—ow!* What was that second one for?" Rex reeled over from another slap from Siris.

"That's for putting up with you for the last hour," Siris said as she crossed her arms.

Thankfully, Kibo stepped in between the two. "Guys! Come on, we have to focus. We don't have time to fight amongst ourselves." He pulled the two of them apart.

"God dammit." Rex sighed. "So, what's your plan, boss?"

"I've learned a while back how crucial it is to have someone at the top."

Rex raised an eyebrow. "I don't follow."

"There has to be someone on the ground coordinating the attack."

"True," said Siris. "These guys are trained and organized. No doubt there's some sort of commander leading them."

"That's right," said Kibo. "All we have to do is find the leader and neutralize him, or impede their communications. The second we cut the head of the snake, the rest of the soldiers will be disorganized and easier to take care of."

Siris turned her attention to Kibo. "Well then, I imagine the great peasant hero Kibo must know where to find this leader."

"Ah, yeah, about that..." Kibo scratched his head sheepishly. "I have no clue."

"Great, now I have to deal with another idiot." Siris sighed. She glanced at the bodies of the soldiers, and it all suddenly clicked. "I have an idea." Kibo and Rex backed up in lieu of another verbal thrashing, to which Siris merely rolled her eyes. "One of them was calling for reinforcements through a radio. If we can find the radioman or the radio, we might be able to track down where the head of this attack is located."

She searched through one of the soldiers as Kibo and Rex watched. She glanced back and saw there were still standing there, confused. "Well, what are you two dolts waiting for? Start searching."

Kibo and Rex begrudgingly followed Siris' command and sifted through the soldiers' things, yet none of them seemed to have a radio on them.

"Damnit, where the hell is that radio?" Rex groaned.

"Right here," Kibo said, but he sounded more anxious than relieved. Rex and Siris turned to see exactly what had warranted Kibo's off-putting reaction. The radio was encased in ice, along with its operator.

"Well, how are we gonna get it out of there?" Rex asked, walking up to the giant tomb of ice.

"I have an idea, but I don't know if it's the best one," Kibo warned.

A large chunk of the ice that Kibo had grabbed immediately shattered into several small pieces when he pulled. Kibo stepped back slowly, now realizing that he couldn't brute force his way to the radio.

"I should have expected that to happen," Siris said as she approached the block of ice. "The ice I create is made from the air around me. Unfortunately, it ends up being incredibly cold and brittle as a result." Siris looked down at the shattered ice.

"Well, guess that means I ain't gonna be able to help with this. Y'know, with how brute force doesn't work and all," Rex said as he leaned on the wall.

"Hmph, I'd be surprised if you were useful at all," Siris said, only making Rex laugh.

"Oh really? I guess little ol' Rex wasn't very useful when I saved you from being shredded by that soldier now was I?"

Rex shrugged and gave such a smug and irritating smile that she marched right up to him and exclaimed, "For your information, I would have been quite fine without your help. The only reason you stopped him was that you were in the way." She flicked Rex in the forehead.

"Ow! Why do ya always have to hit someone when you're mad?"

"Guys! Now's not the time to be fighting," Kibo called out to both Rex and Siris, who seemed they were ready to pounce at each other's throats.

"I have another idea. It might not work, but this is our best shot at getting this thing out of there." Kibo slowly walked up to the block of ice again and closed his eyes. *Arcanus, can you remove the armor around my left hand?*

"Wait, why would you... No, don't tell me you're gonna do that."

Just do it.

"I can't let you do that kid. You'll freeze off your entire hand."

Just do it! Kibo commanded. Arcanus remained hesitant, unwilling to allow him to follow through with the plan. Kibo was determined.

The gauntlet around his hand disappeared, leaving it bare and unprotected. Kibo raised his hand and placed it on the cold, brittle surface of the ice. As soon as he did, he let out a sudden shout, causing both Rex and Siris to tense up. But it seemed that nothing happened. There was no sudden flash or spark of magic.

Then they saw it. A small flame, faintly moving about in Kibo's palm, slowly melting through the ice. Rex looked back and forth between Siris and Kibo, more confused than surprised.

"He can do that? Wasn't that armor stuff his whole thing?" Rex asked Siris. She, however, did not respond, only continuing to stare at Kibo's hand, watching it melt through the ice. The immovable wall was not crushed but slowly melted away.

What happened to him? Siris muttered, stepping away from Kibo. *Where is the boy who could barely light a match? The one who was nothing more than a cowardly child, a meager peasant who looked at me with fear and obedience. No, that boy—*

Kibo ripped out the defrosted radio, fully intact.

Is gone. Siris slowly leaned against the wall and looked at her palms. They were trembling violently, but why? Why was she so afraid? So what if he had become stronger and more daring? Why did it affect her? She knew Kibo would not hurt or harass her, but that concrete belief suddenly started to crack. What if he unleashed the hatred he had for her? Would the years of torment and mistreatment that she had sown finally be reaped?

You are a Vasilyev! Be proud of it!

She would not let him outshine him. She was a Vasilyev! She'd show him the might of her family, that her bloodline surpassed any power his magic and strange machinery gave him. Siris suddenly walked up to Kibo and ripped the radio from his hands, looking at Kibo with a wrathful gaze. For a moment, Siris waited for the look of fear she had expected from Kibo, but simply saw one of irritation.

"Jeez! If you wanted it, you could have just asked," Kibo said, rubbing his hand out of Rex's and Siris' view.

"You good?" Rex asked Kibo. Kibo's entire palm was covered in severe burns for a split second. Kibo quickly drew away from him, but that was all Rex had to see.

"We gotta fix you up right now."

"It's... I'm fine, okay? Don't worry about it. We gotta focus on taking down the head of the pack right now," Kibo said. Yet his frequent and pained pauses made Rex believe otherwise.

"What do ya mean? Your hand looks like they've been through a fryer, for god's sake," Rex exclaimed. "Just keep away from using that stuff for a while. I don't like when one of my buddies hurts themselves."

"Yeah, I know. To be real with you, this hurts like complete hell. But finding their leader is a helluva lot more important than getting this burn treated."

"And speaking of which"—Siris strutted in between the two of them, holding the radio out in front of them—"Look at what I have uncovered."

—Bzzt— "I repeat. We need all remaining men to retreat to the comms room. Protecting the commander is our utmost priority."—Bzzt—

"Well now, what do you two simpletons think? Being the daughter of a noble family doesn't mean I can't use a radio." Kibo and Rex, though refusing to give Siris any gratification, were pretty impressed with Siris' tinkering.

"Well then, I guess we go in and take them down, huh?" Rex asked.

Siris rolled her eyes. "Ah yes, let's go into a horde of insurgents, walk straight up to their boss and detain him." Rex smirked and pointed backward. Siris and Kibo turned and saw Kaze, Max, Hana, and several other examinees marching toward them, all ready for a fight.

"That's exactly what we're gonna do."

"Well, I hope you're happy with that plan of yours," Siris barked at Rex.

"We did beat all of those bad guys though, didn't we, lass?" Max pointed out. And he was not exactly wrong. Behind them lay what seemed like a warpath, a solid line ripping through the middle of the hallway. It cut through several makeshift barricades of chairs, tables, and crates. Along with that also lay the bodies of a few dozen insurgents, all unconscious. Whether they were slammed into a wall, encased in a tomb of ice, or crushed beneath a pile of rubble, they were all clearly and thoroughly beaten. And it ended right behind them, where the collapsed body of Rex lay.

"It looks like we broke through their main line of defense. Just a bit more and we're there."

"Well, if that means having our best bet breaking into the comms room, battered face-down on the floor, then I don't think it was worth it," Siris snapped back.

"Siris! Max! Now's not the time. We need to get Rex medical attention, and fast." Kaze cut in between Max and Siris. "All of this pointless bickering is wasting valuable time."

"Yeah, but what about Artur? He went ahead all by himself. He could be in deep trouble right now," Siris said.

Kaze stopped for a second, mulling over their options. "Siris and Kibo, you two head forward to provide any necessary aid that Artur may need to combat any more of those insurgents." Kaze pointed at the two of them and then immediately turned to Hana. "Hana, I'll need you to cauterize any wounds Rex may have. Max, I need you to cover me while we take him to the medical wing." Kaze motioned Hana and Rex over to help him. Kibo watched the three of them trying their best to patch up and clean Rex's wounds with a sinking feeling in his chest. Siris was not wrong at all. They had planned on having Max and Rex break into the communications room and distract them while they took care of their leader. But with both of them out of the picture, and Artur rushing ahead, he could not think how this could turn out well. What if they take Artur hostage and hurt him? What if they get gunned down before they can even get to their leader? What if—

Kibo felt a hard smack to the back of his helmet. "Ow! What was that for?"

"Didn't you hear him? Get moving! We got ground to cover if we're going to reach him," Siris shouted as she ran in the direction of the comms room. As he turned to run after Siris though, he heard Kaze.

"Stay safe, Kibo." Kibo nodded silently.

"Don't worry, as long as I have *that* Siris with me, I'll be all right," Kibo said, which seemed to reassure Kaze, who picked up

Rex onto his back. And with one last glance at each other, the two groups parted ways.

CHAPTER 20

—*Bzzt*— "We're surrounded. Bastion troops are closing in on us. We need backup right now. Oh god..."—*Bzzt*—

"God damnit!" Ripper slammed her fist onto the desk. "This whole operation is falling apart. I knew they shouldn't have let some rookie lead." Ripper shouted as she flung the radio at the wall, causing it to explode into pieces. However, Halifax just smiled at her and leaned back in his chair, listening to the many voices and sounds blaring from several different speakers, monitors, and radios spread out in the communications room.

"Now, now, there's no need to be so pessimistic. Why, I'd say things are going exactly the way we want." Halifax leaned forward, resting his chin on top of his hands as scanned several different security monitors. "I'd say we've caused quite a stir, haven't we? Wasn't that our grand plan? To show the world the cracks within the fragile system they had put their faith into?"

"Don't you dare use that condescending tone with me, rookie. I've been a part of this group for over fifteen years. I've worked and fought with half the people within our organization to take down those smug bastards at the top." Ripper stood over Halifax menacingly, remaining unconvinced.

"You seem to be in quite a fury, my friend. I'd suggest a small glass of water to cool off."

"Don't act so calm, you damn two-faced fox!" Ripper lifted Halifax by the collar of his shirt, slamming the glass of water onto the floor. "I'm not going to sit idly in some room while the rest of my men get massacred out there!"

Ripper slammed Halifax against the wall, her hands tightening around his shirt, her entire body trembling in rage. Yet, despite his precarious position, Halifax remained calm. He simply put his hands in the air and asked a small question.

"Okay then, explain to me what you plan to do. I don't suppose you plan on just rampaging across this facility, expecting to turn this battle in our favor all by yourself?" Halifax asked. Ripper gritted her teeth in anger, but she was no fool. With a frustrated grunt, she let go of Halifax, falling back down onto one of the office desks.

"Well then, I guess you must have some brilliant plan to get us out of this mess?" Ripper replied sarcastically. Halifax only chuckled and pointed at the monitors. Each of them displayed different areas throughout the facility. Some displayed rooms that seemed untouched. Others displayed hallways and areas that had been barricaded, hastily blocked off by either Bastion or insurgent forces using whatever supplies they could scrounge up. Finally, some monitors were blank, covered in a mesh of static. The cameras connected to those monitors had most likely been either destroyed or damaged beyond repair during the firefights across the facility.

"What about all this, huh? All I see is a facility in complete chaos, with my men being thrown away like fodder," Ripper said as she watched the security monitors, both furious and confused at what Halifax's grand plan was.

"My, my, quite impatient, are we? I imagined that an experienced commando such as yourself would have noticed it right away." Halifax tapped on a few different monitors. At first, Ripper was perplexed, not quite understanding what Halifax was alluding to. Then it all clicked.

"Those are all the locations we have barricaded or taken control of," Ripper exclaimed as she walked up closer to the monitors. "What are you trying to prove? Aren't they just tactical locations?"

Ripper noticed one of the insurgents placing a strange device, planting it carefully inside a box they'd used as a barricade. They turned it on, and a little light on the device flashed on and off. The soldier took one quick look at it before swiftly closing the box and pushing it safely behind other supplies they had.

"Was that a—"

"Bomb, yes," Halifax cut Ripper off, observing the several different monitors as he finally decided to explain his master plan. "Each of the areas our men have fortified is an important structural backbone for the building, and I've had an explosive placed in each of these locations and set to go off with the press of a button." Halifax reached into his pocket and pulled out a detonator, his thumb resting gently on top of a small, bright red button. "With a single tap, I can turn this training facility into ruins."

"And now you may ask, 'Wouldn't that take us down with this whole building?' Well, of course it would. If I was still trapped here, of course." Halifax walked slowly across the room, reaching a small door labeled *Storage*. "My original plan was to sneak in, plant explosives, and rush out before Bastion caught wind of us. Of course, considering the current situation we are in now, I would say that would be nigh impossible." Halifax paused for a moment as he reached for the handle.

"And that's where our bargaining chips will come in hand." Halifax opened the door, the faint light from the comms room revealing what lay inside.

About a dozen or so people were in the room, their hands and legs tied and their mouths covered in masking tape. They let out muffled screams for help, their faces a ghostly pale, their bodies reeking of both fear and hysteria.

Yet, Halifax cared little for his hostages. They were pawns meant to move forward his plans. He watched as they screamed helplessly and did the only appropriate thing for the sorry souls.

He slammed the door, leaving his prisoners once again in the dark. "Every person in that room is either an influential diplomatic official, noble, or businessman that has backed and provided vast quantities of wealth to Bastion." Halifax paused for a moment and let out a quiet chuckle, as though an amusing thought had worked its way into his head.

"Of course, the great and moral Bastion will be forced to let us exit this building scot-free, purely to save the lives of those 'innocent' men and women, and most definitely not because of the sheer loss of support and income that would come with their deaths," Halifax stated, once again drawing his gaze back to the detonator in his hand.

"But I still plan on turning this place into a smoldering pile of ashes, from which the seeds of hatred and divide will be nourished, allowing us to swindle away Bastion's support and power." Halifax pulled out a small shiny object from his pocket and tossed it to Ripper. She caught it in midair and saw that it was a coin.

"And of course, we'll make a hell of profit from all this. We won't give them those hostages just for safe passage. We'll also demand quite a large ransom for these fellows. Enough to fund all our future operations against this corrupt regime." Halifax backed away for a moment and pulled out his revolver, inspecting it. He polished it slightly and, checking to see he had cleaned properly, asked Ripper, "What do you think? I hope it's to your standards."

Ripper was unable to speak. This rookie had put together quite a refined plan, one that would not only help lower the casualties on their side, but also obliterate their target. Furthermore, he had thought ahead, considering ways they could further the goals of their movement in the long term. She had found only one word that could convey what she thought.

"Brilliant."

"Heh, thought as much." Halifax chuckled as he slid the revolver into his holster.

"See, if there's one thing you should take about from this, Sergeant Ripper, it's that you shouldn't underestimate people." Halifax stared at the monitors for a moment, watching the conflict that was raging across the facility, and then suddenly jolted upward, moving slowly toward a small desk in the corner of the room. On it stood a singular microphone, to which several wires and speakers were connected. Halifax leaned on top of the desk and brought the microphone towards his mouth, taking one final glance at the storage room with a devious little grin. "And now I believe it's finally time to initiate our backup plan."

"I wouldn't be so sure about that." Two enormous roots burst from the ground, slamming Halifax into the ground and ensnaring him. Ripper quickly turned in the direction of the voice to see none other than Artur surrounded by a swarm of roots.

"Blimey! Where is it? Where is that damn detonator?" Halifax desperately tried to break free from the roots.

"Looking for this?" Artur held up the detonator in his hand. "I overheard your entire conversation. I know your entire plan in and out now, Halifax. I would have been a bit quieter," Artur said as he slowly started to crush the detonator.

"You fool! If you break that it'll trigger the failsafe on the bombs and bring down this whole damn building" Halifax yelled out, but Artur paid no heed to Halifax's warning. Instead, he dropped it.

"You idiot!"

A pair of vines swooped in from the ceiling and grabbed the detonator, wrapping around it. "Well then, guess I'll have to restrain you two and turn that device in as evidence of your crimes," Artur said as he summoned two giant roots from the ground and turned towards Ripper. She just laughed and cracked her knuckles.

"All right then. I guess it's time I show this rookie what a real soldier does."

"We gotta be getting close to him now," Kibo exclaimed as he ran across the hallway, only for Siris to just roll her eyes.

"As if I couldn't tell that by the several roots and plants that are all around us," Siris stated sarcastically, but there was some truth to it. Ever since passing a broken vent opening, all of the insurgent holdouts they moved through had been covered in a mess of several different and strange plants. Many of the insurgents who stood guard at these locations were either knocked out cold or were trapped in a mass of roots and vines, unable to move. The further they went, the more overgrown the path had become, until the floor was covered in plant life.

"The comms room should be right around the corner," Kibo stated as he and Siris reached the end of the hallway. Kibo looked to both sides, searching for an exit or turn they could take, but all he saw was just a massive cluster of roots and vines covering the wall in front of them. "Oh great, you brought us to a dead-end. I knew we must have missed an exit back there."

"That's not possible, all the markers pointed us in this direction. There's no way this could be the end." Kibo looked around frantically for some kind of exit or doorway that they could take. "Besides, don't you think it's strange that there are so many roots and plants covering this wall?" Kibo brushed his hand against the growth of plant life, curious as to what may have been behind the dense foliage.

A sudden blur swished right past Kibo, narrowly missing him by a few centimeters.

"What was that?" Kibo turned to see what slashed past him. It was a dark brown root twitching in the air, having ripped itself from the wall as a response to Kibo's fiddling. The entire wall started to move, the once-docile plants awakening. Various vines and roots ripped themselves out of the wall, thrashing about randomly, as though they hoped at least one of them would hit their target.

"*I think it would be a smart idea to step right the hell back,*" Arcanus yelled at Kibo.

"Don't you think I know that?" Kibo snapped at Arcanus as he dashed backward, dodging and weaving as best as he could. It would have been nearly impossible for Kibo to dodge all of the vines that swung at him—and of course, it was.

Kibo slammed face-first into the ground as a sudden tug at his left leg pulled him across the concrete floor.

"What the—?" Kibo exclaimed as he looked over his shoulder to see a dark root, twisting slowly around his leg, moving inch by inch up towards the rest of his body.

"*God damnit! Rip that thing off you before more of them pin you down.*"

"I'm trying, I'm trying!" Kibo panicked as he grabbed hold of the root, tearing it off of his leg. Which only drew the attention of all the roots flailing wildly across the room to Kibo. The once hectic room went completely still for a single moment, enough for Kibo to shout, "Oh, shit."

Several spires of ice ripped through the ground with a thunderous *boom*, impaling or shredding the several roots and vines that rushed at Kibo.

"Whoa! Thanks for getting me out of there. That was pretty intense!"

"What did you think a few grasping weeds were going to do anything against me," Siris replied smugly. Kibo rolled his eyes. They had much more pressing matters to deal with.

"Still, I don't think cutting down a few of these is gonna do us any good when there are hundreds of them. We need to hit them at their source." Kibo and Siris' gaze locked onto the mound of plant life stuck to the wall in front of them.

However, Siris seemed unconvinced. "Why do you care so much about killing these plants? This place is just a dead-end, is it not?"

"Don't you think it's a bit strange that he'd sprout up so many to deal with a few insurgents? Why would he plaster all of them against the wall when it would be easier for him to spring them up from the ground?" Siris mulled over what Kibo told her for a moment, and quickly glanced at the wall of tangling roots.

"Unless, unless this isn't a dead end."

"It's the entrance to the comms room!" Kibo jumped in excitedly, much to Siris' chagrin.

"Now, as I was *saying*, that Artur fellow must have covered the entrance to keep anyone from getting in to provide support to their leader," Siris continued.

"And to keep their leader from trying to escape as well." Kibo noticed something else. "That means Artur can't get any support."

But Siris only smirked and raise her hand.

"That's if we couldn't take down this blockade." Siris let out a massive blast of frost from her hand, sending all of the roots and plants flying toward the door, their leaves and features wilting from the cold as they slowly froze over. The plants fought with all their vigor and strength, but the mound of green stilled, covered in a layer of frost.

"Goddamn, that was fast! Thought they would've been a bigger challenge for us, but she took care of them within a split second! Guess that's something else to add to the list of reasons you're scared of her, huh?" Arcanus joked.

Kibo just stared at the wall of ice, both amazed and fearful of Siris. He and Arcanus watched Siris walk up to the frozen wall of ice and stare at it for a moment, as though she was an artist admiring her work. Before it all suddenly broke apart, shards of ice rained down onto the floor, revealing a large, partially damaged door hidden behind it. A metallic chrome label said: *Communications and Surveillance.*

"Well, what are you waiting for? Let's get going, shall we?" Siris called out at Kibo, snapping him back to reality, and ran over to help Siris, who seemed to be struggling to open the door.

"This blasted door won't budge. Some of the plants must be still stuck to it from the inside." Siris tried pushing the door open with all her might. However, Kibo just looked at her, disappointed.

"What's wrong with you? Help me get this damn door open. Aren't you supposed to be the strong one?" Kibo pointed to the side of the door.

"Oh," Siris said, her face turning bright red. Right next to the door's handle, she saw *PULL* in dark bold letters.

"*God damn it,*" Siris muttered to herself as Kibo came up next to her, leaning against the wall next to the door.

"Okay, on the count of three we'll rush in. I'll take the lead while you stick behind me and make sure we don't get ambushed by any plants or insurgents. Got it?"

"Of course I got it! I'm standing right next to you," Siris replied, irritated.

"All right. One…"

"Two…"

"Three!"

Siris swung the door wide open as Kibo dashed into the room, his fists held up high to guard against any potential threats. Siris trailed behind him. However, instead of stepping into what they expected to be a raging battle, they had barged into a stalemate, two different parties in a tense standoff.

On one side stood Artur, the detonator held firmly in his hand, staring down coldly at his opposition. On the other stood Ripper and Halifax, the latter holding a snub-nosed revolver pointed directly at a captive's temple. He'd pulled one of the hostages out of the storage room as one last desperate attempt to stop Artur.

"Called in a little backup, huh? Well, they aren't going to get you out of this situation," Halifax said, giving quick twitchy glances from Kibo to Artur. "You two, put your hands where I can see them," Halifax shouted at Kibo and Siris. Both of them hesitated for a moment, until Halifax shouted, "Put them up, right god damn now, or I swear I'll blow this man's brain across the damn floor!" Halifax shoved the snub-nose into the hostage's head. His captive let out muffled screams in response, tears flowing down his face. Kibo and Siris looked at each other for a second before putting their hands in the air. As they did though, something caught Kibo's attention.

Huh, that's odd, Kibo thought to himself.

"What is?" Arcanus asked Kibo.

I swear I saw that other officer reach for something on her belt. It almost looked like—

"Are you going to do the right thing? Give me that detonator or allow this innocent man to suffer a tragic death," Halifax shouted, disrupting Kibo's train of thought. Halifax glared down at the detonator in Artur's hand, desperately wishing to get it back.

"Come on, you heard him. Give us the damn remote or this whole place will go down in ruins," Ripper shouted.

However, Artur remained indifferent; his cool and stern demeanor contrasted heavily against the panicked and jittery movements of Halifax and Ripper. It seemed as though Artur had the upper hand over the two.

"I do not wish for the harm or death of any civilians or innocents, but I'm also a pragmatist," Artur stated as he took a slight step forward, shifting his gaze to the panicked hostage. "Do you think I'm going to trade you a device that can level this entire building and cost the lives of hundreds, if not *thousands*, of individuals for a single hostage?"

Halifax let out a silent growl, born from a sense of frustration and helplessness. But Halifax suddenly smiled, as though he had found a crack, some flaw in Artur's logic.

"Well then, what could you possibly want from us? If you truly did not care for this man's life, you would have made some sort of move by now. You have no reason to pause, unless you have another motive."

"Pretty observant, aren't you?" Artur smirked, pointing at Halifax with the detonator. "I'm guessing you know what I desire." He turned his gaze toward the storage room door. It took a split second for Halifax to guess what Artur wanted.

"How many—"

"All of them," Artur cut Halifax off.

Halifax's expression changed to one of bewilderment, but he quickly regained his composure. "And what exactly do you plan on doing if I don't?" Artur did not respond, yet Halifax could tell he had gotten Artur right where he wanted him. "Well then, it seems we have ourselves a stalemate of sorts." Halifax looked up at the ceiling and let out a pompous laugh. Artur's fists shook uncontrollably, his cold and stern aura starting to crack. It seemed that the tides had turned against him.

Something snapped from Siris' direction.

"What's going on there?" Halifax quickly shifted his gaze towards Siris, who was looking down at the ground with a look of confusion and disgust plastered on her face.

"Oh nothing. I just happened to accidentally step on something unimportant." Siris quickly shifted her attention back to Halifax, a look of indifference on her face. Halifax narrowed his eyes, not entirely convinced.

But he had more pressing matters to focus on. Yet, when he turned back, Artur's once-cold expression had been replaced by a little smile, much to Halifax's bewilderment. "Why the hell are you smiling like that?"

"'It seems we have ourselves a stalemate' is what you said, right?" Artur asked Halifax.

"What about it? Neither can make an act without losing something desperately important to us."

"Yet, it seems that you forgot one very important thing about stalemates."

"And what might that be?"

"Stalemates are a battle of attrition. A race against the clock to see who can outlast the other." Artur took a sudden step forward. "And it appears that you've run out of time." He dashed towards Halifax, a few roots sprouting from the concrete floor and traveling alongside him.

"Bloody hell!" Halifax panicked, and out of sheer instinct pulled the trigger of his revolver.

"Huh?" Halifax slammed his finger against the trigger again, but it would not budge.

"Take this!"

Artur slammed into Halifax, sending him across the room with a single swing of his root-covered arm.

"Rookie!" Ripper turned to aid Halifax but was blocked by Kibo.

"You're not going anywhere while I'm here," Kibo replied, ready to fight her with every ounce of strength he had.

"God damn it! That was one hell of a blow," Halifax sputtered, holding his side in pain. He slowly got back up, frantically looking around for his revolver. It lay across the floor by a small wooden desk, entrapped in ice except for the grip and trigger. "Kept me focused on you while that brat over there froze my revolver, did you?" Halifax spat at Siris, who managed to grab hold of the hostage and shatter his bindings.

"Of course I did. I'm one of the greatest—"

"Yeah, yeah. Of course, you're one of the best, you noble swine. But even someone like you couldn't freeze something with such control with both your arms up in the air." Halifax stepped back, letting out a few pained gasps of air. "What is your secret, girl?"

A shard of ice barely scraped past Halifax, leaving a thin line of blood across his left cheek.

"I have no reason to answer you," Siris said gravely. Despite her best attempts to hide it, one could tell she was livid, her normally cold blue eyes now burning with anger. Luckily, Artur stretched his hand in front of her.

"We can't let them get to us, otherwise this whole situation might go sideways, Siris. They won't be able to slip away from our grasp, not while we're here," Artur told Siris. Siris looked at him for another moment, before turning back towards Halifax, her rage still clearly visible despite her best attempts to suppress it. Satisfied with Siris' return to form, Artur turned his attention back to Halifax.

"During your little back and forth with your comrade over there, I believe that one of you had shattered a glass of water all over the floor."

"And I am guessing that Ms. Ice Queen over there used the water on the floor as a conduit to freeze my revolver with her foot?" Halifax asked.

"Correct. And your sweat-covered long coat and leather gloves were more than thick enough to freeze without drawing your attention." Halifax turned to look at his right hand and saw a long strip of ice had climbed up to his hand from the bottom of his long navy coat. Halifax turned towards Artur, seemingly impressed by his plan.

"You're a smart couple of recruits, aren't you?" But instead of seeming frustrated or panicked, Halifax smiled. "I have to give it to you, hatching such a plan on short notice is quite genius." Halifax leaned forward with a foreboding grin. "But you aren't the only ones who've thought ahead."

With a single, quick motion, Halifax threw a grenade at the ceiling of the room and dashed underneath one of the desks. For a split second, everyone in the room watched in horror as the grenade stood still in the air, moments away from exploding.

"Get down!"

CHAPTER 21

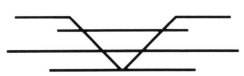

Siris stood above the hostage with large spikes of ice protruding from the ground around her. She'd created a dome above them to take the brunt of the explosion.

"That bastard! Are you all right?"

"Yes." The man looked up at Siris, the palpable fear in his eyes striking directly at her soul. She felt pity for the man and an odd familiarity with his situation.

She knew she could not just leave him here while those two were around. She had to get the man out of here.

Siris looked out the icy dome in search of an exit or escape route. The amount of dust and debris made it impossible to see anything in the room, leaving Siris blind save for one thing.

In the distance, there was a faint red glow, barely visible through the broken room. Despite all the haze of the heaps of dust flowing through the air, Siris could make out exactly what it was. Siris turned towards the hostage. "Listen right here."

"What is it?"

"See that light over there? That's the exit out of this mess of a room." Siris pointed at the lazy glow of the exit sign.

"This whole place is covered in dust and smoke. Now is your best chance to get out of here." The hostage looked at the door hesitantly. Yet every second he hesitated, the more settled the room became, and the cover he desperately needed slipping away.

"Could you stop acting like a frightened little child and get a move on? If you wait any longer, there won't be a way for you to get out of here without getting injured," Siris snapped at him.

The man looked up at her and then back at the exit. After a quick second, he stood and started towards the exit.

"Miss, w-what was your name again?"

"Vasilyeva."

"Ms. Vasilyeva, I-I just want to say if it weren't for you, I'd probably be dead by now. My brain would have probably been splattered across this floor." The man clasped both his hands around her own and looked up at her with gratitude. "Thank you."

Siris stood silently for a moment, her eyes fixed upon the ground.

"Uh, miss...?"

"We don't have time for such acts of gratitude. Get the hell out of here before you get caught in the crossfire," Siris shouted at the man, she was no longer providing him a choice, she was commanding him. The man scratched his head sheepishly before moving toward the door as quickly as he could without breaking his cover under the dust-filled room.

Siris let out a quiet sigh as she slumped back into her icy cover. She stretched out her hand and gazed at it for a moment. She could still feel the warmth of the man's hand.

I don't think a single person ever looked at me like that before. Always, no matter who it was or what position they were in, they all hid their true feelings from her. Her servants—or *friends*—all talked formally to her out of fear or necessity.

But that man did not care for who Siris was or what background she came from. He only displayed what he truly felt: gratitude.

"Damn it, Siris! Now is not the time to get distracted." Siris jolted back to her feet. She stepped out of the safety of the ice dome. The once spotless and well-kept comms room now looked like a warzone. Desks, chairs, and equipment had been damaged beyond repair. The electrical wiring beneath the floor was exposed, with small, sputtering sparks occasionally flashing from their now damaged and uninsulated bits.

Something crunched underneath her feet. A shattered light bulb that had fallen from the ceiling.

"And all of that with one grenade." Siris looked up in awe at the massive hole within the ceiling, revealing a mess of ventilation and piping that spread out in several different directions. However, the ones closest to the ceiling had been visibly damaged, pipes bent or pierced by the explosion, and one of the vents unhinged from the roof and left hanging a few centimeters off the floor by a metal wire. Siris sized up at the true extent of the damage.

"Siris?" She immediately jolted around, having felt the sudden tap on her shoulder. Fortunately, she turned to see it was none other than Kibo, the faint blue glow of his visor visible through the dust cloud.

"You fool! Don't go touching random people in the middle of a fight. I could be an enemy for all you know," Siris barked at Kibo. But despite that, she was relieved to see a familiar face.

"Yeah, you're right. It would've been really bad if you were that Ripper woman," Kibo said with a slight chuckle. Siris raised an eyebrow.

"Oh really?" Siris said as she let out a blast of frost from her hand, freezing Kibo in place.

"What the hell are you doing?"

"Hmph. I don't remember you being so blunt toward me, and neither do I remember hearing one of those insolent fool's names."

"Saw right through me, didn't you?" Kibo stated confidently. "Guess there's no point in hiding it anymore."

Slowly, the right side of Kibo's helm began to melt, followed by the left, until eventually all of his armor oozed across his body, melding together until he turned into a blob of shifting matter. Siris watched him change, unsettled, wanting to look away from the nightmarish being before her, yet her curiosity kept her watching.

Bit by bit, limb by limb, the mass shifted into place, hardening into the shape of something, of *someone*. Halifax. His once-pristine navy coat was in tatters, his clean and well-kempt face covered in dust, blood, and sweat.

"I should have guessed it was you, but it doesn't matter anymore," Siris stated. "You better surrender yourself quietly, or I'll give you a nice bit of payback back for those remarks you so casually spouted against me."

But Halifax paid no heed to her warning. Instead, he asked her a small question. "May I at least have the pleasure of knowing what the name of my opponent is?"

"I could ask you the same thing."

Halifax let out a quiet little chuckle. "Very pushy, aren't we? The name's Halifax Evans, your well-born," Halifax said with a mocking little bow. Siris smacked him right across the face with an expression of disgust. "What wrong, princess? I thought that a noble such as yourself would enjoy being treated in such high regard." Halifax rubbed his cheek, a bright red mark plastered across it.

"Do you think I'd believe a single word from the mouth of a snake like you? Besides there's nothing you can do against me. You're all talk," Siris barked at Halifax. It had become apparent that his taunts against her were working.

Instead of snapping back at Siris, Halifax laughed, but it held no warmth nor joy within it. Siris felt the hairs across her entire body stand up as a dark and unpleasant feeling built up within her, as though this haunting laugh had opened the door to her most fearful memories. With each passing second, Halifax's mocking laughter pulled her deeper into the crevices of her mind, until everything around her faded into darkness.

"Get up, girl." Siris gasped for air. Endlessly shaking from the cold, Siris felt as though several burning scars ran across her hands, unable to hold them still for even a split second.

"What did I say, girl?" Siris quickly snapped her head up, yet she couldn't bring herself to even look him in the eye. She knew she could not stay on the floor much longer. It would only cause her more pain.

"I-I'm sorry," Siris weakly whispered, every word carrying the full brunt of her fear. But he didn't care.

"Of course, you should be. Now get up or I'll show your father what a disappointment you are," he barked back at her, standing as still as a statue. Siris slowly moved onto her feet, despite the immense pain. Finally, she brought herself to look the man in the eye. Every ounce of energy that irradiated from his eyes only carried a mixture of fury and displeasure, almost as if he was wasting his time with her. That he had far better things to do, and all she was doing was simply holding him back.

"What did I tell you, girl?" he demanded. Siris opened her mouth for a moment, but could not say a single word. Her mind was clouded with such fright that she couldn't think up a single sentence.

"That I need to concentrate harder on my spells?" Siris whimpered, almost surprised at the fact that she was able to even say to string together something comprehensible.

"Wrong! You have to further train your endurance. You cannot cast anything but the most basic of frost spells," he yelled at her, making Siris instinctively huddle up.

"Have you ever seen a grenade explode before, girl? It can wipe an entire bunker within seconds. Do you think you can stop something like that?" The man looked at Siris cowering before him with disappointment.

"Tsk, no wonder that father of yours always wanted a boy." Those words were the ones that truly cut deep.

"But I can cast spells! Look," Siris said, bringing her shivering hands together to create a small swirl of snowflakes and ice in front of the man, desperately trying to impress him.

"So can every other frost mage!" With a single motion, the man let out a blast of snow and ice from the tip of his left index finger, covering the entire room in a blanket of ice and snow, blasting away Siris' spell in an instant. "Simply having the ability to cast magic does not make you a good mage. Do you think that comparing yourself to the local commoners and rabble makes you any better than they are?" He talked down to her, waving away the small gust of snow that Siris had made. "Especially that commoner boy. Do you know how weak one must be to bring themselves above someone who cannot properly wield magic?"

Siris did not respond. She looked down at the floor, barely able to keep herself from crying.

"I watched you wow those children, watched you bully that boy who had no power and no magical ability to counter what you did to him. How can you even call yourself a mage when you have to compare yourself to a boy who can barely use magic?" the man questioned her.

"Even after so much training, I can't say anything other than you lack talent. You cannot wield magic that is more advanced than the most novice of spells. And even then, you dare to belittle those who can't even use magic." The man smirked. "If it was not for your family and name, not a single mage or organization would look at you," the man said condescendingly, all while letting out a cold belittling laugh.

It was those words, that laugh, that caused something to snap in Siris. Suddenly, all the fear, all the hesitation, any final attempt to maintain civility disappeared, replaced with a blinding fury.

"How-how dare you say that? Stop—"

"—laughing!" Siris landed a blow with her full might across Halifax's face, only for Halifax to turn and smile back at her.

"What are you?" Siris looked at Halifax in shock, all the color from her face gone. Where Siris had smashed her fist into the left side Halifax's face, the skin fell always to reveal the tissue. His jaw became dislocated from his mouth, leaving it dangling freely in the air. To Siris, he was no human, not even a beast. He was a monster.

"It seems you don't have much experience when it comes to dealing with shapeshifters such as myself," Halifax spoke in a clear and open voice, despite half his face mangled to unsightly proportions. She stepped away from him slowly, yet he leaned closer, bringing his horrific face as close as possible to Siris.

"Unlike you common folk, our bodies are not limited to a single shape or mold," Halifax stated in a mocking tone. "Our bodies can take any shape, fill any cast." Halifax paused for a moment, as though he had an epiphany, and shifted his gaze towards the puddles of water across the broken floor. "You could say that we are like water."

Halifax leaped into the air with all his might, a gust of wind accompanying his grandiose escape, tossing heaps of dust into the air.

Siris shielded her face from the blast. As she lowered her arm, she saw a giant eagle in the air, flapping its wing back and forth with all its might.

"Impossible, that can't be."

"Me? I know. Quite a shock, isn't it?" the eagle cut Siris off. "Halifax, the great shapeshifting magus, at your service."

Despite having shapeshifted into an eagle, Siris could almost still see a smug grin across his beak. Within a single moment, the tides of battle had shifted once again.

I need to maintain my composure against this thing. Siris leaped backward, attempting to put as much distance as she could between the two of them. But Halifax knew in an instant what she was planning and dove towards Siris at incredible speed.

To Siris, he seemed like a dark blur. Fortunately, she managed to dodge the brunt of Halifax's attack. But not completely. She felt a sudden burst of pain across her right arm, so agonizingly brutal it felt as though he had ripped it clean off.

"Damn!" Siris ran for cover under the desk and let a few more deep breaths. She glanced down at her arm to see the extent of her injury. There were three huge slashes across the span of her right arm, cutting deep into her soft flesh down to the bone. Blood stained the right side of her coat a dark red.

That monster's out to kill me! Siris wiped the sweat off her brow and scanned across the broken field for her enemy.

It seems like he is waiting for me to make my move. Siris turned her gaze back to her arm. *But I'll stand no match against him with a wound like this.*

Siris closed her eyes and laid her hand across one of the slashes upon her arm, grunting as she froze her wound shut. Siris let out a few quick breaths and slowly shifted her hand onto another wound. Her skin had gone pale, the pain of such an extreme process starting to take its toll upon her, but she did not stop.

Siris shook her fist with vigor as she slapped her hand onto her arm. The adrenaline rushed through her veins, her body shaking with raw determination as she braced one final time.

"Argh!" Siris fell back onto the desk, sweat running down her entire body as she sealed her final wound, letting out a sigh of relief. But Siris knew she could not rest, not while *he* was watching her every move.

"Come on out, you shapeshifting mongrel!" Siris jumped out from underneath the desk, shouting to the vast emptiness of the desolate room. Yet she received no reaction.

Siris stayed on-guard for any attack or approach against her. She scanned her surroundings, listening for any sound that would give away her opponent's position.

"What was that?" Siris suddenly turned around, as she heard something behind her. But it was only water dripping onto the floor. Still, something seemed off about it.

Why would there be water dripping from above? Nope, the piping above her wasn't damaged from the explosion. It didn't make any sense, unless...

With a deafening roar, Siris summoned a ring of frozen spikes around her, bursting through the rubble straight into the ceiling.

Only to see the blurry form of a hawk suddenly weave away from her frozen death trap. Siris clicked her tongue in frustration as Halifax hovered above her.

"I was cutting it pretty damn close there, wasn't I? That's what I get for shapeshifting back into my original form for even a second!" Halifax looked down at Siris with both concern and contempt. *Yet, for her to notice the frost dripping off my jacket... I can't stay here for much longer!* Halifax turned his gaze up to the maze of wiring and equipment above him. *Besides, I've already completed my objective.*

"No you don't!" Siris threw an icy spear at him with all her might.

Halifax beat his wings, barely dodging the frozen spear, the frosty chill of the spear grazing him as it flew past. It shattered into several shards.

"Did you think I'd let you go so easily after giving me such a lavish gift?" Siris lifted her arm to display the giant slashes he had inflicted upon her. "I still have to repay you for it!"

"Well then, Ms. Vasilyeva, let's see just how generous you can be," Halifax said, somewhat intrigued by Siris' resolve. He stretched out both of his wings, which were so large they covered a vast swath of the area around Siris in darkness. Upon locking his gaze on her, Halifax dove with a powerful flap of his wings, traveling towards her with such speed and energy that it seemed impossible to stop his attack.

"Wait, how do you know my family name?" But he did not respond, instead flying closer to Siris. He noticed that she was not panicking, not trying to aim a counter-attack or set up any defensive shield around herself.

The next thing he knew, Halifax lay on the floor, gasping for air as he frantically looked around for Siris.

"Looking for me?" Halifax turned to the sound of the voice to see Siris leaning against a giant spire of ice, staring down at Halifax with a smug little grin. "Of course, even the great Siris Vasilyeva can't hit someone moving that fast."

"I have a bit of experience dealing with mages like you, thanks to a certain dolt." Siris stepped off the icy tower onto a stairway of ice she formed, walking closer to her dazed opponent.

"At such ridiculous speeds, you're nothing more than a raging bull, unable to turn or slow down, even at the sight of a sudden obstacle." Siris paused, clearly drawing enjoyment from the site of Halifax, who was struggling with every ounce of his strength to crawl away from Siris like an injured animal trying to escape its hunter. "And to top it off, you had taken the form of a hawk. Which, I believe, tends to not have the sturdiest of bodies." Siris turned her vision to Halifax's mangled wings, which had been broken and contorted nicely thanks to the pillar of ice.

"I think you should have made a run for it while you had the chance." Siris lifted the frantic Halifax off the ground by his neck. She watched him sputter and squawk in vain with a maniacal smile.

"*Look at him, gasping and clawing for his worthless little life.*" Siris suddenly froze up, her devious smile disappearing in an instant upon hearing that all too familiar voice.

"*What's wrong? Don't you feel good to have caught your prey? Isn't it great to have the power of life and death within your grasp?*"

Shut up. Shut right now! Siris snapped back at him. With every passing second, she felt her control waning.

"Why are you so afraid to take his life? All you have to do is snap that little twig of a neck he has. How could you let him go after all of that filth he talked about you?"

Shut your mouth! Siris suddenly jolted upright and stared deep into Halifax's eyes. She watched him for a moment, a look of true, unadulterated fear in his eyes.

"Go." Siris dropped Halifax onto the ground unapologetically. Halifax coughed and sputtered for air, slowly shifting back into his human form. As Halifax regained his breath, he looked back up at Siris with a curious, somewhat bewildered expression, confused by her sudden mercy.

"Why did you let me—"

"Leave now!" Siris kicked Halifax in the stomach, sending him back to the ground and gasping for air.

"You don't have to tell me again, princess." Halifax crawled slowly towards the exit, his body shifting to the form of a snake. Right before he left, he turned to take one last look at Siris.

"Guess I should remember that face of yours, since I owe you one now," Halifax hissed with the flicker of his forked tongue. With one final glare, Halifax slithered through the mounds of rubble, twisting and turning through them until he slid into a small crack in the floor, disappearing into the darkness.

I owe you one? Siris pondered Halifax's last words to her. *What could that possibly mean? He is nothing more than the leader of a small insurgent group. What possible help could he provide me? Moreover, there's no way he can escape this building.* Yet, the longer the thought lingered in her mind, the more questions she asked.

Why would he leave the explosive device behind? Why would he risk working his way through this facility and just leave empty-handed? A troubling theory popped into Siris' mind.

Could he have been a double agent? That would explain how they got all of that high-grade equipment and broke in so easily! He was probably trying to bring them out into the open and get crushed in one swift blow by Bastion. The pieces fit together in her mind, but she started to question herself once again. Because what could be the purpose of orchestrating such an event? They could easily end up causing far more harm than good to put an army of insurgents into a building full of civilians. Why not just take them out at their base of operations?

Siris let out a sigh of defeat, unable to come to any solid answer.

Whatever he meant, it's nothing good. Siris brushed the dust off her pants and stared off into the vast emptiness of the broken comms room. "Now then, where are those other two?"

"Kibo, god damnit, get up, kid!"

"Jeez, I'm up!" Kibo climbed out from a pile of broken furniture, all while snapping back at Arcanus. "You know that zapping someone isn't the best way to wake them up!"

"I know."

"Then why did you do it?"

"Because I felt like it," Arcanus said with a muffled chuckle.

"If you weren't wired into me... oh forget it," Kibo said as he rubbed his aching neck. "What happened here?"

Kibo moved around the remains of the comms room, surveying for any signs of Artur and Siris, but the veil of dust made it impossible to see any further than his arm. "Arcanus, can you turn on infrared vision? Can't see a thing out here because of this dust." Kibo's visor whirred to life, its display turning a dark blue, with small pangs of red and yellow dots appearing from the occasional sparks off broken wires. "There we go!"

"My pleasure, kid. See, it's not all bad to have a supercomputer like me around," Arcanus stated smugly.

Kibo rolled his eyes. Out the corner of his visor, red light flashed and quickly disappeared. Kibo searched for the origin of that pang of red but saw nothing save a vast blue ocean devoid of heat. "What do you think that was, Arcanus?"

"Beats me. Whatever that was, be on your guard. Don't know what you can run into here."

Kibo obliged, taking caution for any kind of sudden approach. He slowly walked across the piles of rubble and broken furniture, searching for any signs of movement that could give away the position of that flash of red. He saw a partially broken dome of ice, but Siris herself was nowhere in sight. Just as Kibo's focus waned, something caught Arcanus' attention.

"There, I saw something!" Kibo swiftly spun around.

Someone's arm was sticking out through a small crack in a pile of broken furniture. But something seemed off.

"How could there be a pile of broken furniture mounted on top of each other? And is that a puddle?" Something suddenly clicked in Kibo's mind. "Oh no!" Kibo sprinted toward the mound of wood and metal without thinking.

With every step he got closer, he could see the bright red color of the person's arm slowly becoming darker and darker, the dark puddle below the arm growing larger. Kibo launched himself toward the small gap.

Kibo fell flat on his face, staring at the broken floor, run through by a mix of several different roots and vines.

With Artur sitting right next to him.

"You should have been more cautious. You could have fallen into a trap, you know," Artur replied, taking slow, pained breaths between every few words or so.

"Jesus, man! Your entire arm's been ripped to shreds!" Kibo examined Artur's battered arm, which was wrapped in a mixture of leaves and vines, a sort of emergency first aid. Despite Artur's best efforts, slight gaps in his wounds were beyond fixing with a simple bandage.

"Come on. You can't hang out in a place like this. We have to get you some form of medical attention before one of your wounds gets infected."

"Are you insane? We can't leave this place now, not while *she's* out there."

"Her? Who's her? Are you talking about Siris? I mean, yeah, she's pretty damn scary, but I don't think she'd—"

"Not her, you dumbass! That other woman. The one with Halifax," Artur snapped at Kibo as he looked outside the safety of his cover, scouting for any sight of Ripper. Kibo stepped back for a moment, trying to process everything Artur had told him when something urgent popped into his mind.

"What about the detonator?"

"Right here." Artur opened his left hand to reveal the detonator. Though it was covered in Artur's sweat and blood, it seemed to still be intact. "I managed to take cover under one of the desks here, thankfully, but that damn banshee didn't let up."

"She tried to grab the detonator right before I dropped for cover." Artur glanced at his mauled arm. "I managed to get away from her, but she left this nasty mark right before everything fell apart."

"Do you have any clue where she might be?" Kibo asked, searching for any sign of Ripper.

"Right now? No idea. But there's one thing I can be sure about." Artur let out a sharp breath as he lurched forward, holding onto his bloodied arm. "She won't go down easy."

Artur grabbed onto a bit of furniture sticking out of the mound, trying to get back onto his feet with whatever strength that remained in his body. "I need...to get back...onto my..." Artur collapsed, letting out a muffled scream of pain.

"You can't do anything while you're like this. You'll only make your arm worse if you keep trying to push yourself."

"Then what the hell am I supposed to do?" Artur clutched his left arm.

Kibo weighed several different options and choices he could make. Finally, he replied, "You're supposed to get out of this warzone and get medical attention. You and I both know this. You can't do anything in that condition." Kibo stretched out his hand towards Artur. "You know this is the best course of action to save that arm of yours and get that detonator away from enemy hands."

Artur begrudgingly grabbed onto Kibo's hand. Kibo pulled Artur onto his feet.

"Okay then, let's make our way out of here." As the two of them stepped out from underneath their hovel, Artur suddenly froze up, grabbing Kibo with all the strength left within his aching body.

"Do you hear that?"

"Hear what?" Kibo asked. At first, he did not hear a single thing. As he listened more carefully, he heard a small buzzing sound, similar to an electrical wire fizzing out. But it sounded more chaotic, more violent, as though it were trying to escape from something's grasp with all its might. Before Kibo could listen any further, Artur yanked Kibo back.

"Whoa. What was that for?" Kibo turned to see Artur drenched in sweat, his eyes darting across the room rapidly, searching for the source of the strange sound. "What's wrong?"

"It's *her*," Artur stated gravely, looking off into the vast cloud of dust that hung across the battle-scarred room. Across the room, there was a small, sudden flash of bright light before it was swallowed up by the darkness once again.

"Run."

"Wait, what?"

"Run, dammit!" Up until a moment ago, Artur could barely stand. But now it was as if he had been possessed by a demon, sprinting away from the flashing lights with all the energy left within his body.

Kibo bolted after him. "Hey, wait up! Don't run so fast. you're already pretty banged up."

Kibo dodged a huge blast of electrical energy that came from behind him. Before he could look back, Kibo was pulled away from the scene.

"Ow!" A giant grasping root coiled around his arm, pulling him over a toppled desk. He crouched next to Artur, who had taken cover.

"I hope to dear god she didn't see us hide behind here. We have to stay silent right now. Do you understand?" Kibo had far too many questions rushing through his mind to stay silent.

"Who is she? What the heck was that? Why the hell are they even trying to blow this place up?"

"Lieutenant Tiana 'Ripper' Ivanov of the Russian Brotherhood," Artur replied as he quickly looked over the desk, trying to spot Ripper. "She's part of the most infamous terrorist group in all of Russia. They target and attack diplomats and nobles across the nation, and they'll do anything to accomplish their goals."

"Let me guess, they wanna take down the government?"

"Mostly they wish to see the Tsardom and nobility torn down. They believe that only then will the Russian people truly be free from the tyranny of the elite." Artur ducked back down, his face drenched in sweat. "I don't think we can hide for long from that monster."

"What are we gonna do then?"

"The only thing we can do," Artur stated, stepping over the toppled desk. A pair of roots crawled up from the ground and twisted around him. "Take her down."

However, Artur felt Kibo's metallic gauntlet on his shoulder. "I can't let you go out there and fight her in your condition."

Artur looked over at Kibo. "I don't plan on fighting her. I'm leaving her to you."

"Wait, what do you mean?" Kibo asked.

Artur turned away from several flashes of light and sparks coming from Ripper's direction and looked down at the root that had latched onto his arm.

"I left a small root as a marker by the hostage room, just in case we ended up in a situation like this." Artur jerked his arm back, pulling at a long line of roots that disappeared into the rubble. "Fortunately, I managed to have it slowly grow back toward us, allowing me to head over there and get the rest of the hostages to safety." Artur then turned his gaze back towards the vague figure of Ripper, illuminated within the dust clouds by the sparks radiating off her body.

"That's where you come in."

"Me?"

"I need you to hold Ripper off while I get the hostages clear." Artur tossed something small at Kibo. It was a shriveled seed. "Fortunately, I haven't seen any signs of her other companion. Let's hope he fled from here in the chaos or is busy dealing with that other friend of yours." He then held up another similarly dark and shriveled seed in his hand. Kibo watched as it suddenly sprang to life, roots and sprouts flowing out of its shell.

"This is gonna be the signal for when I've gotten all the hostages out of here. Once you feel or see that seed burst into life, it'd be best for you toget the hell out." Artur looked at Kibo directly into his eyes, his tone one of pure urgency and gravity. "You understand?"

"Got it."

"Good, then hold down that damned monster for as long as possible." Artur dashed off in the direction of the hostages.

Kibo turned towards the sounds of crackling energy.

"You seem kind of quiet kid. You all right?" Arcanus asked.

Kibo looked down at the bright blue triangle embedded in his palm. "This is the first time I'll be face-to-face with someone in a fight all alone." Kibo let out a nervous chuckle. "Probably also the first time I'm going to be fighting someone who wants to kill me."

The two of them stayed quiet for a while, wallowing in the silence of the room, waiting for the other to speak first.

"*Listen, Kibo. I trust you—us—that we can get past her. Don't forget, you got me by your side.*" Kibo looked down at Arcanus, quickly shaping his hands into fists.

"You're right. She won't be any different than the matches."

"*Then let's show that bastard what we've got,*" Arcanus exclaimed. Kibo looked off towards the occasional flashes of sparks coming from across the room, becoming brighter and closer with each burst. He knew that he couldn't run from this fight, that he couldn't turn back now.

It was now or never.

CHAPTER 22

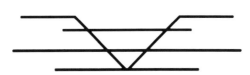

"Ah crap. Watch out, kid!" A blast of lightning hit Kibo in his chest and sent him barreling towards a pile of rubble. And the origin of that blast? Ripper—and she was starting to look quite frustrated.

"Have you tired yourself out yet, boy? Or do I have to keep up with this little game of ours?" Ripper let out an annoyed grunt. Arcs of electricity lashed out from all over her body, ripping through any bit of broken furniture.

How is she still going? Using that much power should have easily fried her to a crisp. Kibo panicked, leaping off the pile of rubble onto his feet. *What the hell is she?*

"Don't let her get into your head, Kibo! Remember, you're not going up against an average soldier. She's a powerful mage. Hell, the fact that she is even being pushed back by you is something."

I guess you're right, but still. Kibo paused. *She hasn't gone after me at all. Why isn't she going all out and just staying back the whole time? Unless...?*

"Unless what, kid?" Kibo raised his fist into the air, staring down Ripper as he slowly edged closer.

"Whoa, Kibo, what's gotten into you?" Again, no reply. But it was clear that Kibo had some sort of plan stirring around his head. Ripper was clearly irritated.

"Coming for another round of blows, are we? You are a stubborn ass." Ripper put out both her hands and let out another blast of electrical energy, creating a shield of a chaotic and violent mess of lightning. "You can't keep it up forever."

Kibo slammed into Ripper at full force. Ripper's eyes flew up in a panic, doing everything in her power to hold Kibo back. The two clashed, Kibo pushing against Ripper's barrier with all his might, and Ripper attempting to control the chaotic energy flowing wildly from her. But, slowly, the cracks within Ripper's once-impenetrable barrier started to show.

Bit by bit, the energy flowing from her hands became more violent, lashing the walls, ground, and herself. Ripper flinched as her power backfired, scorching lines of unbearable heat across her arms and body. "Enough!" With a violent and painful shout, Ripper let out a blast of such power that it shook the entire foundation of the room. Waves of lightning sliced through any piles of wreckage that stood in their path, ripping across the sundered room.

Kibo was struck with such force that even that tight suit of armor couldn't dull the blow. Kibo stared up at the darkness of the room, the faint glow of his visor gone. Every part of his body ached.

Arcanus? No response.

Arcanus! Again, no response.

"Answer me!" A heavy weight crushed his chest in the silence. His heart beat faster, his breathing more irregular by the second.

"Come on, Arcanus, please say something!" Kibo begged, every ounce of him pleading for the return of his companion, but there was nothing.

Oh god, what am I gonna do? Kibo's mind raced, struggling to form some sort of plan. Nothing came to him. His mind had drawn a complete blank. "Please, anyone, help me," Kibo called out into the darkness.

Kibo's visor flickered on. A faint blue glow at first, before a tidal wave of code flashed across his screen. Information flew across his visor within seconds, entire logs and sheets of words and strings passing by. Then they all slowly disappeared until his visor was blank, leaving him alone with his thoughts once more.

Until three small words appeared in the middle of his visor. *Stay focused, kid.*

"Even now he calls me a kid?" Kibo let out a nervous laugh. *Okay, I just have to stay focused.*

Kibo hopped back onto his feet, turning towards Ripper once again.

However, the same could not be said for Ripper. Every part of her body was shaking uncontrollably. What drew Kibo's attention was her hands.

They were wrapped in streaks of seared flesh, her palms covered in burns. He cleared his throat.

"You couldn't handle it, could you?" Kibo called out to Ripper. She looked up at him momentarily but did not respond. This only served to answer Kibo's suspicions. "I was wondering why you were able to release and control so much electrical energy without suffering any sort of backlash." Kibo turned his gaze back down towards her charred hands. "But the truth was, you couldn't. You were doing all you could to control the energy that you were releasing from your body, and you were just barely able to manipulate it to stop my punches. Am I right?"

Ripper only stared at Kibo with a seething look of hatred. Then Kibo pointed back over his shoulder, towards the direction he and Siris had broken in from.

"I was shocked at how much control you had over your powers. But then I remembered spotting a little something on that belt of yours." Kibo glanced down at Ripper's belt. "You've taken some kind of drug, haven't you?" Kibo pointed out. To his surprise, Ripper finally responded to him.

"Quite the detective, aren't you, metal man?" Ripper scowled. "You think that's going to change the outcome of our little brawl? That knowing this detail will give you some advantage over me?"

"No." Kibo glanced down at Ripper's burnt hands. "But the knowledge that the drug you took made you produce more energy than you anticipated, and far more than you can handle? Yes."

Ripper narrowed her eyes. "Do you think that a few small burns are gonna stop someone like me, boy?" Ripper lifted her hands in the air, both shaking violently. Whether in pain or fury, Kibo could not tell. "I've been in countless battles against soldiers, mages, and assassins, and in every fight I've come out alive no matter what wounds or injuries they inflicted upon me.

"Don't think that a boy like you will be the end of the Ripper." Ripper's voice quavered with such fury that it left Kibo speechless. Unfortunately, his silence only amused Ripper.

"What's wrong, boy? Lost for words?" Ripper slapped her palms together and smiled for the first time. "You believe all the stuff they peddle, don't you?"

"What do you mean?" Kibo stuttered out his question.

"Bastion. Do you really see them as some fucking beacon of hope? That they spread peace and order across the globe?"

"Don't you dare speak that way about Bastion," Kibo snapped at her. "They bring hope to the downtrodden and weak. They topple tyrants and defeat rogue mages across the world. They were meant to stop people like *you*."

"Oh, of course. Do they also travel on beams of holy light, flying down from the heavens upon white pegasi?" Ripper spat on the ground. "Let me guess, were those the same exact words that you were fed by some propaganda radio show, where a pair of disgustingly good angels defeat a horde of diabolically evil bad guys?" Ripper glared with unbridled fury.

Ripper laughed at him. "I'll let you go on and keep believing that fantasy of yours. Wouldn't want to spoil the surprise for you down the line. If you make it out of here alive, that is.

"I think it's time I show you why they call me Ripper."

With a vicious crackle, lightning burst from Ripper's hands, lashing in all directions. She pulled them back in, taming the wild arcs of energy. Kibo was blinded by the light radiating from them.

"You're probably wondering how I managed to restrain all this energy in my hands."

"It's because you're storing all that energy in a small area, isn't it?" Kibo answered.

"It seems that you're quite a perceptive young man. I imagine you're already thinking of ways to stop me now." Ripper brought back both of her arms and stepped forward. "But I'm afraid your time's up."

Ripper charged toward him, her hands slicing through everything that stood in front of her. He watched her grow closer, unable to move his body at all.

Move! But Kibo's legs wouldn't budge. Was it the fear of being all alone against another fighter, or was it the fact that he knew his opponent had no mercy for him?

Kibo watched helplessly as Ripper approached, her left arm poised to slice through him in one fell swoop.

But it was in that state of true fear, that moment, Kibo remembered those small three words.

Stay focused, kid.

That was all that he needed.

"What the?" Ripper looked up at Kibo, expecting to have cleaved through his body like a butcher knife. Instead, she found herself in an arm lock, caught in Kibo's grasp. "Why you..."

Ripper lurched backward, her elbow ripped from its socket by that boy. "You bastard!"

"I figured I couldn't take on someone like you head-on, so the best way to beat you was to get rid of your fangs." Kibo imitated Ripper's pose from before. "And with such a wide swing like that, there was no way I could let the opportunity slip by." She stared at him with burning hatred. Every ounce of her body seemed to ooze with rage. He had awakened the wrath of a warrior.

"You piece of brainwashed trash. Don't look down on me!"

With a shout of rage and pain, she popped her arm back into its socket in one clean motion.

"Are you nuts?" Kibo looked at Ripper, bewildered.

"I didn't intend on slaughtering the youth, but you've done much to change my mind." Ripper's hands lit up again. "Pray that God favors you, boy, because you'll be having a chat with him any moment."

Ripper brought down her arm like an executioner's axe, slicing through the earth with all her might. At the very moment she made contact with the ground, a giant crackling wave of lightning sped towards Kibo, ripping its way through the rubble.

Kibo dashed out of the way of the blast. He watched the searing line of lightning crash into the wall, bursting into a blast of electrical energy and leaving only a charred crater, small remnants of electrical energy crackling around it.

"Guess she wasn't lying." Kibo watched as the foundations he stood on shook with every step Ripper took. The energy bursting from her body tore through everything in its wake, but it did not faze Kibo. His sights were set on Ripper, and nothing would break his focus.

Ripper hurled a mote of lightning towards Kibo. As Kibo watched the chaotic ball of energy rush towards him at full speed, several different scenarios raced through his mind.

A massive pillar of ice burst from the floor, crushing the ball of lightning like it was nothing and almost hitting Kibo as it broke through the ceiling.

"Seems a little farm boy needed my help?" Siris stood on top of a pile of broken desks, all covered in a thick layer of frost.

"If by helping me, you meant to kill me," Kibo snapped at her, though deep down, he felt a slight pang of relief. The monolithic spire in front of them shattered into a shower of ice.

"Why do scum always get in the way of everything?"

Ripper charged toward them at full speed, letting out a furious screech. They both leaped to the side as Ripper slammed her fist into the ground beneath them, sending out a powerful shockwave of energy.

"It seems that you're starting to lose your edge. What happened to the seasoned soldier?" Siris taunted Ripper.

"Shut the hell up! Do you know who I am, girl?"

"Someone who's about to be a stain on the floor," Siris responded smugly, only furthering Ripper's frenzied state. "Oh, and before you even ask, Halifax left you to rot. I don't know why you thought he was going to help you."

Ripper looked at Siris, her expression of rage shifted into one of surprise. "He what?"

"You heard me. The man quite literally slithered out of here like the coward he was," Siris answered.

"He ran away? That doesn't make any sense! After all that planning, coordinating, and spending, why would he leave behind all his work for nothing?" Ripper's face contorted into a look of disgust. "I knew I couldn't trust that bastard!"

"Seems like you've chosen the wrong person to back you up." Kibo brought up both his fists up to his chest. "You should hand yourself over."

Ripper charged towards Kibo at full speed, who just barely managed to dodge the full brunt of her attack, stumbling onto the ground. As Kibo fell, he instinctively closed his eyes. He could feel the wind, the dust hit his face as he fell onto the floor.

But wait, why was the dust on his face?

Kibo felt for his visor, only to find his hand rubbing across his face. Kibo opened his eyes. His entire visor was torn off by Ripper.

A few centimeters closer and... The very thought left him nauseous. He got back onto his feet.

"Stop running, boy!" Ripper brought down her arm, one final blow to finish him.

"Stop standing there like a statue and help me fight her!"

Kibo's eyes flew open.

Siris sent waves of ice and snow, pushing Ripper back. But Ripper held her ground and tore through all of Siris' attacks with unsettling ease.

"You think a few ice cubes are going to stop me, girl?" Ripper radiated such a fierce level of bloodlust it seemed as though nothing could stop her. She slammed down her foot and went into a full-on charge toward Siris.

"Oh no!" Siris panicked, throwing more shards of ice in Ripper's way, trying to find any way to stop the charging bull. But it was completely ineffective, all of them either shattering or being bounced off harmlessly from the aura of electrical energy surrounding her. It seemed nothing could stop her rampage.

Kibo charged into her from the side, digging his fist deep into her gut.

Ripper lurched backward, holding her stomach in pain. "Bastard!"

Kibo landed another powerful blow against Ripper and sent her staggering across the room. Ripper's legs buckled. She tried her best to get back on her feet, to regain her composure, only for Kibo to slam his shoulder directly into her face. He punched her again, this time in the stomach.

Ripper collapsed onto a pile of rubble, her consciousness slowly waning. The savage energies flowing through her were tearing her inside out. Yet, if she stopped channeling her powers, she would be crushed by those two pitiful children. She had no chance of beating them, not in this state. There was no other way now. She had to do it.

"If you're going to take me down, I'll take both of you with me!" Ripper ripped out a syringe from her belt while letting out a blast of electrical energy, knocking Kibo and Siris away from her.

"What is she doing?" Siris looked down at the syringe in Ripper's hand. "Do you think that's going to save you from this situation?"

But Siris could tell there was something very strange about this particular drug. It was different from the others she saw. It had not the sickly green glow she had seen some of the soldiers carry, but a dark red miasma. It moved slowly within the syringe, churning up and down its container, despite the frantic speed Ripper pulled it from her belt.

"I'll blow this room and that damn detonator to bits," Ripper shouted one final time, before sinking the needle into her flesh.

The effects were immediate. Her arm bloated with electrical energy which lashed out in several different directions. Ripper let out screams of such blood-curdling agony that even Kibo and Siris could not help but pity her.

"She's going to scorch this entire facility off the surface of the earth," Siris exclaimed. "What the hell are we going to do?"

"Nothing." Kibo had not moved a single muscle as he watched Ripper slowly destroy her body.

"All we have to do is take this one small blast and it'll be over."

"What are you talking about? That damn detonator is still lost somewhere in this room!"

"It's not." Kibo lifted his arm, the metal surrounding his fist slowly dissipating to reveal his burned palm. In the center was a small black seed with bright green stalks sprouting from its shell, wrapping around Kibo's hand like a thin, green bandage.

Huh, now that I think about it, my hand does feel better. Kibo smiled slightly, distracted by the whimsical little vines growing around his hand. *No wonder Artur used them as bandages.* Kibo felt a flick against his forehead.

"Ow, what was that for?" Kibo turned to see Siris planting her hand across her face,

"Why the hell should I care about your little plant project when there is a literal ticking time bomb across the room?" Siris yelled at Kibo, who sheepishly scratched the back of his head.

"Oh yeah, uh, so this thing sprouting means that Artur managed to get the rest of the hostages and the detonator out of here." Kibo turned his gaze toward Ripper, who seemed as though she was moments away from exploding. "So, I guess what I'm trying to get at is that we should run like hell."

Kibo broke into a full sprint from Ripper as fast as he could.

This boy! Siris rolled her eyes as she sprinted after him.

"How much time do you think we have before this place is a crater?" Kibo yelled at Siris, not daring to look back for a single moment. Siris glanced over her shoulder at Ripper to get a quick look, only to be immediately blinded. The sheer amount of energy radiating from Ripper's body made it impossible to look anywhere near her.

"Jesus, she's burning up like a damn inferno!" Siris turned her gaze back onto Kibo. "She's gonna detonate any second now."

A flash of white light blinded them. Siris could not bear to open her own eyes. As quickly as the flash came, it disappeared.

"My god." Siris turned around and saw Ripper staring quietly at the floor. She was not surrounded by a storm of lightning. Rather, smoke rose from every part of her body, which was covered in either horrendous boils or burns.

Ripper snapped her head up, displaying her grotesque face. It was the look of something out of a bedtime story told to children to scare them. Yet none of it struck fear into Siris' heart as badly as did Ripper's mouth.

The boils around her mouth contorted into a permanent unhinged smile from ear to ear. "What's wrong, your Well-Born?"

"What's... What is...?" Siris stammered as she looked at Ripper in fearful disgust.

Ripper let out a maddening cackle and stared directly down at Siris with her malformed smile.

"I pity you."

A massive blast of light burst from Ripper, instantly blinding Siris. The sound created by the raw energy was so deafening that it was as though she had summoned a storm right into the room.

The shockwave resounded through the room, knocking Siris onto the floor, followed by a blast of heat. The last thing she heard was a scream before it all faded away.

Siris opened her eyes, taking a moment to readjust her vision. She tried to get up, only to feel a weight crushing her to the ground.

It was Kibo, holding onto her with all his might as he huddled behind a flipped-over metal cabinet. Feeling Siris struggle against him, Kibo turned back towards her.

"You're finally awake. I was afraid you got hit badly by the blast."

"Yes, I get it! Now your damn arm off me!" Siris squeezed herself out of Kibo's grip. "You almost crushed me with that damn metal arm of yours. I can't tell if you were trying to save or kill me."

"Okay, jeez." Kibo backed off from her, rolling his eyes.

"You think she'd be a bit more grateful for you saving her ass back there, right kid?"

Arcanus! Kibo looked down at his right hand, the familiar blue triangle glowing from the center of his palm.

"Miss me, kid?"

Where the heck did you go? You left me all on my own against Ripper. Speaking of which..." Kibo peeked over the cabinet to view the full extent of the damage. The front side of the cabinet had melted, leaving behind a mess of burnt papers and splotches of metal.

Wow, she did go out with a bang, huh? Kibo looked around the room, taking in the true extent of the damage that Ripper's blast had done. Every part of the room was covered in blackened streaks from the blast of lightning Ripper had let out.

Yet the damage around the room was nothing in comparison to ground zero. Where Ripper once stood, there was nothing but a giant crater that spanned across a large portion of the room. At the very center were the remains of Ripper, a pile of charred bones.

"That damn woman." Siris stepped over the cabinet, taking a look down at the damage. "She meant it."

"Yeah, looks like it." Kibo sat down and let out a sigh of relief. "But we managed to beat her, and that's all that matters."

However, Siris seemed far too engrossed by the scene. It just seemed sad in an odd way. "To think she'd rather end her own life than be taken prisoner." Siris kicked over a rock and let out a deep breath. "Then again, it wouldn't have made a difference. She would have been executed anyway."

"Who would have known there would be people like her, huh? Willing to kill themselves for some stupid ideology. The

idiocy that is, I tell you." Kibo looked down at Arcanus and back over to Ripper.

Yeah, probably. Kibo tightened his fist. But she did teach me something pretty important.

"And what's that?"

I still have more to learn. Kibo looked off in the distance, deep in thought.

"Yeah, well...no shit, kid," Arcanus snapped at Kibo.

Whoa! Kibo snapped back a bit, surprised by Arcanus' sudden pop-off.

"Just because I called her an idiot doesn't mean she wasn't one hell of a tough fighter!" Arcanus exclaimed with a slight chuckle. *"You—no we—both have a lot to learn before we can take on people like her."* Kibo had a feeling as though Arcanus was talking about Siris, as though he was mulling over something within his core. *"We won't always be able to get help when we need it most. And it's in those moments we need to be able to hold our own."*

Kibo looked down at Arcanus for a moment, before leaping back onto his feet, his fist raised triumphantly in a victorious pose.

"Guess that means I gotta start training harder than ever!"

"Is there something wrong with you?" Siris said with a look of suspicion.

"Uh, yeah, I'm okay," Kibo said, stretching the back of his head, his face turning bright red. *Guess that's one thing I gotta to work on. Damn posters.* Arcanus let out a slight chuckle. *"Yeah, I'll say! Didn't think they'd rot your brain that much. Well, what to do now?"* Arcanus asked Kibo, who smiled. "Rex and Artur!" Kibo suddenly blurted out, a panicked look flashing onto his face.

"What about them?" Siris asked, completely indifferent to Kibo's sudden burst of panic.

"We gotta go check on them! They might have ended up getting into another fight or captured by other insurgents."

"I'm sure they're probably fine," Siris said.

"Come on!" Kibo rushed toward the exit, much to Siris' annoyance.

"This idiot is going to get us both killed," Siris muttered to herself as she followed him.

CHAPTER 23

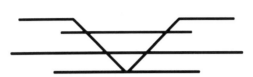

"Rex!"

Rex opened his eyes as he leaped upright, wildly looking around to see where exactly he was. His entire body was covered in a cold sweat, his heart beating so much that it felt as though it was going to explode.

"Calm down Rex." Rex looked to his right to see Kibo, standing by the side. "You all right?"

"Yeah, I'm okay. I was in some kind of forest, there was a crazy fire and... You know what? Forget it. It was a small nightmare." Rex shook his head. "Where are we?"

"We're in the medical ward. You've been knocked out for quite a while," Kibo said, trying to calm Rex down.

Rex sank back into his cot. "Man, that was one hell of a nightmare." Rex wiped the sweat off his face. Numerous bandages wrapped his arm.

"Yeah, the doctors said you suffered a lot of trauma across your entire body." Kibo glanced at Rex, able to tell he was quite a bit surprised. Almost every part of him was covered in a bandage or cast, as though he would fall apart if a single piece was removed. "You suffered some internal bleeding, multiple fractures, and other stuff I can't remember," Kibo recalled. "It's amazing that they managed to patch up all of your major injuries up so quickly, considering how swamped this place is."

"Huh, guess you're right." Rex turned his gaze to the rest of the room. Almost the entire wing was full to the brim with doctors, nurses, and other medical personnel rushing from bed to bed, trying to treat as many patients as possible. Additional soldiers and staff poured in constantly, bringing in more wounded or supplies. Rex

"No wonder I was knocked out." Rex chuckled softly. Rex stared up at the ceiling, looking up and down its whitewashed concrete texture. It looked almost like it was covered in a layer of snow.

Don't think about it, Rex. It's just some crazy dream. Rex thought to himself, but the more it swirled around in his head, the more troubled and infuriated he became.

"Aren't you gonna ask what happened while you were out?" Kibo interrupted Rex's troubling train of thought.

"Oh yeah, what happened?" Rex asked, clearing his head.

"After you got knocked out, Akira and Hana carried you back to the medical ward. And before you ask, don't worry. Other than a few small bruises and cuts, they're fine," Kibo answered before Rex could ask the question.

"Guessin' you're all right, too. You know, on the inside and all that?" Rex asked, looking down at Kibo's hands, clearly recalling the burns from his attempt at magic.

"Oh no, don't worry about my hand. They healed all of the burns in an instant." Kibo brought up his hand and stretched them out before Rex. Just as Kibo stated, Rex could see that his palms had healed completely.

"What else you expect from the docs here, huh?" Rex whistled, impressed. "Well, how about ya tell me everything that happened while I was knocked out cold?"

After a long and winding explanation, Rex thought over everything he was just told. "Damn, sounds like you three had one tough fight."

"What's wrong?" Kibo asked.

"I don't know. What if things went south? What if you guys were up against someone even tougher?" Rex looked down at his bandages. "I just wish I'd been there, you know? Things could have gone better for y'all."

"What do you mean?" Kibo looked confused. "We got out just fine. We took out the commander, saved the hostages, and got back all in one piece."

"Yeah, yeah, I know. I can't help it. Hell, even when I was pummeled into a pulp and carried over here, I still couldn't help but feel ashamed. Get what I'm saying?" Rex sighed. "I don't wanna see my friends get hurt, that's all."

"Well, neither do I," Kibo said. "When I saw you in that state back there, I felt terrible. I mean, I was just a couple meters away from you. I could have—should have—come to help when you were fighting your way through that many soldiers. But we can't always be there to help our friends. In those moments, you just have to hope and believe that they can handle it," Kibo said.

Rex looked at him for a moment, "Eh, guess you're right." Rex smiled weakly.

Kibo put his hand on Rex's shoulder. "I'm here for you, and I'll do my best to make sure that's always the case."

"Yeah. Thanks, man." Rex smiled.

"Anytime. Think I'll check up on the others," Kibo said as he got up and stepped away from Rex, turning back towards the rest of the room.

"Gotcha. I think I'm gonna dose off for a bit. Still got pain in my arm."

That went even better than I expected, Kibo thought joyfully. *Nice to be able to cheer someone up for once.*

"*Yeah, I imagine. Especially when you stick that close to the script, kiddo,*" Arcanus mused. "*Must be nice having me feed you all the nice and uplifting words, huh?*"

Oh, shut up. Kibo blushed.

"*It's okay, kid. That's what I'm here for.*" Arcanus chuckled. "*Let's check up on the others, shall we?*"

Yeah, let's.

"A group of militants held hostages and threatened Bastion, but the examinees, one of which was a Vasilyev, valiantly fought them back. While their motives are still unknown, we must still congratulate Bastion and the Russian military's successful effort to"—*kkrt*—"Boris, they used British-made rifles. Some of the bodies were identified as private military company mercenaries. It does raise some questions on Commonwealth involvement"—*kkrt*.

She flicked the television off. "As you can see, the political objectives were accomplished. Approval ratings are up, and support for the bill among the Red members of Parliament is increasing," the administrator said. "Our Russian friends are certainly happy."

Members around the table nodded in approval. Though one in the back seemed a bit worried.

"Yes, that should keep the Reds and Whites in Parliament happy with us. Do you have a plan that'll keep the Brits from feeling slighted?" one of the officials asked.

"Oh, we do. We'll have our men back in London to make sure to turn this into some sort of benefit, or at least something not harmful to the Commonwealth." The head commander cleared his throat. "It should keep both sides happy with us, and we'll keep operating without any more interference from the Reds."

"What's the status of the rebel group, Chameleon? I'm sure your infiltration went well. Great performance on that 'stage' by the way."

Everyone turned to the undercover agent. Instead of a tall, gaunt, bearded Halifax, he was a clean-shaven, bald fellow with a permanent smirk plastered on his face.

"Thank you, sir. Thanks to my infiltration under the guise Halifax, I was able to convince the rebels to go all in." Chameleon leaned back lazily on his chair. "Which, of course, made it easy for our boys to run in and take care of their now-understaffed holdouts. All of their ringleaders are in prison or dead. The Russian Liberation Front is effectively dissolved."

"Good man. And lose the accent, you're not undercover anymore." The old man chuckled. "But that's only two out of three objectives." He turned towards the officer across from him, who had been silent the whole meeting. "Batros, I'm sure the extra data on the students helped your recruitment decisions."

No answer. Batros stared blankly down at his folder.

"Batros, report."

He suddenly snapped his head forward. His eyes were intense. "Sir, about fifty wounded, but thankfully only around ten casualties."

The commander rolled his eyes. "I am aware, but it's irrelevant. What's the report on the recruits?"

"I have my selection. But again, these men were badly hurt. My second in command, Sidorov—"

"Oh, that runt? I apologize for shooting him," Chameleon said, half-sincerely. "But I did what I had to do. The rebels were beginning to believe I was a mole."

Batros' voice deepened. "I had to send him home on a stretcher. I'd just like to say that we must be wary in the future."

The agent shrugged. "Acceptable losses."

The veteran stood up and was beside Halifax in a flash. He lifted the agent by the neck with one arm, a revolver in the other. Fear flashed on Halifax's face. Batros shoved the snub-nose onto his temple. Batros was furious.

"Those were my men. My soldiers!"

"Enough. Batros, stand down," the commander shouted. He was standing up. "Everyone, you are dismissed. Except for you, Batros."

Batros turned to the commander in fury, thoughts racing through his head. But he brought his revolver down, backing off from Chameleon. Chameleon fell to the floor gasping for air, gazing up at Batros with a look of validation.

Batros kept his eyes on the commander, never once moving his gaze from him as everyone filed out the room. Eventually, there were only the two of them left staring at one another, waiting for the other to speak up.

The ceiling fan slowly whirred above them, the only sound in the now-empty room. His blood boiled from sheer rage. "You and I both saw the footage. He shot his fellow man without the slightest bit of hesitation."

"Did you expect him to let your subordinate go and botch this entire operation?"

"He could have done something else. He could have—"

"He already went out of his way to make sure nothing fatal happened to the private. The most he'll endure is a few days in the medical ward." The officer picked up a certain file from his desk before turning toward Batros. "You know this better than I do, Batros. Sometimes sacrifices must be made in the name of security."

Batros just stared off into the distance. "Thanks to him, both Bastion and the Russians got a huge boost of support from the masses, and we've gotten rid of one of the biggest thorns in our side." The commander smirked. "That's a win-win situation if I've ever seen one."

Batros remained silent, not responding to the commander remark. Despite knowing everything the commander was right said, that final look, the one Sidorov gave as he headed out of the room, haunted him. he could not help but feel a pang of guilt deep in his chest.

The commander cleared his throat. "It's about time we get back to what is important."

The commander put down the file he was sifting through in front of Batros. Of course, he didn't need to look twice to know who exactly the commander was talking about.

"Kibo Kozlov, born January 4, 1951." The commander pointed at the picture of Kibo attached to his file. "I imagine you and I both know why Bastion has taken an interest in this boy?"

"I can't see who wouldn't be." Batros picked up the picture of Kibo and stared at it sternly.

"Born to Fyodor Kozlov, one of the most talented operatives among the ranks of Bastion. I believe you went on a few missions with him before he went MIA." The commander chuckled. "It'd be hard to imagine that the son of such a talented mage wouldn't follow in his father's footsteps.

"He joined the Russian militia at the age of fourteen and showed great discipline and drive for someone of his age. He would have made a good soldier for either the Russian military or Bastion." The commander sighed. "Of course, if it wasn't for one fatal flaw.

"The boy was born with a genetic defect, hampering his ability to manipulate any form of magic," the commander said, reading from Kibo's file. "It would've been impossible for him to ever join or become part of any high-ranking unit in Bastion. A boy like him would probably have worked his way into a cozy office job for some company and lived out his days in a relatively boring, but safe environment. But something very interesting happened.

"Two weeks ago, a group of workers contracted for a building project in a nearby town found a giant cavern below an old well that was set to be demolished." The commander pulled out a collection of photos from his front pockets. "What they found was beyond anything we could have imagined."

Batros picked up the photos, staring at them in awe. They displayed images of a vault consisting of otherworldly technology and artifacts. The walls were made of a metallic material with bright blue lines of light moving through them. Each part of every wall was marked with several different runes and imagery that seemed out of this world.

"My god." Batros placed his hand across his forehead. "This is the vault the higher-ups were talking about?"

"I think you can imagine which examinee running through all these trails happens to also be from this town?"

"Kozlov." Batros nodded.

"Affirmative," the commander exclaimed, grabbing another image of Kibo, this time within his combat suit. "We believe that this machine, weapon, or whatever it is, is most likely from this vault." The commander pointed at several photos of Kibo that were specifically zoomed in on his right palm. "In a scenario like this, we would have immediately brought in the boy and the artifact for examination, doing as many tests and experiments as we could to understand what this machine is.

"However, we ran into something very interesting." He pulled out several photos of Kibo during the first part of the exam, each one displaying Kibo in a different stage of armor development—from gauntlets to metallic boots and finally full combat form.

"It's evolving," Batros said, staring at the images of Kibo.

"I think you and I both knew that."

"What are you trying to get at, commander?" Batros narrowed his eyes.

The commander let out a chuckle. "Nothing ever gets past you, does it, Batros?"

"As you probably guessed, we believe this device evolves in moments of dire pressure or strain. While we can't be sure, that's most likely the case based on the numerous recordings we have collected of Kozlov during his examinations. And from the looks of it, the evolution isn't done yet." The commander pulled out large log files containing several lines of data. "As you can see, it seems that even after completely covering himself within that suit, his power still increased.

"That's where you come in." The commander glanced at Batros. "I believe you already placed Kozlov on your team, no?"

Batros looked at the commander and smirked. "You think I'm going to let an amazing recruit like this slip by me? I might as well retire."

"Well said!" The commander laughed. "Keep watch over him and report back on how he's developing. Think of it like a field study."

Batros looked at Kibo's papers for a moment, going over the commander's proposal. "All right, you've got yourself a deal, commander," Batros replied, shaking hands with the commander.

"Get to it, then." The commander smiled. "I'll be waiting to see what kind of team you put together."

"Oh, you won't have to wait long. I've already made my decision."

CHAPTER 24

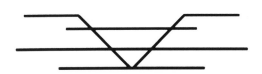

"Why'd ya think they called us here?" Rex asked, looking up at a large set of doors labeled *Conference Room 2-B*. Kibo, Kaze, Rex, and several other examinees stood near the entrance to the conference room, talking about the insurgent attack, small bits of gossip, or whether they passed or failed the exam.

"Well, it must be something important." Kaze looked down at a tiny slip of paper in his hand that had the room number on it. "Considering they handed these little slips out to everyone who was an examinee, it probably has something to do with the Bastion exams."

"You think they're gonna announce who passed?" Kibo asked Kaze, who sighed.

"Because of all the crazy stuff that happened yesterday, I can't tell for sure." Kaze fumbled with the slip in his hand nervously. "We won't know until we head in, will we?"

Kaze took a deep breath and stepped towards the door. "Looks like we're heading in." Kaze put his hand onto the door handle and then...just stood there.

"Uh, Kaze. You all right?" Kibo asked Kaze. No response.

You think he's nervous? Kibo asked Arcanus.

"Of course the kid's nervous," Arcanus exclaimed. *"Every single examinee here must be shitting their pants right now."*

Kaze looked as though he was frozen solid from the swirl of conflicting emotions inside his head. *Should I go? No, no, no. It's too early to go in. But standing here won't miraculously change the results.*

"Hey, man, you all right?"

Kaze jolted upright. "What? Oh, yeah, I'm okay."

"You sure?" Kibo asked. "Because from here, you look pretty nervous."

Kaze sighed. It seemed to him like any other set of doors. But now that he was up close, he could see just how big the set of doors was. They must've been at least twice his height, towering over him like the gate of a battle-hardened keep.

"I traveled here from my hometown of Osaka." Kaze 's hand shook uncontrollably as he gripped the door handle. "I spent so much of my time and earnings to scrap my way here. I-I don't want it all to go to waste, goddamn it!"

"Who said it's going to waste?" Kibo replied.

"What do you mean?"

"All this time we've been fighting, you always took the lead, always tried to figure out the best plan or way to get over any obstacle." Kibo chuckled. "And even when your plans managed to go wrong, you always had another one ready to go."

Kaze thought about what Kibo said for a bit. "So, what you're saying is—"

"I think you're the last person here who'd fail this exam. And if you did... *pfft*... I'd seriously doubt Bastion's selection process."

Kaze let out a small laugh. "Thanks, Kibo. Oh, and you can call me Akira."

"Oh, uh, gotcha, Kaz...Akira," Kibo said.

Akira smiled and grabbed the door handle. "Here we go!" Akira swung open the door, stepping into the conference room.

"Huh, it's a lot more normal than I expected it to be," Kibo said, somewhat disappointed.

The room was like any ordinary conference room, consisting of white-washed walls, fluorescent lights, and long rows of metal, foldable chairs set out for the audience. At the end of the room was a small stage, no higher than a meter, with a wooden podium that had a flimsy microphone sticking out from it. It truly was unremarkable.

"Looks like we have time before the speaker, presenter, or whoever's gonna talk comes in." Kibo looked around the mostly empty room. "Let's try to grab a few seats before this place gets packed."

The three of them picked a spot near the middle of the room, sitting at the back of the row to get a good view of the entire room. It wasn't long after they sat down that more examinees filed in. Kibo watched as examinees took up whatever seats seemed to be the best to them, with a few small groups bickering over a few key spots.

"Heyo! Mind if we sit next to y'all?" Hana tapped his shoulder, Siris and Max standing next to her.

"Oh yeah, sure," Kibo said, motioning to both Rex and Akira to scoot over to the next seat for all of them to fit.

"Feels great to finally relax after all this crazy stuff," Hana said, stretching her arms up towards the ceiling.

"Yeah, we've been through quite a lot these past few days, haven't we?" Kibo thought back to everything that happened throughout the exam. From barely passing the written test to battling strange and exotic creatures to fighting toe-to-toe with Siris.

"Crazy, isn't it, kid? You've made it through hell to get to this point." Kibo looked down at the familiar blue triangle in his hand and smiled.

I wasn't the only one, Kibo thought. Everyone in the room had worked their way through the final exam, fighting tooth and nail to reach this point.

"Yeah, that's true. But these people probably had years of experience using, shifting, and improving their magic. I've been with you for only a little under two months."

Well, I did get stronger, I guess, Kibo said sheepishly to Arcanus.

"A bit? You came here with nothing but a pair of metal gauntlets. Now you've unlocked my full combat form. think you're more than a bit stronger now, don't you think?"

Kibo let out a stifled laugh. *Yeah, you're right. But still, it's crazy to think about how fast all of this is happening.*

"It may seem like that, but I can assure you, kid, this is only the tip of the iceberg." Kibo looked down at Arcanus, puzzled.

What do you mean?

"You've unlocked my full form, but you still aren't close to utilizing me to my full capacity."

What are you talking about?

"The power you're using right now." Suddenly the image of the visor popped into Kibo's head.

I'm still only able to use a small portion of the suit's power, right? Kibo asked, thinking back to his fight with Siris.

"Yup. You see, kid, your body is a..." Arcanus paused for a moment, as though he was thinking about how exactly he was going to explain the machinations of the suit. *"Think of it as a battery and the suit like a generator. The more energy you*

pump from the battery into the generator, the more powerful it gets, right?"

Yeah, okay. But what does that have to do with the suit? Kibo asked.

"Well, the more power you pump into the generator, the more power it's gonna make, but it's also gonna burn through that battery faster. Sooner or later you're gonna have zero power left. But there is one thing that separates you from your average chemical battery. You can improve."

So if I train my body, I'll be able to use more of the suit for longer, right? Kibo said before he looked up and smiled.

"That's the plan."

"What's your plan?"

Kibo turned to see Hana staring at him, and upon realizing that he had just blurted out, his face turned bright red. "Oh, um... I was just planning what to do after getting into Bastion," Kibo said.

"Reallllly?"

"Yeah! I'm really excited. After all, we just been through a lot, right?"

"Right," Hana said, still unconvinced.

"Listen, if you want to know what I'm thinking, it's about what happened in the comms room," Kibo muttered.

"What about it? The three of you came out alive, didn't you? And not only that, you guys took down the boss and saved the hostages," Hana said cheerfully. "You should be proud of what you did there."

"Yeah, I know. But I can't help feeling like I was kind of lost, that I had to rely on others to help me get through there," Kibo said, looking down at the ground with a sober expression.

"I think that's normal."

Kibo glanced up at Hana, confused. "Being overwhelmed is normal?"

"Well, think about it. You're up against some super tough guy and you don't know what you're gonna do." Hana glanced at Akira "So the best thing to do is just learn from it and get better," Hana exclaimed.

"That's what I was thinking too." Kibo smiled.

"That's the spirit, kid!" Arcanus exclaimed. *"If you keep up this attitude, we'll manage to push the suit to its full potential in twenty, maybe fifteen years."*

Twenty? Are you kidding me?

The sudden loud shrieking of a microphone blared through the room.

"Ahh!" Kibo slammed his hands onto his ears from the horrid shrieking. "Don't you think they could at least stop that with some kind of magic? Almost like they're doing it on purpose."

Thankfully, the sound stopped after a short while, letting Kibo and the rest of the group see who exactly was handling the microphone. It was the same Bastion official who had guided them through the physical portion of the exam, now standing on the stage. After fiddling with the microphone, he gave it a few final taps before speaking.

"Hello? Seems like this thing is working," the official said, before turning his gaze to the examinees. "Well, then, hello and welcome to the conclusion of the Bastion entry exam."

I knew it, Kibo thought to himself. *They're gonna tell us who passed.*

"Before we go any further, I want to applaud all of you who have made it this far," the official said joyously. "Originally, the conclusion to the exam was going to be held a week after rigorously matching and ranking of each of your talents and skills.

"However, the crisis that occurred yesterday threw everything out of order, and we've been working for the past twenty-four hours to help the many unfortunate individuals who were injured during the insurgent attack on the facility," he stated gravely, placing his hand across his chest. The soft bickering in the room disappeared as everyone went dead silent. "Thank you all for this moment of silence and to those who gave their bodies and lives in the battle against the insurgents." The official rummaged through some papers that he had placed on the podium, reading the jotted notes.

"An urgent order came from the top ranks. Command has already selected the candidates they would like to see join Bastion," the official said, picking up one paper in particular. "The list in my hand has the names of those who have successfully passed the exam. I will announce them now."

Kibo sat at the edge of his seat, looking at the paper in the official hand with every bit of focus he could muster. He could feel his heart pounding with the fury of an earthquake, every pore across his body sweating with the might of a ferocious river.

Every bit of effort and determination had led him to this moment. This was his life's desire, everything he had worked toward. Within moments, he would know what years of turmoil and torment brought him. He grabbed the edges of his seat in burning anticipation, closing off all his other senses as he waited for his answer.

"All examinees who received a paper stamped with the official magi seal of Bastion has been accepted into the magi corps."

All of the examinees looked at the official for a moment, unable to believe what he had just said.

"Are you saying that everyone in this room passed?" Akira spoke up, asking the question every person in that room was thinking.

"I repeat. All examinees who received a paper stamped with the official magi seal of Bastion has been accepted into the magi corps," the official stated. "Yes, every single person in this room has passed the exam."

The room exploded in a storm of voices, each carrying a different emotion. Kibo looked down at the floor. The examinees around him were either shouting, praying, or crying with joy.

None of that mattered to Kibo. He felt as though he had just climbed the tallest mountain, that he had achieved what had seemed impossible.

Yet, there was another emotion inside him. It was small, yet he could feel it, digging into him like a thorn.

"What's wrong, Kibo? Wasn't your greatest wish just granted?" Arcanus asked, sensing that something was troubling Kibo.

I'm really happy right now. Every part of my body feels like it's about to explode from excitement, Kibo responded quickly. *But...*

"But what?" Arcanus asked.

Kibo looked up from the ground for a moment and pulled out the slip that he had placed in his pocket. It looked worn beyond belief, folded and opened many times from Kibo's constant fiddling. He held it up before him and gave it one long look. *I was thinking about my father and whether I'll be able to find him now."* Kibo paused. *"The more I think about you, about how we got through this exam, I realize how more much I need to find out.*

Kibo placed his arm across his chest and closed his eyes. *I swear to you, father. Wherever you are, I'll find you.* Kibo swore to himself. It was as though nothing could stop him.

"Damn it! Again with that mic!" Rex shouted as the horrendous sound of a microphone screech filled the room, bringing the crowd's unbridled energy and chaos to a halt. All braced against the blast from the microphone.

"Again, I'm sorry about the noise. I've never been quite good at using these sorts of devices. Anyway, most of you will be sent home if you don't require any major medical attention. After which you will be put through a few months of basic training as a way of seeing what division you will be best suited for based on your overall talents, skills, and abilities," he stated. "However, a few of you have already been selected to join a division."

This sudden revelation sent another wave of commotion across the room. The examinees whispered amongst each other.

"Already selected? I thought it was crazy we all passed this quickly, but to have also been selected."

"It's probably some rich kid or one of the stuck-up nobles that got picked already. Probably just bribed their way in."

"This is crazy. I wonder who they picked."

"As I had stated, a few among you were selected to join Bastion's elite division." The man smiled. "And I believe those lucky few will know within a few short moments."

Huh, wonder what he means by that. The slip of paper in Kibo's hand grew warmer, as though it was going to burn through his palm. "Whoa! What the hell?" Kibo tossed the piece of paper onto the floor out of instinct. *"Was that you, Arcanus?"*

"Hey, don't look at me, kid. If I was tryna mess with you, I'd at least be letting out a few small snickers by now."

"Ow!" Rex jumped to his feet.

"What's going on?"

"It feels like my ass is on fire," Rex shouted as he shoved his hand into his back pocket, desperately trying to pull something out of it.

"Ow!" Rex pulled his hand out of his pocket as fast as he could and dropped something onto the floor. "Jesus, the damn thing burned my hand!"

"Wait, your slip too?" Kibo looked down to see an identical slip of paper to the one Rex dropped onto the floor. Kibo and Rex watched their slips on the ground, engrossed by the two small slips of paper.

Slowly, the very edges of their papers burned away, until all that was left was two black playing cards, each with a swirling purple void right in the center.

"That...was not what I was expecting." Kibo looked at the cards, utterly baffled. "Guess we check 'em out."

Slowly, the two of them reached for their cards, as though something was going to happen if they picked it up. They could feel the pressure building on them, bodies starting to drip sweat. Their hearts beat faster, wonder just what terrifying thing could—

"Come on, you two, just pick it up already."

"AH!" Both Kibo and Rex suddenly jolted up out of their seats, turning to see Siris, holding the same pitch-black card in her hand. "Come on, Kaze is already headed out. And yes, before you simpletons ask, he got one too."

Kibo and Rex looked at her for a moment, still somewhat reeling from the shock, before turning back again to their cards.

"Let's just pick them up and go," Kibo mumbled. They both took one final cautionary look at their cards before grabbing them. Quickly turning them around, they both saw an odd string of words and numbers that marked a location.

Floor 2, Wing B, Office 162.

The four stood before office 162. The same purple void on their cards swirled on the door to the office. Above the void sat a plaque with the following engraved upon it: *Leere, Batros. Bastion Operative.*

"I have a feeling we're at the right place." Akira smirked "You all ready to check out this Batros guy?"

They nodded and Akira stepped forth, opening the door to see a normal office. It had a well-polished and laminated oak wood floor, along with whitewashed walls. It had two small windows in the very back that peered out over the testing facility into a large winding forest. Two brown bookcases held several different old books and files, all of which are organized and labeled in alphabetical order. Lastly, in the very center of the room stood a dark oak desk atop a red and white carpe. A middle-aged German in a pair of fatigues sat behind it.

Batros Leere.

"Well, it's good to see you've all finally arrived." Batros smiled, pushing away a pile of paper from in front of him to get a good look at the group. "Even after examining and watching your performance during the exams, it is still quite different to be face-to-face with you all."

He gazed at them, taking his precious time to inspect them one by one. They all watched him silently, occasionally fidgeting uncomfortably in the silence, but nothing more. They just waited, all of them wondering: What does this man have in store for us?

Thankfully, after what felt minutes had gone by, Batros spoke up at last. "I imagine you all know what you're here for now?" Batros asked them all, the warmth in his voice replaced by a more serious tone.

"It would be to recruit us, sir?" Kibo spoke up from the back of the group. Batros turned over to him and smiled again.

"Ah, if it isn't Kibo Kozlov. Like father like son, they say." Batros walked over to the front of his desk. "Yes, that is what I wish. I have watched every one of you during the exam. I watched you all work together in teams and hold your own during your fights. Not a single one of you disappointed me.

"But still, the road ahead will be tough. You will face several difficult and sporadic challenges, from guerillas to corrupt failed states, from smugglers with magical artifacts to rogue magi anarchists. You will see some of the most bitter fighting imaginable."

"Then why would we join you?" Siris asked, somewhat mockingly.

"Because I believe all of you can take it, that you can further improve upon your weaknesses. I offer you an opportunity to become stronger, to turn into some of the best damn agents Bastion will ever see!" Batros shook his fist in the air.

He stepped away from the desk, slowly walking towards the group. They all watched him, knowing exactly what his next words were to be.

"Now then, I ask all of you: Will you join me?" he asked them, the question they were all waiting for.

Yet when it was answered, it was not by the royal, nor the wind mage, nor the fighter. It was answered by the boy in the back, the one who could only light a fire no bigger than a match.

"Yes."

This was the moment Kibo had imagined hundreds of times. The moment he had waited years for. It was finally here.

"Welcome to Bastion."

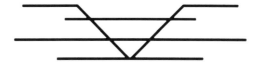

The End

ABOUT THE AUTHOR

Ali K. Eke is a young author with a love for all things fantasy, science fiction, and alternate history. Residing in New Jersey, his many hobbies include reading and writing books, and playing Dungeons and Dragons and video games. He's currently working on acquiring his degree from Rutgers University and finishing the sequel to *Arcanus*, his debut series.

Printed in Great Britain
by Amazon

32578669R00151